CW00616123

CLEANING UP

Gerry O'Brien

Copyright © 1998 by Gerry O'Brien

First published in 1998 by Colin Smythe Limited,
Gerrards Cross, Buckinghamshire SL9 8XA

The right of Gerry O'Brien to be identified as the author
of this work has been asserted by him in accordance with
the Copyright, Designs and Patents Act, 1988

British Library Cataloguing-in-Publication Data

A catalogue record for this book is available from
the British Library

ISBN 0-86140-416-5

Produced in Great Britain
Printed and bound by the Guernsey Press Company Ltd.
Vale, Guernsey GY1 3BW

To Eleanor
And not just because she asked first...

1

The shabby old woman tapped on the window of the shiny, new, red Mercedes.

'Could you please think about not parking on the pavement,' she said, 'it's for people not cars.'

The pock-marked, pale-faced driver of the new car wound down his window, took the cigarette from his mouth, looked at the old woman and blew smoke into her face.

'What?' he said.

'Would you please not park on the pavement, it's for people not cars.'

The driver smiled. Slowly.

'Eff off,' he said, 'silly cow.' He turned back unfussed into his car and wound the window up again. The old woman shrugged and shuffled off down the road.

Twenty yards further on a young man was climbing out of a battered, old Ford Cortina which was also parked on the pavement. The old woman reached him as he finished locking his door.

'Excuse me,' she said, 'would you please think about not parking there, it's for people, not cars.'

The young man looked at the old woman as if she was mad.

'What?' he said.

'Would you please...'

'Yeah, alright, I heard.' The young man was large and crop-haired and he sounded aggrieved.

A few shoppers in the busy High Street overheard the exchange and stopped to see what would happen.

'Stupid bag,' whispered a soft voice, 'what's it to do with her anyway?'

'Seen her at it before,' replied a loud, gruff voice, 'silly cow. Wants to change the world, or something.'

To change the world; it is a simple enough thing to want yet the gruff voice's words were laden with sneer like a hot dog with mustard.

The young man looked at the gruff voice. He looked at Dot. Trapped in uncertainty he looked up and down The Borough High Street and caught sight of the red Mercedes.

'Okay, right, but what about him then? Why bother me and not him?'

The old woman too looked at the red car.

'I tried him,' she said. 'He told me to eff off.' She looked back at the young man and her gaze was steady. 'But that doesn't mean you've got to, does it?'

The old lady nodded at a yellow sign a short way off in the opposite direction. 'There's a car park down there. You can park there safe enough.'

The young man looked at the sign and then again at the old woman. She smiled at him. Hugely.

'Go on,' she said, 'be a love.'

Among the bystanders a woman giggled. Amusement sprang to life and ran around the small crowd until, crushed by a glance from the young man, it slunk off, hurt, into a nearby doorway. The young man looked uncomfortable.

'Okay then,' he said at last, 'it's a fair point I suppose.' He unlocked his car, climbed in and drove off without another word. The watchers were silent.

'Good for you love,' said a woman's voice suddenly.

''Sright,' said the gruff voice without a trace of shame,

2

'bleedin' well done.'

'Only wish I had the guts,' said the woman, 'then I'd tell them.'

'Never mind.' The gruff voice nudged the woman in the ribs and leered at her. 'Tell me instead. What're you doing for the next hour?' He laughed.

'Gaah, push off.'

'No harm in asking.'

'Oh? No? Well let me tell you...'

The old woman shuffled on. The Borough, she thought, my Borough, god bless it and all who sail in it. She raised her head, looked on down the High Street and smiled. There was work to do yet, a task without end.

Of all the people who have written about London, Charles Dickens is king. The Dickensian metropolis is a masterpiece of degeneracy. His gutters reek romantically, his facades decay decadently, his blind alleys keep watch from under the lid of their one good eye and his dead ends are not dead at all – they are just laying low till danger has passed when they will get on with inflicting some damage of their own.

One place that Dickens never wrote about is The Borough. This does not make The Borough the... well, the borough that Dickens forgot. Far from it. He wanted to forget it. He tried to forget it. Most people who have been there feel the same. But it is a place that keeps coming back, mostly in nightmares.

To the thousands of people passing along it every day, to and from the City, The Borough's High Street is unremarkable. The good architecture has all given way to bad architecture and the process has not yet gone into reverse. The retail chains monopolise the shops and the Council has done its bit of ineffectual tarting up to attract outsiders to come and spend money.

But leave the High Street and the air grows thicker and

3

darker. Walk the side streets and the pavement grows greasy underfoot. Listen, and occasional screams of terror will come drifting out of blind alleys until, meeting the lank luminescence that passes for daylight in The Borough, they flee swiftly back to the dark.

At the mid point of The Borough High Street was a shop. Inside, beyond the showroom and right at the back, there was a small office and in the office was a safe. It was quite a safe. It had locks like Chinese puzzles and walls like Fort Knox. It was waterproof, fireproof and bombproof. In short, it was a safe that the makers had fussed over.

With a safe like that, only someone unreasonably determined, unthinkably stupid or terribly mad would install extra booby traps. But then, only someone unreasonably determined, unthinkably stupid or terribly mad would open a jewellery shop in The Borough High Street in the first place

Inside the safe the Diamond was not happy. Although it had been through a lot over the years nothing had ever troubled it much. Earthquake, flood and avalanche had left it unscathed. Murder, war and rape had simply made life that bit more worth living and sinking with all hands to the bottom of the sea had widened its horizons marvellously. But now, for the first time that it could remember, it was really unhappy.

The Diamond stared at the dynamite beside it and the dynamite stared back with a gaze that was dangerously detached from its mind. The Diamond tried to look tough, which should have been easy for something made from the hardest substance on earth, but its heart was not in it. It was distracted by the oldness of the dynamite, by its greyness, by its oily sweat and by the stench of marzipan that filled the airtight safe.

'You're a diamond, aren't you?' said the Dynamite, pleasantly enough.

4

'Er, yes,' said the Diamond, remembering regretfully that when dynamite sweats, it sweats nitro-glycerine.

'Thought so,' said the Dynamite. 'I see them all in here. Diamonds, sapphires, emeralds, rubies. Even knew a moonstone once. Never seen a stone as big as you though. And that's a funny thing, isn't it? I mean, when people like big stones so much.'

'I only started out as a tree,' said the Diamond, trying to sound like nothing very special. 'Long time ago that was of course.'

'I mean, if they like big stones more than little ones, why not have more of the big ones?' The Dynamite sounded immensely reasonable.

'It was a pine tree,' said the Diamond.

'No one likes me,' said the Dynamite. 'They only use me.'

Beyond the old woman, a tweedy middle-aged woman in a Volvo estate was forcing a young woman with two small children out into the traffic of the High Street. Beyond that again there were more malefactors and transgressors and, it was not a new thought to the old woman, there always would be, in spite of everything she could do.

Caught suddenly in a reflective mood the old woman stopped to peer down the length of a spectacularly dismal canyon of a side street called Angel Pass. Far away she could just make out two child-sized figures locked in ritualistic combat. Other small figures clustered around them.

'Have his eyes out,' volunteered one gnomish spectator.

'Gut him,' offered another.

The old woman smiled and thought of the dim distant days almost beyond recall when, slender and elfin, she too had engaged in The Borough's childhood pursuits. Angel Pass had been hers then, monarch of the glen.

In the end, the old woman pictured the distant days, she had left it all behind. Like the generations before her she had simply walked away. The younger children had followed for a while, trying to land half-bricks on her head to bring her back. But no-one ever went back.

Half-bricks. The old woman turned away. It had always been half-bricks. Like half-truths they seemed to shape a more convincing argument.

To the Diamond, the Dynamite looked so unstable that it probably thought it was Hitler. Or Napoleon. The Diamond had known both. But compared to the Dynamite, Hitler and Napoleon looked as dangerous as Sooty and Sweep.

There were guards in the room outside the safe. The Diamond had seen them when it was brought in and it had been trying for hours to contact them. Telepathically. It had been trying since the moment it discovered that the dynamite was eight years past its explode-by date.

Memories. The old woman was trembling so much with the burden of them that she needed to sit down. There was a bench nearby but a tramp was sleeping on it, filling it and snoring like a road drill.

The tramp was huge. He was vast. His trousers legs would have made cocktail frocks for the old woman, not that she needed cocktail frocks, and his coat would have made her a ball gown. The old woman had been to a ball once, never to a cocktail party, but to a ball, yes, she had been to one of those. That was all so long ago though. Could she really be that old?

That she was old she knew very well, in theory. She had been old for a long time. But although she had been happy to play with the idea, to use it and scorn it and abuse it, she had never felt its truth before. The terrifying novelty of it made her weaker by the moment. Her vision grew dim and there was a roaring in her ears.

But the roaring was not just in her ears, it was behind her, shaking the air. She turned to look.

It was a car, a red Mercedes, at speed in low gear. It was screaming straight towards her.

The passenger window was open. A woman leant out of it. A brazen woman. A woman made up to the nines. A woman with hair frizzed into a beehive. An angry woman, raging and roaring through scarlet lips above the roar of the car.

'Rude cow!' The woman shook her fist in the air. 'Bleedin' rude cow!'

It was certain that car would hit the old woman, that the breath she drew now was her last. Then at the first fraction of a moment beyond certainty the driver finally spun his wheel and the car plunged off the pavement, out into the High Street traffic and away.

Shocked by the wind of the car's passing the old woman fell back onto the bench and, landing awkwardly on the sleeping tramp's foot, she tumbled to the ground.

In the car the brassy woman screamed.

'Jesus wept! You've killed her.' She buried her face in her hands and screamed again. The pock-marked man laughed.

'Never touched her,' he said coldly. 'Only scared her.

'You see,' he said as he slowed to the speed of the High Street Traffic. 'She wouldn't be worth the trouble. Would she?

'You can look now,' he added. 'We're okay now.'

The brassy woman uncovered her face and looked nervously at the man beside her. He reached out and patted her thigh below the hemline of her short scarlet skirt.

'Give us a smile then,' he said and she did.

'You were wonderful,' he said and she tried to believe it, to feel that her anger was not really fear. She smiled bravely.

'Well, you told me to shout,' she said as she dried the tears from her eyes. He gave her knee a squeeze and she

7

smiled again, winningly.

And so they leave the story altogether, he in the driving seat and she his passenger. For ever and ever. Amen.

'Dear lady.' The tramp's voice was sweet and low. 'You're not hurt, I hope.' He rose from the bench like the birth of a young mountain and crouched beside the old woman. 'It didn't hit you at least. Now, are you ready to sit up here, do you think, or should I just leave you alone for a few minutes?'

The old woman was too shocked to speak but she reached up with a hand that trembled, and patted the bench. The tramp caught her under the arms and lifted her gently onto it. The old woman reached out again towards a large black handbag that lay on the ground but she was unable to reach it and the tramp picked it up for her and gave it to her.

'There,' he said. 'Anything else?'

The old woman cradled the bag on her lap and shook her head mutely.

'I'll just stay with you for a while then, shall I? While you get your breath back.'

The old woman nodded shakily and the tramp sat beside her and held one of her small, cold hands in his own massive paw.

'I don't suppose they'll be back,' he said. He looked away up the High Street in the direction the red car had taken but it was nowhere in sight. 'It's better to be safe than sorry, though.'

Now, for the first time, the old woman looked directly at the tramp. His hair was shaggy like the fearsome disorder of a lion's mane. His beard from his cheekbones to the middle of his chest was thick and black and silky. His forehead was tanned and creased by the extremes of English weather but beneath it his deep-set eyes were dark and calm, like peaceful nights over winter snow. The old woman smiled.

'Thank you,' she said. Then suddenly, in spasm, she muttered 'Excuse me!' and was violently sick on the ground.

Back in the jewellery shop the Diamond was becoming panicky about its failure to reach the guards in the room beyond. It was not the safe that was blocking its telepathic powers, since a diamond's allure can reach over thousands of miles, it was something about the guards' minds. If it could just...

'Talking about trees,' said the Dynamite, 'I knew one once. Nice bloke he was too. Till he burnt.'

'Oh yes?'

'Do Diamonds burn?'

'Only in small spaces. If things go bang,' squeaked the Diamond. It laughed, desperately.

'Bang!' shrieked the Dynamite and the Diamond rolled up its eyes, in a manner of speaking, and collapsed in a faint.

The old woman and the tramp were talking too.

'Yes, well,' said the old woman as though she were surprised to hear herself talking about it, 'it's certainly the first time anything like that's happened.'

'But other things?'

'Not often, no, mostly not at all. I suppose they're too surprised. And I am a little old woman after all.'

The tramp laughed sardonically.

'You should still be more careful though. You could end up in a lot of trouble.' His expression clouded over and he reached across and took the old woman's hand. 'Believe me,' he said, squeezing gently. 'I know.'

It was the old woman's turn to laugh.

'What, you? Who'd touch you?'

'Ah, appearance isn't everything.' The tramp seemed to fold into himself. 'I'm just a baa-lamb really. They soon find out.'

The old woman squeezed the tramp's hand in return and then started fumbling underneath her handbag.

'Well look, there's no need to worry,' she said, 'I know how to look after myself. I really do.'

From a sheath hidden in the gusset of the bag she drew out a police truncheon and handed it to the tramp.

'You learn when you grow up round here,' she explained. 'I never used to bother carrying anything, did it all with my bare hands, but now I'm older...'

The tramp handed the truncheon back and she put it away.

'Alright then,' he said, 'I'll stop fussing shall I?' The old woman patted his knee.

'That's best,' she said briskly. Then, more thoughtfully, 'Yes, that's best.'

In the depths of its faint the Diamond imagined that it was seeking to enslave the minds of two huge security guards. It sent out images of its immense fire, sparkle and hard cash value but the guards just laughed and laughed and laughed and...

The Dynamite's voice penetrated the Diamond's faint. 'You didn't burn.' It sounded disappointed.

The Diamond dreamt, as it rose nearer to consciousness, that, however hard it tried, it would never reach the security guards. They had no minds. No minds. No minds.

'What's that?' said the Dynamite as the Diamond woke up fully. 'No mines? That'll be the day.' It laughed. 'No mines. No artillery. No bombs I suppose?' It laughed again.

The Diamond had heard that laugh before, from a Corsican in Russia late in the day, and it began again its frantic signalling to the unresponsive guards.

'I don't think I caught your name,' said the Diamond placatingly as it urged the guards to open the safe. 'You must have led an interesting life though.'

It was hard for the Diamond to do two things at once but it had to try; try and keep on trying until it was outside the safe.

Outside the safe. It was so near, yet it sounded like Paradise. But then maybe Paradise is never so very far away.

'You're a diamond,' said the Dynamite. 'Josephine's got diamonds.'

Oh god, thought the Diamond. Please no.

'I've got bombs. We won't take Moscow without bombs you know.' The sweat was pouring off the Dynamite now. Neat nitro-glycerine trickled down its flanks and formed puddles on the shelf beside it.

'Of course not,' said the Diamond. 'Bombs are a must.' But that was not what it was thinking. It was thinking about what happened to Diamonds inside pressure tight safes when pound sticks of Dynamite explode beside them.

'Do Diamonds burn?' the Dynamite had asked and the Diamond had blanched at the question.

Do Diamonds burn? Under those conditions? Hah! Do they ever.

'You realise,' the tramp said after a while, 'that you're just beating your head against a brick wall, don't you? You can't change people.'

'If I thought that,' said the old woman, 'I wouldn't bother.'

'But you'll never change them all.'

'Maybe not. But that's different, isn't it? I'm only after better, not perfect. And you've got to start somewhere.' She became thoughtful.

'A better place to live,' she said, staring off into space. 'Better for all of us.'

'That sounds like you've got children.' The tramp smiled. 'Or grandchildren?' The old woman did not reply. There was an uncomfortable pause.

11

'Sorry,' said the tramp. 'None of my business.'

'No. No, it's alright. I just never got married. That's all.'

The old woman looked away then sat up straight, bristling with indignation.

'Now will you look at that?' she said tartly.

A little way down the street a nondescript car with a surprisingly deep and throaty noise to it had climbed up onto the pavement and parked. Two heavy men in dark coats climbed ponderously out and walked away.

'The driver's still there,' said the old woman standing and straightening her coat. 'Blessed cheek. I'll have a word with him.' The tramp stood too.

'Let me come with you,' he said. The old woman looked doubtful.

'Well... Only if you want to,' she said. The tramp nodded.

'I'd like to. And by the way. I'm Vernon. Vernon Carpenter.'

'Oh, er, and I'm Dot. Dot Coulson.' She looked unsure what to do next until Vernon held out his hand. Dot took it. They shook.

'I'm pleased to meet you, Dot.'

'Yes, well,' Dot turned in the direction of the car. 'Can't stand here yakking all day, there's work to do.' She bustled away down the street. Vernon stood watching for a moment then he smiled beautifully and started off behind her. There was work to do, she had said. There was work to do for once.

The Diamond concentrated its whole attention on the guards. There was no point any more in trying to humour the mad thing beside it. If the Dynamite went bang then it went bang. But the Diamond would not be around when it happened. Not if it could help it. The air hummed with telepathy. The safe bulged and vibrated. If it could just concentrate...

'Sweet guards. Sweet, sweet guards. Just one little look.'

12

The Dynamite had gone into a trance.

'Come on. Pretty guards. In here.'

A new sound filled the safe.

'Moscow,' muttered the Dynamite. 'Moscow! I'm coming, I'm coming, I'm coming...'

The Diamond screamed. Silently.

'LOOK IN THE SAFE! YOU BEGGARS!'

Two men approached the front door of the jewellery shop. One of the men was called Axe and the reason why was under his coat. The second was called Sailor Simkins and he was carrying, with less nominal justification but with equal deadliness of purpose, a twelve pound sledge hammer.

One guard looked at the other guard.

'IN THE SAFE!'

The front door of the shop was always kept locked. It gave way with violent ill will to the combined pressure of the Axe and the Sailor and their instruments of destruction.

The two guards never knew until the moment they died quite why they decided to take the huge diamond out of the safe, but they did it anyway. They were standing in the middle of the room looking at it when the door from the shop fell in.

'You needn't have done that,' said the first guard, who was hypnotised by the glittering gemstone. 'It wasn't locked.'

'Oh shit!' said the second who was not.

'I'll take that,' said a voice.

'Thank god,' the Diamond exulted as the Axe carried it out of the shop into The Borough's so-called fresh air.

'Thank god, thank god, thank god.'

Being a mere animate and mortal object the Axe did not

hear the Diamond, although he would have done if he had been a paving stone.

'Christ!' said the first guard, crawling to his feet. 'We're right in it now. Did they leave anything?'

'Only this,' said the second guard reaching in to the safe.

Outside in the street the Axe was baffled.

'Where's the car?' he said. He looked at the place where his getaway car had stood only a minute before but all he saw was an empty space and, beside it, a little old lady arguing with a truck driver. The driver looked as though he would gladly have torn the throat out of the little old lady but for a huge, dangerous-looking tramp who seemed to be protecting her. The Axe had no time to consider the impossibility of this. He had other problems.

His chief problem, in common with the Sailor, Dot Coulson, Vernon Carpenter and the driver of the truck, though not with the guards who had no problems any more, was the ball of flame belching and tearing its way out of the wrecked doorway of Harry Devine, Bespoke Jeweller.

Riding the fireball could clearly be heard, by paving stones and diamonds at least, a final, drawn-out scream of unfettered fury.

'MOSCOW!'

2

An hour or so later one of Dot's pavement parking transgressors was getting a hard time from his Boss.

'Once more. It's easy, right? You'd gone from outside the shop by the time they came out. You'd gone to the car park. So tell me. Why were you in the car park?'

'Look Boss, I, uh, I really can't say.' Hubcaps's voice was strained. This was largely because he was hanging from the ceiling of the Boss's office by his thumbs. With his chest stretched tight up and down and with his head slumped forward constricting his throat, breathing was something of a trial.

'Why were you in the car park?'

'When I, uh, when I got back, right, there was, uh, like nothing to see. People all, uh, all over, and bits of, uh, like, things, and no sign of any diamond.'

'The car park!'

Hubcaps was uncomfortable. But if he told the Boss why he had been in the car park instead of waiting outside the jeweller's then he would be a jolly sight more uncomfortable. A chap had a chap's professional reputation to think of, after all. He shook his head regretfully.

The Boss advanced a pace closer and stared into Hubcaps's eyes.

'The car park.'

Again Hubcaps shook his head.

15

The Boss was a simple man. His ideas were few and far between, but what he had he held on to furiously. One idea right at the front of his mind was that he did not like Hubcaps Henry.

To begin with, Hubcaps was a foreigner. He was not born in The Borough.

And another thing was; Hubcaps should never have been a villain at all. His Dad was never a villain. His Dad was an admiral who thought Henry was dead. Or hoped so anyway.

And another thing was; As the top driver in the metropolis, tales of Hubcaps's skill and daring were legend. He was, in fact, a bleedin' clever dick.

And another thing was; Hubcaps had only been in the game five minutes yet here he was, fully employed with advance bookings to Christmas. It was disgraceful when men with long years of experience who were worth two, no, ten of him, were hardly working at all.

And another thing was; two of the Boss's best boys were in hospital because of Hubcaps.

And another thing was that the Boss wanted that diamond.

And that was probably the main thing, now that he stopped to think of it.

The Boss wanted the Diamond a lot and it wanted him. It was calling to him with this, like, small voice in his head. This was stupid of course but that must be Hubcaps's fault. Right now everything was Hubcaps's fault.

The voice of the Diamond spoke again. It was telling the Boss that it wanted to make him rich. It was telling the Boss that it wanted to give him... But now it had changed to pictures, beautiful pictures, and the Boss had no words he could use to think of beauty. He gave up on the voice in frustration.

'Take his shirt off, boys,' said the Boss. The boys leapt to do the Boss's bidding and reduced Hubcaps's shirt to rags around his waist.

Hubcaps's torso was stringy. The hair in his elongated armpits was thin and gingery. Exposed even to the excessive warmth of the Boss's office the whole ensemble shrank back, looking for shelter. It wasn't used to air.

'Okay,' said the Boss. 'Now shave him. And don't forget the talcum powder. I want those armpits as smooth as...' He groped for an adequate simile. 'As smooth as freshly shaved armpits. Right?'

While the boys obliged, the Boss smoothed a long feather between his fingers.

'Right then,' he said. 'To business. And don't think you can hold out against this.' He flourished the feather under Hubcaps's nose. 'I've had stronger men than you laughing. Laughing and singing their hearts out.'

Mad Harry Devine sat on an upturned packing crate on the pavement outside his erstwhile jewellery shop. Where the upturned crate had come from was a mystery. It was not a normal part of the furnishings of his shop. But then, he was only sitting on it because the normal furnishings had gone. Perhaps packing cases always turned up just when they were needed to complete a picture of misery and dejection.

Harry considered the idea. He found it strange but not surprising. This was usual. For Harry to find strangeness surprising would be like Everest finding bigness strange. The only thing that surprised Harry was normality.

A police car crept unwillingly onto the scene. Policemen slid out, trying to look inconspicuous. They mingled with a small crowd which had sprung up from nowhere.

A crowd, police and a mysterious packing case; there was fitness to it, thought Harry. There was fitness to everything, if you could only find it.

'Keep these people back lads, keep them safe,' whispered the sergeant in charge of the police. The lads obliged.

17

Working carefully so as to avoid any sudden sounds and movements they urged people back to an official safe distance. For once the crowd moved willingly. After all, the boys in blue had more experience of Harry than anyone else, so they must know, mustn't they? For once they must know.

The Borough thought Harry was mad. Harry thought this was wrong since he did not think The Borough was mad in return. He had thought about it though, long and hard. He had looked at madness from every possible angle to see whether or not it applied to The Borough.

Looking at madness was like looking at cotton wool. From a distance you could see what it was. But the closer you got, the less easy it became to see what was wool and what was empty space in between. Surrounded by the stuff you had no idea of anything. Finally overwhelmed by the imprecision of the whole idea, Harry had decided that The Borough was just normal.

'What happened Harry?' shouted the sergeant.

Absolute stillness. The High Street waited for Harry's reply.

With pain like a sleepless night Mad Harry raised his head. Several people made gestures to ward off the Eye.

Then Harry spoke.

'It went bang,' he said.

'Oh, right. That's alright then,' said the sergeant. 'Any problems?'

'None for you.'

The police sergeant turned gratefully away.

'Nothing for us here boys,' he whispered.

There was a blur of activity and the police were no longer of the party. A pall of blue exhaust fumes hung over the motionless crowd. It was a getaway to gladden Hubcaps's heart.

Harry Devine threw back his head and laughed. Any problems? Any problems! Who'd be normal?

Beneath Hubcaps's swinging feet was a litter of broken feathers.

'Another one boys, this one's broken,' said the Boss and yet more swan's down hit the floor as the boys rushed to oblige.

'Look, uh, Boss, I, uh, I tell you, uh, I, uh, I'm not ticklish,' said Hubcaps, 'I, uh, never have been. It's a fault, I, uh, I know. Upbringing and uh, like, all that. But uh, there it is. Uh, okay?'

'There's no rush,' said the Boss smoothing the new instrument of torture between his fingers, 'I'm a patient man.' He lied. He wanted results. Right now.

'Okay boys, we'll try something different.' Hubcaps winced. 'Tell him a joke.' The Boss pointed at one of the boys. 'You start him laughing and then I'll keep him going.'

Hubcaps groaned. 'Please, uh, uh, uh, no.' The Boss laughed but Hubcaps's prayer was answered regardless. The telephone rang.

'Get it,' said the Boss and he sat down while the telephone was picked up. Hubcaps raised his eyes gratefully to Heaven until he caught sight of his thumbs. There was not that much to be grateful for, really.

'It's for you, Boss. Says it's Rupert.' The boys tittered.

'Shut up,' hissed the Boss, hoping that Rupert had not heard. 'You don't know RUPERT.' The boys fell silent.

'I do,' said a voice like tide-washed gravel. No one paid it any attention. 'Don't I just,' added the voice bitterly.

Robber Rupert had been one of the boys until retiring to Spain at half the Boss's age. He kept up his old connections though, and the Boss spent a fortnight at his villa every Autumn. They were very relaxing, those fortnights, if you could put up with Rupert.

'Rupert, hi! ... Yeah, hit it today. You were right. Pain in the arse for too long ... ... Oh? ... How'd you know? ... ...

19

Is that right? And why ... ... Oh yes? ... ... A little old lady huh? ... Really? ... Yes yes.' The Boss stared coldly at Hubcaps who felt his skin crawl for the first time. 'Of course I knew ... Oh yeah, I'm still coming ... No, no, I'm looking forward to it ... Really ... Really. It'll be great ... Tomorrow then ... Yeah, twenty four hours.' The Boss hung up. He had forgotten how sarcastic Rupert could be.

The Boss stood and crossed to where Hubcaps was hanging.

'So. A little old lady, huh?'

'She, uh, she had a truncheon Boss. I could, uh, like, see it. Uh, under her handbag.'

'I see. She had a truncheon. In her handbag. So when she says, 'Don't park on the pavement...''

'And there was, uh, this, uh, like, tramp with her.'

'Oh really? A tramp, was he?'

'Hell Boss! This is The, uh, The Borough. Uh, anything might have happened.'

'She says jump and you jump.'

'She said 'please' for Chris'sake!'

'What about when I say jump!'

Hubcaps whimpered.

'Jesus!' said the Boss from between clenched teeth. 'A little old lady.'

When Harry's laugh had finally chased away the crowd, it died. No one mourned its passing. In fact people hoped that its end had been exquisitely painful. Revenge may not be justice but that makes it no less sweet.

This was a sentiment shared by the Diamond.

Mad Harry fell forward screaming. He writhed on the ground. He beat his head on the paving stones. He babbled. There were perfectly good reasons for this, seven of them, all pictures. None of them were beautiful.

By beating his head on the ground Harry might shake the pictures loose. By denying their existence he might make them go away. It seemed to work. The pictures went. In their place was the Diamond's voice.

'I hope you liked them.' The Diamond knew that Harry had not. It could read his mind. This was unnerving, even for the Diamond.

'The circles of hell,' said the Diamond, 'though a colourful interpretation I grant you.' Harry stored away the information that sixty-nine shades of black was what the Diamond called colourful.

'I shouldn't bother with that. It was only a figure of speech.'

'I know where you are,' telegraphed Harry.

'I know you know,' replied the Diamond.

'I know you know I know.' The air trembled with telepathy.

'I know you know I know you know.'

Harry rolled onto his back, stared up at the sky and began laughing. Between them he and the Diamond had the most sophisticated two-way bio-communications mechanism in the history of the universe and all they could send was rubbish.

'Yes, stupid isn't it?' agreed the Diamond. 'But it's only the inverse law of communications at work. The more sophisticated the technology becomes, the easier it is to use, so the simpler are the people who use it and the more trite is what they say.'

'I know,' said Harry.

'I know you...'

'I expected you to be surprised, that's all.'

'Nothing surprises me...'

'Then we're alike.'

'...except normality. And please let me finish.'

'Alright, if...'

'I agree.'

There was a long pause. Harry picked himself up from the ground and sat down on the packing crate.

'By the way,' he said, 'take a look at this.'

A piercing scream cleaved the air which trembled audibly, rattling the windows in nearby houses. The Diamond started babbling, much as Harry had done.

'It doesn't exist. It doesn't exist. It doesn't exist.'

Harry switched off the image.

'The centre of the sun,' he said. 'Though a colourful interpretation, I grant you.'

'If you call sixty nine shades of white "colourful".'

'A figure of speech.'

There was a long pause.

'What next, then?' said the Diamond. 'A truce?'

'No. You still have to die,' said Mad Harry Devine. 'You are a danger to mankind.'

'Ah. And there was me just thinking the same about you.'

'And I'm the only one who'll do it. You know that.'

'And again, ditto.'

'I know.'

Neither of them knew what to say next.

'Then may the best... thing... win,' said the Diamond eventually.

'I hope so. I really do.'

'Cocky aren't you? For a mortal.'

'Closing down on this channel now. Over...'

'And out.'

Hubcaps swung gently in the draught from the open door. He listened to the dwindling sounds of the Boss and his boys.

'I want to know who this old lady is, right? I want to know who she's working for. I want the Diamond and I want her dead. In that order. By tomorrow. Got it? By the time I go to Spain. Oh,' The Boss's final words faded fast behind a door swinging shut. 'And someone see to that bastard back there.' The door banged.

Silence.

The door opened again. Brisk, business-like footsteps approached. Hubcaps's eyes widened with fear. And the footsteps came nearer. And nearer. And nearer.

The packing case was empty. The remains of the jewellery shop still smouldered, sending thin plumes of smoke up into the clammy Borough air. The only sound was the busy hammering of shopkeepers and householders boarding up their windows.

The boards were not intended to stop the windows from rattling when there was no wind or other reason for it. They had stopped all by themselves five minutes before. They were going up because of the lone howling that had sounded just after that. It had come from Harry Devine.

Mad Harry had stood on his packing case, raised his arms to the sky and howled like a wolf. He had also roared like a lion, quacked like a duck and sounded off like a rooster on heat. All of which meant only one thing to the wise of The Borough. Mad Harry was going adventuring. So the wise were boarding up their windows, as were the half-wise. The simple folk were just hiding and watching. They had boarded up their windows as soon as the bomb went off.

3

Dot Coulson sat beside Vernon Carpenter's bed and watched the enormous, courteous man as he slept. It was right, Vernon sleeping, it was how he had been when they met. She smiled at the thought. When they met. It was not an hour ago.

A courteous man. '"Courtesy costs nothing," said the Irishman as he bowed to the bullet.' The old saw ran round and round in Dot's head, never tiring. Courtesy costs nothing. Dot had never known much courtesy, only what she had had from social workers really. And theirs was not real courtesy. It was a veiled threat.

Courtesy costs nothing. Which was just as well since Vernon had no more than that to spend on it. Yet he had done her the courtesy of shaking her hand. She looked at it, wrapped in bandages now into a fist. He had done her the courtesy of saving her life.

If Vernon had not been standing between Dot and the unexpected fireball then she would never have withstood it. That was what the doctor had said. And if he had not been wearing six layers of wool, if he had not had such a thick mane of hair, if he had not had on his bobble cap...

Vernon had lost the wool and the hair but they had saved his skin. And without the lion's mane, without the beard and whiskers, he was just a baby really. A great, innocent baby.

Who snored.

'Aunty Dot,' said a brisk voice.

Well Vernon did not need the wool.

'Aunty Dot,' said the brisk voice, more briskly.

Dot's hand clenched tighter inside its bandages. It clenched round something that sent warm messages direct to her heart.

'Aunty Dot!'

Vernon would never need for anything again.

A brisk hand shook Dot's shoulder.

'Aunty Dot!' said the brisk voice one last time.

Dot turned to look at the young nurse standing behind her. She was the youngest of Dot's nieces and nephews, the runt of Dot's sister's vast litter of children.

'I'm off duty now,' she said.

'Then for heaven's sake, relax, Runt,' said Dot. 'I'm staying till he's awake.'

The Runt bridled. Everyone called her 'Runt'. She spent a lot of time bridling.

'You can't,' she said.

'And it's no use telling me he's under sedation...'

'He's under sedation.'

'Or that he won't be awake till morning...'

'He won't wake up till the morning.'

'Because I'm...'

'And they'll probably discharge him then. There's not much the matter with him.'

'I'm staying.'

The diamond in Dot's fist suddenly became bitingly cold. Equally suddenly she was aware of it not just as a diamond, but as the Diamond. It had become immense. She was more aware of it than she had been of anything before. And suddenly waves of a strange feeling were washing over her, a new feeling, a feeling she had never even imagined. It was panic.

Dot's breathing became irregular. She half rose to her

25

feet. She sat down again. She tried to speak. She spluttered. Spit dribbled down her chin. She held up her hand imploringly to the Runt.

'Aunty Dot?' said the Runt. She bent down over her aunt and caught hold of Dot's wrist. The old woman was in a bad way. Her eyes were staring. Her breath was coming in short gasps. As the Runt felt her pulse she tried to speak but could only whisper.

'Get me out of here.'

'But...'

'Get me out.'

'I think you should stay, Aunty. You need to see a doctor.'

'You wanted me out. Now get me out!'

'But...'

'Do it!'

All eyes turned to watch as the young, caped nurse escorted the tottering old lady out of the ward and into the wide, sloping corridor beyond.

The Boss's office door swung wide.

'Right you,' said a voice like tide-washed gravel, 'I'm here to see to you.'

From where he hung, Hubcaps looked down into the tight face of one of the boys. The face was misty. Something to do with pain, thought Hubcaps. And fear. But even so, the boy seemed to be fifty. Fifty at least. And he had a tic by his right eye.

'Any last requests then?' growled the boy. He unsheathed a long-bladed knife.

'Requests?' said Hubcaps struggling to sound jovial.

'Yeah,' said the boy. 'Requests. What they give dead men before topping 'em.'

'Oh. Yes. Uh. Well. That's uh, decent of you, I uh, I must say,' said Hubcaps. He thought of the kinds of thing he might want. And of the kinds of thing he was likely to get.

26

'You couldn't, uh, manage to sprinkle me, uh, on Hampstead Heath, could you? I've, uh, I've always had a soft spot for, uh, Hampstead Heath.'

The boy considered Hubcaps's request seriously then shook his head.

'Nah, sorry, it's outside our parish. It'd only lead to grief, planting corpses on other geezers' turf.'

Hubcaps gave up on joviality and had a go at nonchalance instead.

'Of course, there, uh, needn't be a corpse at all.'

Again the boy considered Hubcaps's proposition seriously.

'Nah, there's got to be a corpse. "See to him," that's what he said, see. And that's corpsing. I'm dead if I don't corpse you.'

'Oh well. Uh, fair enough,' said Hubcaps.

'And don't you try nothing on neither,' warned the boy. 'Or else.'

Nonch beggar, he thought. It was out of order, geezers hung out for corpsing coming on nonch.

'You're the boss,' said Hubcaps. The boy flinched at the idea. 'So, uh, better get on with it, eh.'

'Yeah,' said the boy, 'better had.'

He raised his knife to strike.

'Only...' said Hubcaps.

The boy sighed and lowered his knife arm.

'Come on,' he said, 'do me a favour. I thought you was in the trade. Giving me "Only...". Just forget it, okay?'

'Alright.'

'Okay. Where were we then?'

'You were...' Hubcaps nodded at the knife.

'Yeah. Right,' said the boy. He raised the knife, then lowered it again. Compassion crept warily across the dangerous landscape of his face.

'Look,' he said, 'I'm not saying your "Only..." wasn't a fair enough try-on. I wouldn't want you thinking that. Not when it's your last thought, like. Only, I've had your "Only...'s" before, see.' The boy sounded tired. 'I know all about your "Only...'s." He perched on the edge of the Boss's desk and poked with his knife at the blotter.

'There was this bank manager once...'

Hubcaps coughed, violently. The boy twitched, startled. A chunk of the blotter fell to the floor.

'Sorry mate,' he said, 'I'm forgetting myself. You'll be wanting to get on.'

'No, er, uh, not at all. Just a, uh, tickle in my throat.' Hubcaps coughed again. 'I'd, uh, I'd like to hear,' he said. 'Really.'

'Well, alright,' said the boy settling again. 'But only if you feel up to it.'

'Uh, sure.'

'Well there was this bank manager see. And we've had our little chat like, "There needn't be a corpse," all of that. And now it's, time, like. So I'm just about to see to him, when out he comes with it. "Only...".

'It's good too. It's like, hesitant, suggestive, alluring you might almost say. Better than you. But then he's more comfy. He's lying down.

'Anyway, he's got me going proper.'

Hubcaps coughed savagely.

'You really alright?' said the boy.

'I'll, uh, I'll survive,' said Hubcaps. The boy laughed, then looked uneasy.

'Where was I?' he said.

'He's, uh, he's got you going.'

'Yeah, that's right. He has. Got me going proper. I mean, this "Only..." What's it mean, eh? Well I'll tell you what I think it means.

'I think it means; "Hang about." Right? "Hang about, let me live and you won't believe your luck."'

Hubcaps nodded.

'I can see that,' he said.

'I think it means; "Give me this chance and I'll empty my bank into your pockets." You see what I'm saying?'

'Ah ha.' Hubcaps nodded again.

'I think it means; "If you want to retire to Spain and live like a pig in muck for the rest of your life, if you want to be like that bleedin' wonder-boy Rupert, then this is the moment for you, my lad."'

'And, uh, did it mean, uh, all that?'

The boy sighed.

'Did it hell.' He winkled with his knife at the grime behind his nails.

'Er...' Hubcaps nodded in the direction of the knife.

'Oh, right you are, sorry mate.' The boy wiped the blade on his trousers. 'We don't want you getting blood poisoning, do we?'

'Quite,' said Hubcaps. 'There is a code.'

''Sright.' The boy laughed wistfully. 'The Robbers' Code.'

'About the, uh, the bank manager...'

'I unlocks his chains and off he runs. Bit of a bastard eh?'

'Yes,' said Hubcaps. 'Selfish sod really.'

The boy nodded.'Yeah,' he said, 'spoils things for the rest of you, doesn't it? I mean, it's not like I want to tar you all with the same brush.'

'Of course not.'

'It's just, I have to, see. Once bitten twice shy.'

'Quite.'

'So that's alright then, is it?'

Hubcaps nodded.

The boy felt the edge of his knife then took a small piece of whetstone from his pocket and stropped the blade gently against it.

'And no hard feelings, eh?'

In the corridor Dot could at least breathe again. But the Diamond was still bitingly cold.

29

'Are you alright?' said the Runt.

'What do you think?'

'You seem alright. Now.'

'It's this, thing.' Dot held up her hand.

'Well you wanted it strapped in there,' said her niece.

When Dot picked it up, as she was lying in the gutter outside the devastated jewellery shop, the Diamond had been warm, welcoming, inviting. Now it was, not hostile exactly but... Dot groped for understanding.

'It's gone cold.'

It went colder still. It was trying to be more than cold, it was trying to be not there, to be nothing. The cold of nothing is beyond belief. It is also beyond description. Dot did not try.

'Very cold,' she said. 'It wants me to take it away from here. It's hiding from someone.' She was surprised at the thought, which had sprung up from nowhere. 'It's frightened.'

'Look, Aunty...' The Runt was baffled but before she finished, Dot was gone.

'Aunty!' wailed the Runt after Dot's fast disappearing figure.

'It's promised me my hand back,' came one last despairing cry. The Runt gave chase.

Hospitals have more corridors than any other buildings on Earth. Corridors twine through hospitals like worm holes through rose beds of well-rotted manure. And hospital corridors never have stairs, they simply slope, sometimes steeply and sometimes gently but always uphill.

The Runt was toiling up a particularly treacherous gradient between X-ray and the Princess Eugenie Tropical Diseases Wing with Dot nowhere in sight when Harry Devine came slogging uphill in the opposite direction.

Mad Harry was out of breath and he did not know where he was. He knew where he wanted to get to. He had read it in the Diamond's mind. It was just over there, not fifty

30

yards away. But the Diamond's mind had held no map to show him how to get there and the corridors had made him completely confused.

Now into Mad Harry's confusion entered the Runt. He glared at her.

'Burns and General Surgery. Which way?' he said in a voice that made the Runt wish, when she had heard it, that she never had.

'Er, first left, second left, first left, first left, second left and it's second on the right. Not far,' she croaked.

Harry looked away down the corridor, struggling to picture the maniac maze of The Borough hospital. There was something about five lefts in a row that seemed complicated, even to him. He turned back for confirmation but there was none. The Runt had gone.

And who could blame her? thought Harry. These corridors, they just weren't safe.

'So, uh, you knew Rupert then,' said Hubcaps as the boy worked at sharpening his knife.

'Oh yeah, I knew Rupert,' grated the boy.

'He's, uh, been gone quite a while now, hasn't he?' said Hubcaps. 'Years, I, uh, I heard. Soaking up the sun.'

Hubcaps felt quite chatty. At least, that was the impression he was trying to create. But it was difficult creating any kind of an impression when breathing was such hard work. Except an impression of breathlessness. Hubcaps watched the boy carefully.

'I don't want to talk about Rupert,' said the boy. He felt the edge of his blade again, looked happier and carried on sharpening.

'Shan't be long,' he said, 'then we can get on.'

'You were with the Boss then, were you? All those years ago.'

'I've been with the Boss thirty three years,' said the boy, 'come Christmas. Longer than the Axe. Longer than the

31

Sailor, even.'

'Ah,' said Hubcaps. 'Loyalty. Nothing, uh, nothing like it.'

'A fat lot you care about loyalty.'

'Uh, true enough.'

'Being a freelance.' The word was filled with a world of scorn.

Hubcaps bridled.

'They, uh, have their uses, surely?'

The boy thought.

'Nah.' He shook his head. 'None that I can think of.'

'So you wouldn't, uh, like, fancy it yourself then?'

'Nah. There's the security for one thing.' The boy laughed, 'I mean, look at you.'

'You wouldn't, uh, fancy doing a, uh, Rupert, then? Uh, clean up for yourself. Live in the, uh, sun.'

'Look. Leave Rupert out of it, eh?' The boy felt his knife again. 'He was a one-off.'

'Just as, uh, well, from what I've heard.'

'I said, leave him out of it!' The boy glared at Hubcaps then put the whetstone back in his pocket.

'I mean, if they were, uh, all like him, you'd be...'

The boy leapt to his feet and thrust the knife point at Hubcaps's throat.

'Leave Rupert out! Right!'

'But he, uh, he robbed you,' gasped Hubcaps.

'Leave it or I'll...' The boy flourished his knife under Hubcaps's nose. 'I will!'

'Then, uh, then do. My thumbs are killing me.'

'Right then, that's it!' The boy was red with fury. He swung the knife high.

'Only...'

'And don't give me your "Only...'s"!' The knife carved the air in a wide, glittering, backhanded arc. Or it would have done if it had been a more showy and less purposeful knife. In fact it had a black blade, good for night-time use,

32

which had been hollow-ground, good for terrifying sharpness. It whispered through the air like a shadow of the night and what it did was nothing half so crude as carving. Hubcaps's thumb strings parted gratefully under its kiss.

The Runt finally found Dot in the car park.

'You should keep right out of sight, Aunty, if you're hiding,' she said to the pair of feet that was sticking out from under her car.

Dot emerged, scuffing her knees on the gravel as she crawled out backwards. By rights she should have grazed them badly but her stockings were made of sterner stuff than gravel.

'I don't know what got into me,' she said, 'hiding. I've never hidden in my life.'

'Yes,' said her niece, 'but then that's always been the problem, hasn't it?'

Dot scowled.

'So people say, anyway,' added the Runt quickly.

'Look, stop wittering.' Dot held out her hand. 'And get this thing off me.'

The Runt sighed and began to unwrap her aunt's hand.

'I don't know why you wanted it there in the first place,' she said as she worked. 'You could have just put it in your handbag.'

'You're right of course,' said Dot. 'Now just get on with it, eh.'

'So why didn't you then? Put it in your handbag?'

'Oh I don't know,' said Dot. Then she said the first thought that came into her head. 'Paranoia, maybe.'

And where, she wondered instantly, did she get hold of a word like that?

The boy had moved, obviously, since he was astride Hubcap's chest and the knife was back at Hubcaps's throat, but he had moved so fast that Hubcaps never saw a

33

thing. He looked surprised. The boy smiled.

'Gosh,' croaked Hubcaps. 'You're good, aren't you?'

The smile broadened. Without humour.

'Yeah. Very good.'

The smile faded.

'But that's enough about me. I want to hear about you. Tell me about your "Only...".'

4

'Poppy!'

'Yes Woopert?'

'I've decided. I'm going to London.'

'But Woopert...' Poppy came out from the kitchen and leant against the door frame which shimmered as though it was melting. It was the effect Poppy had on most things. In Spain, with the heat, most things were about to melt anyway.

Poppy was pouting.

'You've spent all morning on the silly old telephone, and now you're going to beastly London.' She sighed. 'And I suppose you want me to look after your wotten old Boss tomorrow. Or had you forgotten he was coming?'

'I'll be flying back with him. This really won't take long,' said Rupert. 'A little matter of helping him find something he's lost.'

Or at least, thought Rupert, of finding something that the Boss had lost. And finding it first.

'And anyway, you know you like him really. He's very fond of you.'

Rupert fled towards the bedroom.

'Where did you put my suitcase?'

Poppy followed Rupert to the bedroom with a sinuous motion that had more cat in it than most felines possess in nine lifetimes. A second door frame shivered in the sultry air.

'It's under the bed. Don't you wemember? When we...'

Rupert remembered. There were some things he just couldn't forget, even with all the rough and tumble of life alongside a sex-goddess. He shivered and for once it had nothing to do with Poppy, even though her personality was coiling across the floor at him from the doorway. He was thinking.

Too much honey, he thought, that was his problem. There was probably a name for it. But a short sharp dose of The Borough would sort it all out. And getting one over on the Boss. Rupert smiled. More ruthlessness and less amour would remind him that he was still a gangster.

Hubcaps and the boy had come a long way together, though not in any literal sense. The boy was in the Boss's chair and Hubcaps was stretched flat on the floor with his arms above his head, still too stiff to move.

The boy's name was Rudge. Hubcaps knew this. They had come a long way. Rudge was talking.

'Let me get this straight then. You get the diamond from this old lady you saw...'

'And it was only me saw her, remember. No one else knows what she looks like.'

'...and you give it to me and I give it to the Boss and he's, like, grateful.'

'Or you could...' Hubcaps hesitated to suggest it.

'Or I could go freelance. Clean up for myself. Retire to Spain. Do a Rupert. That's what you're saying, isn't it?'

'Er. Yes.'

'Retire to Spain.' Rudge raised his head and looked into the future and for once the future lay beyond the Boss's office wall. Then his face saddened. There was a cloud on the horizon. There always was.

'But how do I know you'll give me the diamond?' he said.

'Because,' Hubcaps sighed deeply and it was a great

luxury. 'Because a chap has given his word. And a chap has a code.'

Hubcaps's name was not Henry Hampton de Villiard for nothing.

'Ah,' said Rudge, 'I see.'

'You sound doubtful.'

'Well, yeah.'

Hubcaps was only too well aware that chaps called Rudge mistrust chaps called Hampton de Villiard. They had reason to, in Hubcaps's opinion, since times were when de Villiards had hunted Rudges for Saturday afternoon sport. And the chief difference between Rudges and de Villiards was that de Villiards knew this for certain where Rudges could only guess at it. Their ancestors, after all, had not survived to tell the tale.

'I meant, of course,' said Hubcaps, 'that a chap observes the Robbers' Code. Honour among thieves and all that.'

To Rudge this did not sound much better, but maybe he knew more about robbers than Hubcaps. Or maybe he did not. It was time to make up his mind.

He thought of Rupert and he thought of getting even.

'Alright,' he said, 'you're off the hook. For the time being.' He put away his knife and knelt to massage Hubcaps's shoulders.

Rudge had strong hands. They worked Hubcaps's stretched muscles knowledgeably and it felt exquisite. Hubcaps permitted himself the luxury of another sigh.

'Aaah!' It was a great sigh. A sigh to remember.

'Shut up!' said Rudge. 'You don't think I'm doing this for your benefit, do you?'

'Oh yes?' Hubcaps didn't really care. 'Well why then?'

'I'm getting your arms working.' Rudge's fingers dug deep into Hubcaps's trapezius muscles. 'You don't suppose that I make deals without shaking on them, do you?'

'Aaah.' Hubcaps sighed again, and again it felt wonderful. 'I see. The Code.'

The hospital corridors might be a maze, but at least it was a maze with direction signs. Even the Boss and the boys were able to follow the signs from Reception to Burns and General Surgery without too much difficulty. Yet three times as they made the long, uphill journey their path had been crossed by Mad Harry Devine. Each time the Boss shrank back into a doorway behind a discreet screen of boys. It seemed to make sense.

The Boss knew, of course, that it was impossible for Mad Harry to have found out yet who was behind the destruction of his shop. But then the Boss also knew that it was impossible for spilt salt or broken mirrors to have the slightest effect on his future happiness. Somehow just knowing didn't make much difference.

The Boss and the boys sat beside the beds where the Axe and the Sailor had been lain to sleep off the effects of the fireball. A nurse was with them.

'It's no use trying to talk to them, sir,' she said in the standard issue brisk voice. 'They're under sedation. They won't wake up till tomorrow morning.'

The Boss turned and gave the nurse the kind of look that put the boys in mind of thumb strings and feathers.

'Is that right?'

'Yes sir, that's right. So if you wouldn't mind...'

'I can wait.'

'But sir...'

'They might talk in their sleep.'

'Look. Sir. Whatever you want, it's just going to have to wait. These men have experienced severe trauma and what's best for them right now is a good long sleep.'

'That's fine by me.'

'Undisturbed.'

'Undisturbed eh?'

The Boss cuffed the nearest boy, who had just sniffed.

'Undisturbed, you hear?'

The nurse sighed. She had a good feeling that she was beaten but she wasn't ready to leave the battlefield yet. She became conciliatory instead.

'But you know, they really were terribly lucky. And the other gentleman over there, too.' She looked in Vernon's direction. They all looked in Vernon's direction.

'Why,' said a boy, 'what happened to him?'

Smack! went the Boss's hand.

'Ouch!' went the boy.

'Shutup!' said the Boss. 'You want to get us thrown out?' He turned back to the nurse. 'So. What did happen to him?'

Hubcaps and Rudge shook hands. They walked to the door.

'So tell me,' said Rudge. 'Out of curiosity. How did you know about Rupert?'

'I didn't.' Hubcaps smiled. 'I guessed.'

Rudge looked assessingly at Hubcaps and his face was tinged with respect.

'Long odds those, then,' he said. 'To bet your life on.'

'Maybe,' said Hubcaps. 'But high stakes too. Worth playing for, wouldn't you say?' Rudge did not reply. 'So tell me,' Hubcaps went on. 'What exactly did Rupert do to you?'

Rudge looked pained.

'Well. Remember that bank manager I told you about?'

Hubcaps nodded.

'Rupert got him in the end. Squeezed the beggar dry.'

As the nurse finished telling Vernon's story, the Boss dragged his gaze away from where the big man lay in his bed.

'You're right nurse,' he said. 'That's luck. Isn't that luck boys?'

The boys all nodded hard.

'There's been a lot of luck around today, one way and

39

another.' The Boss's voice was gloomy.

'Oh yes? Doesn't sound like much has been coming your way.' In her newly conciliatory mood the nurse tried hard to sound interested but she had been on shift for eighteen hours and, frankly, interested was a bit of a strain. She had been happier on the whole with brisk, but brisk had not had much effect on the Boss either. So maybe she should try bossy. Bossy was often best, in the long run. Bossy got results.

'And now, sir, I really must ask...'

'This old lady...'

'If you would like to come back...'

'The one he fell on.'

'Don't call that luck,' sneered a light, boyish voice in the background. He raised a few sniggers but the Boss chose not to notice. He was trying to think and talk at the same time.

'They'll be waking up in the mor...'

'What did you say her name was?'

'Who? Mrs Coulson, sir?'

'If that's the old woman.'

'She's aunt to one of the staff nurses here. Now I really think that...'

'You don't happen to know where she lives do you?'

'No. And since visiting...'

'It's alright love, the boys are just going. Got that did you boys?' The Boss looked meaningfully at his junior associates.

'Er...' said a chorus of voices.

'Yes Boss,' said the light, boyish voice. 'I got it. Come on lads. No peace for the wicked.'

The light, boyish voice led the rest of the boys off towards the corridor. The Boss was thoughtful as he watched them go. He was good, that one, he was bright. But bright wasn't always best. It needed too much watching.

'And now sir...'

The Boss returned his attention to the nurse. A fifty pound note appeared as if from thin air and hung in front of her nose.

'Look love, I really need to be here when they wake up, alright? So relax, eh.' But he was talking to thin air. The nurse was gone and the air was thick with the reek of disapproval.

The Boss shrugged and the money disappeared as suddenly as it had appeared. A small sigh of relief could be heard from the Boss's wallet. At least it could have been, if the Boss had been a paving stone.

The hired limousine whispered away from the front door.
'Woopert!'
Rupert looked up as Poppy blew him a kiss.
'Love you!' she called.
'Love you too,' said Rupert. His tone was grudging and so was his brief wave out of the window before he instructed the driver to close it. He settled himself comfortably in his seat and did not look back. A day away in London! The prospect was heaven.

Poppy closed the front door and leant back on it with a sigh. Unheard by her, the door sighed too. She contemplated the time she had ahead of her. Twenty four hours of peace. And how she needed it.

'Right,' she said to herself, dropping the sex-goddess speech impediment. 'Let's get on with it then.'

She trailed away towards the bedroom discarding her few clothes on the way. Mini skirts and skimpy knickers were all very well in their place, but their place was not around the human form.

Five minutes later a baggy object in crumpled overalls emerged into the hallway. It paused, lost in thought. The spanners for the Ferrari, where had she put them?

Hubcaps slipped his car gently into gear and, gripping the

steering wheel gingerly on account of his sore thumbs, he eased away from the Boss's office. There had been faster getaways, there had been more dramatic getaways, but, as far as Hubcaps was concerned, there had never been more welcome getaways.

Like Rupert, Hubcaps did not look back. He had successfully given Rudge the slip and it was a well-known fact that looking back has disastrous effects on people who have just made dramatic escapes. So Hubcaps was looking ahead. A long, long way ahead. As far from Rudge, the Boss and the boys as he could get. He smiled at the thought. And the smile widened as he thought of Rudge's trusting faith in him.

If Hubcaps had been Rudge, then he, Hubcaps, would have accompanied him, Rudge, into the lavatory. But Rudge had not. He had trusted to Hubcaps's better nature. And to the Robber's Code. Which just went to show how little he understood either.

Robbers have always been reputed to set great store by their code, but in fact there is nothing very special about it. It is simply an all-purpose, off-the-shelf professional code used by everyone and it says; look after number one because, in this profession, no one does it for you.

In practice there is one tiny detail that distinguishes the Robbers' Code from, say, the Solicitors' Code, the Doctors' Code, or the Double-Glazing Salesmen's Code. It is a tiny detail of cost arising from the fact that robbery is the only profession that didn't actually buy its Code off-the-shelf. At least, that's what the doctors, solicitors and double-glazing salesmen say.

Hubcaps slowed down as he approached a T-junction. Poor old Rudge, he thought. He stopped. Trust was what did it. He looked right. Too much trust held a man back. He looked left.

'Hullo,' said Rudge. He was sitting in the passenger seat.

'But I... You never...' stuttered Hubcaps. 'How did you...'

Rudge smiled.

'Like we said earlier,' he said. 'He's good, the boy, very good. And so.' He looked round brightly at the scenery. 'Where are we off to now, then?'

Dot and the Runt were driving home. The Diamond nestled in Dot's lap, catching the light and shattering it with cold precision like children plucking the wings off flies.

'It was Mad Harry,' said Dot, 'the man you saw. It's his diamond. At least, it came from his shop.'

'But he couldn't have known where it was already. Could he?'

'He knew alright. And the Diamond was scared.' Dot looked into the Runt's eyes. ' That's Harry for you.'

'So you should throw it away, if he's that dangerous.'

'Uh uh. How often does one of these fall into your lap?'

Dot gazed lovingly at the Diamond and the Runt laughed.

'And this is the woman who got into all this by deciding to clean up The Borough. Pavement parking. I ask you. When it boils down to it, you're just as bad as the rest of them.'

'It was something I could manage, at least. And as for cleaning up The Borough. Just think how much polish this thing would buy.'

The Runt glanced across at her Aunt.

'You mean that you'd...'

The old woman nodded.

'It's a thought, isn't it?'

'No one would thank you.'

'Maybe not,' said Dot. 'But they'd know.'

The two women drove along in silence for a short while. The silence was broken by the Runt.

'So.' She glanced across at her aunt. 'What happens now?'

Dot gave her niece a long, thoughtful stare.

'You're in then, are you?' she said.

The Runt shrugged.

'Someone's got to look after you.'

Dot laughed.

'Then make sure you do.'

A fresh silence was again broken by the Runt.

'Well? What does happen now?'

'We begin,' said Dot, 'by keeping one step ahead of the opposition. Whoever they may be.'

In Burns and General Surgery everything was still. Patients dozed or lay watching the ceiling, turning cracks into nightmares that would return to haunt their sleep.

The Boss remained close to the Axe and the Sailor but he was watching Vernon Carpenter. This was more fascinating than watching the ceiling but it was also more worrying. At least, it was with what the Boss had in mind. Even asleep Vernon Carpenter was as plausible a nightmare as any cracked plaster.

The Boss was hesitating. Someone who had been at the scene of the explosion must have the Diamond. It could just as well be Vernon as anyone else. So somewhere in or around that bed the Diamond might be hidden, waiting for him to rescue it.

The Diamond wanted the Boss. It had told him so. And it was a neat fit since the Boss wanted the Diamond. And maybe all that was needed to make everybody happy was for the Boss to search Vernon's bed. Everybody except Vernon of course. But tramps weren't meant to be happy. It wasn't in their job spec.

The thing that made the Boss hesitate was the possibility that Vernon might wake up. The longer he waited though, the more likely that was to happen.

'Nothing ventured, nothing gained,' the Boss reminded himself. His feet did not move.

'He who hesitates is lost,' he assured himself. His back-side sullenly refused to rise from its chair.

'Faint heart never won fair jewel,' he said, more loudly. And now, finally, he moved.

There were screens at the end of the ward. The Boss arranged them around Vernon's bed only to discover that, shut in and at close quarters, the sleeping giant was more intimidating than ever. He exuded strength like a lion. Casually.

The bed shook. An arm was hoisted out from under the sheets and flopped onto the coverlet. Vernon sighed. The Boss froze. So much arm, so little effort. But also, you don't break omelettes without wasting eggs. He took a step forward, reaching out for the bedclothes.

'Nothing hesitates never wins,' he mumbled.

Not far away Mad Harry Devine was slumped in a small, pitiful heap in a corner of a distant, deserted corridor. A constant mumbling noise came out of the heap.

'First left, second left, first left, first left, second left and second on the right.

'First left, second left, first left...' Harry looked up. There was the sound of approaching footsteps, the first in what felt like hours.

Harry held his hand out in an imploring gesture.

'Burns and General Surgery, which way? Please?'

The Boss's boys stopped and stared at Mad Harry. As one man they shrugged. Then a light, boyish voice said,

'Why not follow the signs? We did.'

The boys disappeared along the corridor and Harry watched them go with a sour expression on his face.

Follow the signs! Why did everyone tell him to follow the signs? Fools. Didn't they know about signs?

'Look, can't I drop you off somewhere?'

Hubcaps spoke with circumspection. He may not have

known Rudge for long, but he knew enough to know that Rudge had a forceful personality – the force being ten inches of razor-sharp, matt-black steel. Put a few hundred miles between him and Rudge and he could take a relaxed view of a personality like that. But while he was sitting right beside it, circumspection was definitely the thing.

'After all. You must have, er, things to be getting on with? Places to go, people to see to?'

Rudge reached into the inner recesses of his jacket and took out an empty fag packet. He read one side of it, turned it over, read the other side and shook his head.

'Nah. All I've got here is, "dispose of corpse." See?' Rudge held the empty packet out to Hubcaps but Hubcaps was concentrating on driving and took Rudge's word for it.

'And I wonder whose corpse, eh?' Rudge grinned and the fag packet disappeared back into the inner recesses. He patted his jacket.

'Marvellous thing that, you know. Personal organiser. I'm lost without it. And the blokes what sell them make a packet, they say.' He waited for Hubcaps to laugh but Hubcaps didn't feeling like laughing.

'Never mind,' said Rudge. 'Where was I?'

'Dispose of corpse,' muttered Hubcaps.

'Oh yeah. Well.' Rudge gave Hubcaps a long hard stare. 'You're the liveliest corpse I ever saw. But then, it's never too late, is it? To slow a corpse down.' He patted Hubcaps's arm confidingly. 'Never too late.'

At the touch of Rudge's hand, Hubcaps shut his eyes. There was something about being touched by a hand that only shortly before was going to kill you that...

'Look out, eh!' said Rudge. The touch on Hubcaps's arm disappeared. Hubcaps opened his eyes.

A red light shone threateningly at the side of the road. A pedestrian was stepping out on the rash assumption that cars stopped at red lights. Other cars were pulling across the junction ahead. Hubcaps hit the brakes. Rudge laughed.

'Steady! We don't want the cops taking an interest.'

Normally Hubcaps's carelessness would have angered Rudge. It would have been one more example of the fecklessness of freelances. But not today. Today, for the first time in his life, Adnan Rudge was going places and his heart was young and gay.

He looked around at the scenery, again. It was the usual Borough bleakness but there was one bright spot in it.

'Cor,' said Rudge, 'take a look at that.' Hubcaps looked. On the other side of the lights a battered old car was at the head of the queue. It had grimy wheels, grimy paintwork, grimy windows and so many corners knocked off that its builders would no longer have known it.

Hubcaps noticed all this because he had a professional interest in cars. But Rudge?

'Look at what?'

'Her! Just look at her. Shining out through that windscreen like a beacon in a wicked world.'

'Eh?'

'Her!'

As far as Hubcaps could see, the girl that Rudge was talking about merely had what are politely called 'regular features'. Hubcaps himself wouldn't have given her a second glance if it hadn't been for... He glanced a second time, more closely. If it hadn't been for the old woman she was talking to.

'You like her then, do you?' he asked calmly.

'Like her!'

To Rudge in his new found optimism the Runt was the glory of creation. She was laughing. Her eyes sparkled. Her skin glowed. Her full lips were parted to show teeth of translucent pearl. But there was a lack of approval in Hubcaps's voice that somehow implied criticism.

'You know what your problem is? You don't know class when you see it. That's your problem. She's class.'

Hubcaps did not reply. Rudge became less certain. He was embarrassed now by Hubcaps's indifference.

'You don't think so?'

Hubcaps shook his head and at that moment the Runt looked across towards them. She saw two pairs of male eyes fixed on her, and one male head shaking slowly and positively.

'Hey, look out, she's looking.' Rudge's embarrassment grew. He looked away. 'No call to stare like that,' he mumbled

Behind them horns sounded and voices began to shout. In front of them the lights were green. The Runt drove past Hubcaps's car and he watched her dwindling in the rear view mirror.

'Come on,' said Rudge, 'are we going?'

'Oh yes,' said Hubcaps, 'I think so. Hold on.'

There were two dull thuds – one as the accelerator hit the floor, the other as the steering wheel hit the limits of its lock – then no more. All sound was lost in the upwelling of noise that was Hubcaps's car being given its head.

Rudge saw hands frozen on horns that had been impatient for progress only seconds before. He saw terror in the faces of oncoming drivers as Hubcaps swung wide in a U-turn across their path, saw the world spin around him and felt power thrusting him back in his seat. He saw all this and felt all this but...

'Hey! She wasn't that great,' was all he said.

No one heard him.

5

Mad Harry Devine had found a small, dark hole to crawl into and he was taking the opportunity to lick his wounds. The wounds were all psychological, but there was still comfort in licking them.

Harry had spent the afternoon failing to unlock the secrets of the corridors and the wasted hours felt like a lifetime. He had a brilliant mind and he knew it, so to be defeated by a corridor was wounding.

It was more wounding still that the corridors were man-made. Merely man-made was a better description. Made by mere men. After all, who the hell builds hospitals? Architects, dammit. And Harry had met architects.

He curled up more tightly and the dark warmth of his hidey-hole was comforting, womb-like, primordial.

The midwife in the delivery room noticed a slight twitch of the bed cover where it hung close to the floor. She lifted up the thin cloth to investigate and found herself looking straight into Mad Harry's startled eyes.

Many women would have fainted or screamed. But the souls of Scots midwives are forged from billets of iron.

'Oh no you don't. I know your sort. So out you come my lad!' The words were delivered with that peculiarly loving firmness of tone which is reserved exclusively to the profession of midwifery. But there was nothing firm or loving about the hold the midwife had on Harry's leg as she dragged him kicking and squealing into the harsh light of the delivery room.

'And you can thank you lucky stars,' she went on as she dragged him into the corridor and flung him away like a curling stone, 'that I've other things to be doing than seeing properly to you.' She turned back quickly and shut the door as a terrifying scream sounded from inside.

'Now then my lass.' The midwife began and at the sound of her voice the screaming died away. 'We don't want any more of that, thank you very much.'

Harry rose to his feet, wrapped his arms across his chest and looked around. He was cold, disorientated and uncomfortable but then birth, he reflected, is always hell.

Birth was the thought furthest from the Boss's mind right now. He was at the other end of life's continuum. At least, he was afraid of ending up there, any minute now.

The Boss's little adventure in Vernon's bedspace had gone hideously wrong. He was unsure about quite how it happened, but he had ended up with his head locked under Vernon's arm. Vernon was still asleep and nothing the Boss could do would wake him. With his face crushed into Vernon's sweaty armpit, the Boss was suffocating. Or maybe drowning. And he was frightened. Frightened as hell.

The Boss did not really believe in hell. At least he did not want to. The afterlife he wanted for himself was very empty and very still and very unlike the afterlife that everyone promised was waiting, just for him.

But whatever the afterlife was, he would be experiencing it quite soon unless he did something about it. The thought made him want to scream. But he could not. It made him want to gouge Vernon's eyes. And he could not. Finally it just made him want to panic, and even that he could only manage with difficulty.

He blacked out. Or maybe just died. It was a simple transition.

Fires roared, demons danced and the wailing of lost souls filled the air with a sound very like 'Abide With Me'.

'Oh well,' muttered the Boss as he took in his new surroundings, 'can't win every time.'

The screens around Vernon's bed were thrust efficiently to one side. A crisp, starched figure rustled up to the bedside.

'Now then,' she said in a voice which could never be surprised by anything that patients got up to, 'what on earth is going on here then?'

The Runt's shapeless little car drew nervously to a halt outside Dot's house. It had mixed feelings about stopping there.

Fifty yards back down the street Hubcaps's car eased to a halt with even greater reluctance. This was understandable. It had more to lose than the Runt's car. Life still owed it some fun.

The cars looked cautiously around. All around them the bones of other cars sprinkled the ground like mechanical confetti, but that wasn't what they were looking at. That was too painful. What they were looking at were the corners, the low walls, the little alleys between the houses, the places where the do-it-yourself mechanics lurk. Judging from the state of the street, the place must be thick with them.

They wouldn't actually see them, of course. No one sees the DIY mechanics. Only their handiwork. If they can bear to look.

Nothing moved.

'Well?' said Rudge.

Hubcaps said nothing. He watched the Runt's car. Rudge watched him.

'Is this it?'

Hubcaps shrugged.

'You could ask her to dance,' he suggested.

Rudge went red in the face. He wanted to express his feelings but years of subservience to the Boss and politeness to clients, so necessary in those precious final moments, had robbed him of the words for outrage.

Hubcaps watched him sympathetically. Freelances never lose the words for outrage. Freelances use them all the time. This was the wrong moment to discuss this with Rudge, though. He tried something else.

'I thought you liked her,' he said.

'Yeah well.' Rudge looked out of the window. 'Maybe. But she's not what we're after, is she?'

'Oh I don't know,' said Hubcaps, 'seems to me like...'

Hubcaps stopped talking and stared at the Runt's car. It had started rocking from side to side. It carried on rocking, more and more until, when it seemed certain the car would roll over, a door flew open and Dot burst out onto the pavement.

'A bit of oil on that wouldn't hurt,' she said as she slammed the door. 'See you later then,' she shouted.

Dot stood and watched as the Runt turned her car around, in what Hubcaps noted was a six-point turn, and drove away. Watching in his mirror, Hubcaps could have sworn he saw the car skip as it disappeared round the corner at the top of the road.

'Well?' Rudge turned back from watching the car go. There was a dog-like expression on his face. 'If we're following her, shouldn't we...'

'Uh uh,' said Hubcaps. He smiled. 'Though later maybe. If you want.'

Dot was entering one of the narrow-fronted houses.

'You see, we were actually following her.'

Rudge looked puzzled then his face lit up. Not a pretty sight.

'The old lady?'

Hubcaps nodded.

'But how...' Rudge was relieved and impressed. 'How'd

you find her?'

Hubcaps looked nonchalant.

'Skill. Determination. And knowledge of the game.'

'Ah.' Rudge nodded. 'Pure luck then.'

Hubcaps eased the car into gear.

'Come on,' he said, 'we're going visiting.'

The Boss's boys clustered around a telephone box, trying to hear what was going on inside.

'I still don't get why we couldn't just go to the office,' said a plaintive voice.

'Sssh!' said a chorus of voices, 'we can't hear.'

'It's cold enough out here to freeze the balls...'

'Sssh!'

'Now there's an interesting thing,' said a deadpan voice, 'I don't suppose you know where that say...'

'Ssh!'

'I was only...'

'Shut up!'

Inside the telephone box the light, boyish voice hung up looking pleased with itself.

'Gah! Now look what you've gone and done,' said the chorus of voices, 'He's only gone and finished hasn't he? We never heard a thing.'

The light boyish voice came out and stood smiling at its colleagues.

'Right boys,' it said, 'we're going visiting. Follow me!'

The light, boyish voice set off along the road at a brisk trot and the boys began to follow. They were brought to a halt by the deadpan voice.

'Just a minute, what's all this "boys"?' Who's he think he is?'

'Yeah. 'Sright,' said the chorus thoughtfully, 'It's lads to him. Who's he think he is?'

'And all this "follow me" lark. Giving orders. Who's he think he is?'

'Yeah! Who's he think he is?'

'And he never said "please",' said the plaintive voice getting in on the act.

''Sright,' said the chorus. 'And he never did.'

'And what's the hurry anyway?' said the deadpan voice, 'We're not bleedin' greyhounds.'

'Yeah,' said the chorus, ''Sright. We're not.' There was a long pause.

'He's gone now anyway,' said the deadpan voice. 'He'll probably get that diamond and keep it for himself.'

'Yeah,' said the chorus, 'he'll probably...' and then it woke up.

'Bleedin' hell!' The chorus looked wildly round but the light, boyish voice was nowhere in sight.

'It's only what we all had in mind anyway,' said the deadpan voice. It took a compact sub-machine gun from inside its coat. 'Only none of you got onto the winning team.'

For once the chorus was speechless. It stood in a deeply offended huddle in the middle of the pavement while the fast developing rush-hour crowd flowed silently round it at a respectful distance. Resentment crackled through heavy clouds of thought sparking occasional murmurs of ''Sright!' and 'Yeah!'

The mood was broken by the plaintive voice.

'So what do we do now then?'

The deadpan voice indicated the telephone box with the barrel of its gun.

'You play sardines,' it said.

The doorbell rang again. Impatiently. And who could blame it? It had rung six times already, each time longer than the time before, and it wasn't its fault that Dot hadn't come. So where, it wanted to know, was the point in ringing again?

Dot was not surprised that the door bell was ringing. She had expected that it would. Old women don't go lifting expensive diamonds without expecting that, sooner or later, someone will come looking for them.

She wished they hadn't come quite so soon, though. She wasn't ready for them.

'Coming,' she called weakly, standing in front of the mirror in the hall. 'Coming.'

On the other side of the door a thumb rested on the bell push yet again.

'Right, that's it,' said the doorbell. 'I've had enough.' It bit the thumb, hard.

Hubcaps leapt backwards.

'Bloody thing!' he said. 'It bit me.'

'Eh?' said Rudge.

'Electric shock or something, I suppose.' Hubcaps sucked his thumb. 'Bloody thing.'

Rudge sighed deeply. If you wanted a job doing... He pushed Hubcaps gently to one side and held his thumb out towards the bell.

Dot inspected her appearance critically.

'Hmm. More tomato sauce, I think.'

She shook a blob of sauce from the bottle in her hand, rubbed it into the front of her blouse and checked the overall effect.

'Perfect. That's the stains done then.' She hurried into the kitchen, put the sauce bottle away, and returned to the mirror.

'Now for the hair.'

A muffled scream came from outside.

'Are you alright?' said Hubcaps.

'Little bleeder!' said Rudge. 'It bit me.'

With exquisite care Dot dragged long, straggling strands from out of her neatly arranged hair and hung them in studious disarray around her face.

'That'll do.'

Dot assumed a cronish posture in front of the mirror and twisted her face into a terrifying mask.

'Mirror mirror on the wall, who is ugliest hag of all?'

She laughed and started limping heavily towards the door.

'Coming,' she called weakly. 'Coming.'

'So what was the point in asking,' muttered the mirror to itself, 'if you don't even wait for the an answer?' It sighed. That was life as a mirror all over.

Outside, Rudge was nursing his thumb.

'Break it down!' He nodded at the door. 'Just break the bleedin' thing down.' Hubcaps coughed gently and stepped forward. He glanced over his shoulder at Rudge and then knocked, gently.

The door swung open to the limits of its chain. Dot's head appeared at the crack.

'Yes?' she said in her most piteous old lady's voice.

'Er...' began Hubcaps.

Rudge sighed, straightened his tie, pushed Hubcaps aside and bowed.

'We're from the council, ma'am,' he said, 'may we come in?'

'Got your identification, have you?' said Dot, ageing ten years with every word.

'Identification ma'am?' Rudge looked puzzled.

'Your card. Saying who you are.'

'Er.' Rudge fumbled in his pockets and shrugged. 'Not as such.' He looked to Hubcaps for support. 'Card?' he said.

'I can't speak to you then, can I?' said Dot. She shoved the door to shut it but it would not budge. Although Dot had seen nothing move the door was blocked by a foot. She looked at Rudge with respect and he twinkled knowingly back at her. He was good, the boy, very good. And he knew it.

'Be a good girl and act your age, eh,' he said. He gave the door a shove. 'Just open up.'

There was a sudden movement as Dot's heel came down on Rudge's toe. The pain was appalling.

'Lor'!' Dot leapt backwards, clutching her foot. 'What have you got in there? Bricks?'

Rudge smiled. Whoever invented steel toecaps deserved a medal for service to industry. His knife appeared in his hand.

'Hey! Hold on a minute!' said Hubcaps.

'Stand back!' said Rudge. 'We're coming in.'

The door chain was tough but it was no match for Rudge's knife. It gave up the unequal struggle with a sigh and tumbled in fragments to the ground.

Rudge turned to Hubcaps. 'Okay? Ready?'

Hubcaps looked at the knife.

'Er,' said Hubcaps, 'I usually wait outside to, er, look after...' He nodded at the car. Rudge laughed, bittersweet, and shook his head ruefully.

'Freelances,' he sighed. The knife disappeared and Rudge swung the front door fully open.

'Get inside,' he said. 'I don't want you disappearing again, do I?'

Hubcaps managed to look insulted.

'And anyway,' said Rudge, 'you may learn something.'

'Right,' said the light, boyish voice. He started the engine of the minibus as the deadpan voice climbed up in front beside him. 'Any problems?'

'No,' said the deadpan voice flatly. He turned leaden eyes on the light, boyish voice and the light, boyish voice felt them weigh on his soul.

'Shall we go?'

The minibus rolled forward and stopped, waiting to join the heavy High Street traffic. The deadpan voice smiled coldly as he caught sight of the chorus. They were crammed into the telephone box, which had a thin, steel chain wrapped tightly round it.

'On then,' said the light, boyish voice. 'On to fame and fortune.' There was a chill pause.

'Yeah, well,' he said, embarrassed by his outburst. 'Fortune anyway, eh?'

The deadpan voice said nothing. He only smiled. Beneath his coat the sub-machine gun nestled against his leg and the smile warmed at the thought of it.

In the telephone box the mood was tense. The voices of the chorus no longer sang in unison. Instead they had taken on a rat-like quality, something to do with stress.

'Get your bleedin' foot off my...' The instruction expired in a gasp of pain.

'When I get hold of them I'm going to...'

'What? You're going to what? Smart arse.'

'If we get hold of them. Where have they gone? Does anyone know?'

'They've gone to the old lady's, haven't they, to get themselves a diamond.'

'Oh! Smart! Well done Einstein. But where's that, eh?'

'Anyone know what her name was? The old lady?' said the calmest of the rat-voices. 'We could ring directory enquiries, like they did, couldn't...'

'Look, can't we just...'

Somewhere in the middle of the crush a body began to struggle furiously. Very furiously. It was, it suddenly realised, fighting for life. Those closest to the furious body tried to move away but there was nowhere to go. The walls of the box bulged under the strain. The chain creaked and groaned and... stretched. A small gap appeared round the edge of the door. Fresh air trickled in, unwillingly. Willing or not though, it had a soothing effect. At least on those closest to it.

'Anyone got any bolt croppers?' said a reasonably calm rat-voice. 'I think I might just be able...'

'The old lady's name. Someone must know.'

'Bolt croppers? Anyone?'

There was a last tempestuous struggle from the heart of

the crush and then stillness. The boys observed a few moments of respectful silence. Then, 'Bolt croppers?' said a small voice and at last someone responded.

'Here mate. They're only little though.'

Ten pounds of case-hardened steel slipped between struggling bodies on its way to the door.

'Pass 'em along!'

'Pass 'em along.'

Elsewhere lips moved painfully slowly as a boy struggled to read a notice on the wall with his nose pressed against it.

'Is it, Di-rec-tor-y En...'

'Yeah Einstein. What's the number? And pass the phone this way, eh. And does anyone remember her name?'

Beside the door a boy was labouring to get the bolt croppers onto the chain.

'Oi, stop shoving, I'm nearly...'

There was a deeply satisfying crunch as the chain parted and the boys exploded onto the street. The relief was wonderful.

Two bodies remained on the floor. They had stopped breathing. Their relief was permanent.

Only one body remained standing. It clutched the phone and looked surprised. The phone squawked at it.

'Directory enquiries, what name?' The body was startled.

'Er...' he said in his rat-voice.

'What name please?'

'Er...' Rat-voice poked his head out of the telephone box. 'Oi! Anyone! What was her name?'

The Runt swerved her car violently to avoid a flood of bodies tumbling unexpectedly from a telephone box. They were men. Most were large though some were small and rat-like and they spilled out in an unstoppable stream. They poured onto the pavement until the pile of bodies had created a dam and the last of them rolled in a foaming backwash out across the road.

Horns sounded, cars swerved, tyres screeched and drivers sat with their hands over their eyes wishing they were somewhere else, somewhere safe and peaceful, like Silverstone say, during the Grand Prix.

In spite of the confusion there were few real crashes. Most cars are well up to the job of keeping themselves intact. Left alone they do nothing else. So it is mostly drivers that cause accidents. But only when the cars cannot prevent it.

The Runt's car watched as one of its brethren hit a lamp post and another went through the boarded-up front of a tobacconist's shop. They would be blamed, of course.

'On Wednesday evening,' the paper would say, 'a car hit a lamp post while another left the road and entered a tobacconist after...' But would the cars that stopped take any credit?

'Most drivers remained calm,' the report would go on. 'They halted their vehicles safely, avoiding serious injury and further damage.'

The Runt's car stood looking at the mess and considered the yet-to-be-written news story. It was not fair, it thought, but then life was not fair, was it? It had not made the Runt's car a Rolls-Royce for starters.

'Gee up!' said the Runt. The car sighed. Not a Rolls-Royce was one thing, but 'Gee up'? Was that really what it all came down to?

'Clip clop,' it muttered as it pulled away. 'Clip bleedin' clop.'

The Runt was thoughtful too. She glanced at the seat beside her where Aunty Dot's bag sat, solidly immobile. Inside the bag was the Diamond.

If the Runt had read the gleam in Aunty Dot's eyes correctly that diamond was worth a fortune. And not a small fortune either, but a great, big, hulking, serious-minded fortune.

And now it was the Runt's. Or it could be. And oddly enough, once the thought had surfaced it seemed to grow and fill her head with pictures. And the pictures were not about nursing.

There were worse things than nursing of course. People who weren't nurses never tired of telling her so. But there were better things too.

There was, for instance, sunshine. There was sunshine in Aunty Dot's bag and one little peek wouldn't hurt, would it? Not just one little peek.

'Whoa!' said the Runt quietly.

She was not sure whether she had really wanted to speak. She was not sure whether she really wanted to open the bag and take out the Diamond and look into its inner fire. She would be captivated by it. That was the problem. And she was not sure if that might not somehow be wrong. So she said 'Whoa,' quietly. And if anyone heard, then it wasn't down to her.

The car heard all right. Some words it heard before they were spoken. Anything, for example, that meant something like 'stop'. It pulled quickly into the side of the road before the Runt could change her mind. She was good at changing her mind.

Carefully, very carefully, Dot put her foot back on the floor.

'Shut the door,' said Rudge to Hubcaps. Hubcaps pushed the front door but it jammed against the fragments of chain that littered the carpet. He tried to sweep the bits of metal to one side with his foot but they caught in the shaggy pile and he had to go down on his hands and knees to pick them up. Rudge hissed impatiently.

Dot's foot hurt like hell but otherwise it seemed all right. She sighed with relief, quietly, no bones were broken. Feeling comforted about her foot she turned her attention to other matters more pressing. The most pressing was the man in her hallway who had used a knife to get in. He looked extremely dangerous.

The other man was not such a problem. Any villain who so carefully tidied her carpet, Dot felt, was more of a pussy cat than a tiger.

Dot even felt a little sorry for Hubcaps. If he tried shutting the door now, she thought, it would probably go but there he was, still patiently picking at little bits of metal. She wondered idly how such a nice looking boy had got involved in all this, but there was no time for much idleness. The main thing at the moment was to make sure what 'all this' was about. As if she couldn't guess.

'What do you want?' she quavered in a frail, elderly voice. 'I'm only a poor old woman. There's no money in the house. Nothing worth taking at all.'

'Oh that's alright love,' said Hubcaps looking over his shoulder, 'we're not after money.'

'Shut up!' said Rudge. 'Shut the door and shut up.

'And you.' He glowered at Dot. 'Quit cowering. I've met your sort before.'

'Oh yes?' quailed Dot. She had no intention of dropping her camouflage yet.

'Yeah!' Rudge advanced till he was nose to nose with Dot. 'All sweet little old lady to your face, and stab you in the back soon as look at you.'

Rudge looked straight into Dot's eyes. Dot looked back. Rays of understanding lanced from eyeball to eyeball. Dot sighed and straightened up.

'Yes, well, alright,' she grumbled, acknowledging Rudge's victory. 'Not that I'd stab you in the back myself. You must be thinking about a friend of mine. I use a truncheon.' She smoothed down her dress and looked regretfully at the stains, now drying hard on the front of it.

'That's better,' said Rudge. His hand was still hovering, ready to reach for his knife. 'And don't go trying anything on. Right?' He cast a quick glance in Hubcaps's direction. 'There's been enough people trying things on for one day.'

Dot smiled and hoped it was disconcerting.

'Yes alright,' she said. 'Relax.' She held up empty hands. 'You're the pro after all and I'm just the enthusiastic amateur. And that knife of yours.' Dot allowed awed respect to enter her voice. 'That's something else.'

The flattery relaxed Rudge immediately. He even smiled. 'You think so?'

'I know so.' Dot rubbed her hands together. 'Now, how about a nice cup of tea while we talk things over?' She turned to Hubcaps. 'And shut that door eh, there's a dear. The draught here's something wicked.' Hubcaps looked uncertainly at the last few fragments of metal in the carpet.

'Oh, leave those, I'll get the Hoover to them later,' said

Dot Rudge caught Hubcaps's eye and shook his head gently. There would be no time for hoovering. Hubcaps sighed and bent again to his task. Who would have guessed, he thought, that a broken door chain could be so awkward. It was as if, in death, it was continuing to serve its mistress as it had in life. Only it was keeping the door open now, for the easier ejection of intruders.

Hubcaps's thought came nearer the truth than he knew. Security devices have an almost canine loyalty built in. All of them. Except the renegades.

'Tea then,' said Rudge. 'Kitchen this way, is it?'

'Sugar?' Dot handed Rudge his tea.

Rudge sipped.

'No, thanks, I'm sweet enough already.'

He put his cup down carefully.

'Aah, there's nothing like it, is there?'

He looked around the kitchen.

'Nice little place you've got here. Very nice.'

'You think so?'

'I know so.'

Dot smiled.

'So it'd be a shame, wouldn't it, if anything happened to it.'

'Yes.' Dot sounded thoughtful. 'It would at that. I'd be upset. Really upset. You're not thinking that anything will happen to it, are you?'

Rudge picked up his cup, sipped again and set it down.

'Well now, that all...'

From the front of the house came the sounds of the front door opening then closing. Rudge dashed for the hallway.

Hubcaps watched with wide-eyed innocence as Rudge appeared from out of the kitchen, knife in hand.

'Anything up?' he said. He swung the front door to and fro. 'It's alright now, all done. See?' He shut the door. 'And I hope,' he said, wandering past Rudge into the kitchen, 'that there's still tea left for me. It's been quite a day, what with one thing and another.'

'Yeah.' Rudge put his knife away and followed Hubcaps. 'And it's not finished yet. Mate.'

In the kitchen Hubcaps shook the fragments of chain in his hand and looked enquiringly at Dot.

'Oh, just put then in the rubbish,' she said. 'There look, in the corner.'

'Proper little mother's help,' Rudge snarled. He sat down again.

'Yes,' said Dot innocently. 'I like that in a man.' She turned to Hubcaps.

'Why don't you just sit there look, and I'll pour you some tea. Now you take sugar, I know.'

Hubcaps smiled pleasantly.

'Yes please. Two.'

'There you are you see.' Dot turned briefly to Rudge. 'Two sugars. Sweet as he is.'

'I need to keep my strength up,' said Hubcaps. 'You never know when you're going to need it.'

'Shut up!'

Rudge stood up, violently.

'Shut up the pair of you! I've had a-bleedin-nough of this.'

'But...' Dot looked startled.

'I said 'Shut up!''

Rudge picked up his cup and flung it at the wall. The thick liquid smeared down in an orange-brown stain to the floor. Dot stared at him in amazement.

'What did you go and do that for?' she said.

Rudge leant forward and his knife was suddenly pointing at Dot's heart.

'A cup of tea, you said, not a bleedin' tea party. Chat, chat, chat. We didn't come for a tea party. Right?'

No one said anything.

'Right.' Rudge relaxed slightly. 'And now. About this diamond.'

'Diamond?' said Dot. But she was too quick. She cursed herself immediately. Of all the things she could have said, 'Diamond?' was the stupidest. And of all the expressions she could have made, that pathetic, wide-eyed innocence was the worst. Rudge would know now for certain that she knew what he was talking about. And, after this pause, he would know that she knew he knew.

'That's it.' Rudge nodded, smiling. 'Diamond. I see you know the score.' He paused. 'Well?'

He was good. She had to give him that. He was very good. But she was good too. Or she would be, if she could think straight. But there was this air about Rudge, and about Rudge's knife, that was surprisingly off-putting. Dot picked up her tea, took a sip and put the cup down again. The sipping was meant to give her time to think, but all it did was leave her upset at the way the cup rattled when it hit the saucer. She took a deep breath.

'So what's your interest in it then?' she said. 'After all, it's not like it's yours or anything, is it?'

Rudge took the knife away from the area of Dot's heart and, very, very carefully, laid it across the side of her neck.

'No,' he hissed. 'It's not mine.' He looked at Hubcaps. 'And it's not his neither. But we've been sent to get it. And what we do with it then is our business. Alright?'

'Alright,' whispered Dot, resisting the impulse to nod vigorously.

'So. I'll ask you again. What about it?'

'Well...'

'Yes?'

'You'd like me to be honest I suppose?'

Hubcaps eyes sparkled as he watched the scene in front of him. Rudge may be good, but this old woman was something else. Nonchalance. How did she know that Rudge's weak spot was nonchalance?

'Yes. Be honest. It's best.'

'Well, I haven't got it.'

Rudge considered this. He smiled.

'But you know where it is though, don't you?'

'Er...'

'The truth, okay?'

'Okay.' Dot swallowed and felt the blade kiss her throat more warmly. 'I don't know where it is,' she said.

She stared hard at Rudge and prayed that he could not tell the difference between a whole truth that was only half true and a half truth that was wholly true. If there were such things. If she had got them the right way round. If she... She was rambling.

The Diamond was in her handbag and her handbag was in the Runt's car and Dot certainly didn't know where the Runt's car... A thought suddenly struck her and she was so horrified by it that it took her mind right off her present predicament. She sat bolt upright.

'The little minx! She wouldn't dare.'

But she would, thought Dot. At twenty two Dot would have had the Diamond away for herself and the Runt was born of the same blood. She had been cast in the same mould. Dot sighed. She could say goodbye forever to her idea of cleaning up the Borough. Ah well. Easy come, easy go. And perhaps, just perhaps, it was all for the best. The Runt was young. The money would be more use to her in the long run. And it was useless crying over spilt milk. Suddenly warm with a flood of generous sentiments, Dot wished her niece well and then allowed her mind to return to her kitchen. Warmth. That was the thing. And then she was puzzled. Warm was all very well, but should she be feeling moist too? She looked down. Blood covered the shoulder of her dress and was beginning to stain the top of her sleeve.

'Oh God,' sighed Dot and she fell to the floor in a faint.

Rudge's knife was so sharp that Dot never felt a thing

when it cut her. But Rudge and Hubcaps both reacted with horror to the blood oozing from the long shallow wound on Dot's neck.

'Silly cow,' said Rudge, going into a panic. 'What did she want to do that for?'

'Pass me that tea-towel,' said Hubcaps urgently. He had one hand pressed firmly against Dot's wound and was cradling her head with his other hand, trying to make her more comfortable. 'And now find me some more.' He sniffed at the dirty rag that Rudge had passed him. 'Clean ones.'

Rudge went round the kitchen, pulling drawers onto the floor and scattering the contents of cupboards.

'There aren't any more,' he said eventually. 'I've looked everywhere.'

Hubcaps took in the destruction and sighed.

'Then try upstairs. There must be an airing cupboard or something. Bring sheets, towels, anything.'

When Rudge came back Dot was awake and sitting up.

'Is she going to be alright?' he asked.

'No thanks to you,' said Dot. 'Playing silly beggars with knives.'

Rudge looked sheepish.

'Never had no accidents before,' he muttered. 'Must be what comes of working with amateurs.' He passed Hubcaps an armful of assorted laundry and sat to watch as the freelance dressed Dot's wound.

'You've done that before,' he said.

'One of the perks of driving,' said Hubcaps distractedly, 'putting robbers back together when things go wrong.' He patted Dot's arm.

'You'll need some stitches in that. We'll take you to hospital, unless...' He turned to Rudge. 'Unless you've got any objections?'

'Boss has gone to the hospital,' muttered Rudge who in any case felt out of place when it came to putting people back together.

'Then we'll have to keep out of his way, won't we?' Hubcaps turned back to Dot. 'Are you ready to go?'

'The sooner the better dearie,' said Dot weakly. 'The sooner the better.'

'Good.' Hubcaps patted her arm again. 'That's it, we'll have you there in no time.'

Rudge opened the front door and stood back to let Hubcaps pass with Dot leaning against him. The procession crept only a little way down the garden path before coming to a complete stop. They all stared at Hubcaps's car, what was left of it.

'But we've not been quarter of an hour!' protested Rudge in outrage. Hubcaps looked at his car. What was left of it. A tear trickled down his cheek.

'I said I should stay and watch it,' he muttered. 'Bloody do-it-yourselfers.'

Hubcaps's car had been the hottest getaway machine in the Metropolis. Now it was just a wreck. The complete job. A total write off.

He turned to Rudge.

'So. What now, then?'

'Um,' said Rudge. He was thinking hard. 'Call a taxi?'

At the far end of Dot's street a minibus hurtles noisily round the corner and into sight. Its tyres squeal, its engine howls and its suspension complains as it does its best to prevent the driver turning it over onto its side. With an effort the van rocks back onto four wheels and scorches on down the street towards Dot's house leaving blistered tarmac in its wake. Rudge hears it, looks up and tracks its progress. There is something familiar about it that he can't quite put his finger on, something that bodes no good.

'Oh dear,' says Hubcaps but Rudge has got it too now and he understands what he's got. It is a crisis.

Rudge can spot a crisis at a hundred yards. It is not difficult, to be honest, because the world suddenly shifts into slow motion. And it does not matter to Rudge that slow motion is merely Nature's way of allowing his brain to keep pace with fast moving events. He is proud of his talent.

Rudge watches intently as events unfold, incredibly slowly.

The white minibus is a hundred yards away and Rudge is thinking. What is it that is so familiar? he asks himself.

The bus is fifty yards away. Rudge is still thinking. Ah yes. Got it. Familiar faces are behind the windscreen. It is the Boss's bus for the boys.

Forty yards. They're beggars, those two. Of all the Boss's boys – good lads most of them – those two you could never call 'friend'.

Thirty yards. Funny though. The faces look nastier than usual.

Twenty five yards. And another funny thing. Why are they looking at the old woman?

Twenty. Rudge's head turns. The old woman sees them looking. She is frightened.

Fifteen. Turn head back. And another funny thing. Why only two?

Ten. There is greed in their eyes. The beggars are free-lancing.

Five. Contempt fills Rudge's eyes.

Four. His face creases in a hungry smile.

Three. Beggars. Well he can show them.

Two. Draw!

One.

'FREEZE!' A deadpan voice. 'Don't even dream of moving.' A voice to freeze hell.

Rudge's hand is half-way to his knife, but there is a sub-machine gun at the minibus window. It has a dirty barrel. Rudge can see right up it. He thinks. Long odds. Fight on? Or run away?

Hands up, very slowly.

Live to fight another day.

'Good, Rudge. Good boy. Slowly. You've got it.'

The minibus door swings open. The gun stays pointing at Rudge's chest. The deadpan voice descends to the ground. His movements are calm and smooth, like a snake preparing to strike. The minibus door slams shut.

'Now. Turn round. That's the way. And walk. Back through that door. Right. And you two as well.'

Old woman and freelance behind me. Hall darker than outside. So, silhouettes in the doorway. Okay. Go for knife, drop to one knee, then one throw, only one chance, past old woman, past freelance... Difficult. Yes, a bitch. But not impossible.

Now!

The light boyish voice enters last. The front door slams. After the outdoors, the house is silent. And dark.

In the darkness a darker point of night sighs through the air in a deadly straight line.

A single shot from the gun lights the hallway in its flash.

Tumbling figures are seared onto reluctant retinas.

A howl of pain sounds restrained after the gunshot and then there is silence. Again.

Across the Borough the early dusk was deepening. In her little car the Runt sat looking at the Diamond in her lap and she was amazed by it. It was only a crystal, after all, and no larger than a golf ball. How could it have such immense value?

She carried on gazing into its depths. At first she could feel the Diamond's magic working on her. It was only a crystal, she told herself again, as if words were a charm that could keep magic at bay. But the Diamond was more than a crystal and it had bewitched grander souls than the Runt's.

How, wondered the Runt as the Diamond's spell grew on her, could people part with such a jewel at any price? And by then she no longer felt the magic. She was inside it.

She would have been interested, and frightened, to know that in all the times it had changed hands, the diamond had never been sold. It was proud of this record. It was unmatched, so far as it knew, by any other gemstone. To hold the Diamond was to own it and the price was paid in blood, not gold – usually in arrears.

The Runt held the jewel up again to the weak interior light of the car. The crystal was clear – flawless she supposed was the proper name for it – and yet that cold, empty, white space was haunting and bewitching and ... old. It was so old.

Even before the first cut was made to wrench the diadem

73

from its natural grey-stone coat, the perfection had been there. Even before man, it had been there. Even before life, maybe.

The Runt turned the jewel in front of the light. And it dazzled her. She shut her eyes and still it dazzled her. It amazed her and fascinated her and took her breath away.

Now the Runt was not naturally greedy. She was bright, pretty, lively and quick to learn. She could have been almost anything she wanted to be and yet she was a nurse. So, clearly, getting money was not her first desire and if her thoughts now were avaricious, then they were thoughts that were born outside her skull.

The Diamond was hers.

The Runt closed her hand around it. Who holds it, owns it, she thought. And the thought entranced her.

The Diamond was hers and, cradling it in her hands, the Runt knew that anything she wanted she could have and hold, just so.

The Diamond was hers and, holding it before her face with its beauty falling on her, the Runt knew that she was no longer merely pretty. She had become more than beautiful. She was... She groped for a word and found one ready to hand. Flawless.

The diamond was hers. Pressing it to her breasts she shared its warmth and the coldness of uncertainty was gone. Pressing it to her belly she shared its heat and the liquid fire of it flooded her and filled her until she knew she could never be cold again – not lonely cold, nor sad cold, nor frightened cold, nor old cold, nor ever, ever, dead cold. This thing had lived for ever. And it was hers.

In Dot's hallway the light came on. People blinked in the cruel electric glare and looked at the chaos around them.

The light boyish voice was pinned to the door by the knife through his arm. Rudge lay on the carpet with a lump the size of a small egg standing out on his forehead. The

74

deadpan voice sat with his gun pressed into the base of Hubcaps's neck watching for the slightest sign of escape. His heart was not in his work though. The single shot that he had managed to fire had gone off prematurely and he had shot away the little toe on his left foot.

There was probably, the deadpan voice thought vaguely, other damage to his foot as well since he was wearing industrial shoes. All the Boss's boys wore industrial shoes. They kept feet safe at times of stress and excitement but, still, they had their drawbacks. One drawback arose when the steel toe-caps were torn into by high velocity bullets. Then there were complications that no British Standard had been designed to cope with.

Dot stood with her hand still on the light switch and took in the scene in front of her.

'Oh dear,' she said. 'Dear, oh dear, oh dear.' She walked calmly down the hallway and looked at the deadpan voice's foot. It was bleeding into the pale grey pile of her carpet.

'We'll have to do something about that.' Her voice was kindly and warm. 'And.' She touched the light boyish voice on his arm. 'About this.' Carefully she eased the knife out of the door but left it in the wound, not knowing what else to do. The light boyish voice sighed and slid slowly to the floor, smearing blood all down the white paintwork.

Dot went back to the deadpan voice who had said nothing. His face was very grey and he continued to stare sightlessly at Hubcaps lying in front of him. Hubcaps was concentrating on staying very still.

Gently, with enormous care, Dot took the gun from the deadpan voice's limp hands and put it into the umbrella stand.

'There,' she said briskly when she had finished, 'what we all need now is a nice cup of tea.'

At the sound of Dot's familiar words, Hubcaps started giggling. The deadpan voice appeared to pay no attention and Hubcaps rolled onto his back, his giggle became a laugh and the laugh became full and wild. It was not a happy sound. The day had been too much.

Rudge groaned and sat up, clutching his head.

'We didn't come here for a bleedin' tea party,' he muttered. Then. 'What happened?' He looked around and focused on Hubcaps. 'And you can shut up too,' he said. Hubcaps carried on laughing and Rudge leant across and slapped him hard. There was silence.

'I said 'Shut up!' didn't I?'

Looking round further, Rudge saw Dot.

'Oh. You. And how are you doing?' he said. Dot fingered the dressing that Hubcaps had put round her neck.

'It's stiffening up but...' She nodded at Hubcaps. 'If that's the medicine, then I think it'll be alright.'

'She needs stitching.' Hubcaps sat up. 'She needs hospitals, doctors, nurses.' He nodded towards the now silent voices. 'And so do they. And no tea either, by the way. Nothing by mouth. In case they need operations.'

'Hark at him eh? Doctor bleedin' freelance.' Rudge stood up unsteadily and clutched at his skull. 'So what do you recommend for heads then?'

'Aspirin?'

Dot laughed.

'He'll make a good doctor yet.'

'Yeah,' snarled Rudge. 'Make a good doctor weep.' He stumbled against the still shape of the deadpan voice which rolled over onto the floor.

'He's passed out,' said Dot unnecessarily.

'Forget about him.' Rudge pushed at the fallen man with his foot. 'And about him too.' Rudge yanked his knife from out of the light, boyish voice's arm. Hubcaps and Dot winced as they imagined the pain and they turned their eyes on Rudge. The light, boyish voice fainted and the unplugged wound began to bleed.

'What are you looking at me like that for?' said Rudge, 'Like I was some kind of criminal or something.'

Dot sniffed and looked away towards Hubcaps.

'That arm.' She nodded briefly at the light, boyish voice. 'Shouldn't you do something for it?'

'Er.' Hubcaps was still looking at Rudge and was momentarily confused. 'Oh. Yes. Yes, I'll tie it up. There's still some stuff left in the kitchen.' He hurried away to find the remains of the laundry that Rudge had collected from the airing cupboard.

Now Dot had Rudge by himself, she eyed him speculatively. Feeling that he had somehow lost ground, Rudge braced back his shoulders, took a step forward and cleared his throat ready to speak but Dot got in first.

'Now look. I really don't know where it is,' she said firmly. 'The diamond I mean. So since there's nothing I can do for you, perhaps you should just go now, eh? I'll sort out all this.' Her glance took in the chaos around her. Rudge was again about to speak but Dot ploughed on unregarding.

'And as for him.' She nodded in the direction of the kitchen. 'Why not just forget him, eh? Let him off the hook. Whatever hook you've got him on. Go home. No stone's worth any more of this.'

Rudge shook his head.

'I already let that beggar go once today. And I don't believe you can't do nothing for me neither.' He wagged his knife at Dot as he stressed what he was saying.

'See. Maybe you don't know where the diamond is, but you know who's got it and so do I. It's that bird you was with earlier.'

Hubcaps came back into the hallway carrying an armful of laundry. Neither Dot nor Rudge paid him any attention.

'Look.' Dot's firmness turned bitter. 'You heard your friend. We need to get these men to hospital. And me. It's important we get stitched up.'

'All that's important,' said Rudge, 'is that one bloke round here doesn't get stitched up. Me.'

He turned to where Hubcaps was binding up the light,

boyish voice's arm. 'You finished yet?'

Hubcaps nodded reluctantly.

'He'll live, I s'pose.'

'Right then.' Rudge hauled the light, boyish voice to one side and opened the front door. 'Into the minibus. The old lady's taking us round to see that bird she come here with. It's her that's got the diamond. Isn't that right?'

Hubcaps glanced at Dot. She was slumped now, as though the backbone had gone out of her.

'You see?' said Rudge. He jerked his knife in the direction of the door. 'So outside. Both of you. I'll be right behind.'

'But what about these two?' There was real concern in Hubcaps's voice.

'They can look after themselves. Now come on, move!'

Hubcaps, Rudge and Dot went out through the front door. Behind them, in the hallway, a fallen figure groaned. And moved.

Beyond the front door the early dusk was thickening rapidly into a dark and murky evening which the street lights did little to break up. So it was not until Dot and Hubcaps were right beside the minibus that they were able to see the state it had been reduced to. When they saw it though, Hubcaps was immediately angry.

'Beggars,' he said. 'It's no way to treat decent vehicles.'

Dot caught Hubcaps's eye.

'Yeah, little bleeders.' She smiled. 'You got to look on the bright side though, haven't you?' Hubcaps looked puzzled.

'What you waiting for?' said Rudge coming up behind them. Then, as he saw the state of the minibus for himself, 'Bleeders! Evil-minded, poxy, little bleeders!'

'Right enough,' said Dot gently. 'But what now then?'

'Back inside,' said Rudge. He was thinking fast. 'We'll call a taxi and wait.'

Dot laughed.

'Catch a taxi coming round here?' she said.

'We can try,' snarled Rudge. He turned back towards the house. 'Come on! Inside!'

Rudge walked into the brightness of the hallway.

'FREEZE!' said the deadpan voice. 'Don't even dream of moving.'

The Runt was captivated by the Diamond. She could hardly bear to put it down. But she could not sit here for ever, either. She needed to get away. She needed to think. There were practical considerations involved with suddenly becoming rich.

Without really understanding how it had happened, the Runt's decision had been made. The Diamond was hers. She put it carefully onto the seat beside her and took control of her car again.

'Giddy up,' she said and, with a sigh, the car pulled out into what was now the streaming traffic of the evening rush hour.

Around the Runt's car horns blared and headlights flashed, startling her. She looked round to see the danger that had alarmed the rest of the traffic but she failed to understand what the problem was until a car pulled alongside her and a brutally attractive young man wound down his window.

'Lights!' he yelled.

With her window shut the Runt could hear nothing. So she wound down her own window.

'Lights!' yelled the young man again. He was driving with one hand and pointing aggressively with the other. 'Lights, you stupid cow!' Then he saw the Runt's face clearly for the first time.

'Cor!' he leered. 'What are you doing tonight, lovely?' He laughed savagely and the Runt wound her window back up and turned on her lights. She was shivering with anger and fear.

Behind her a blue light started flashing on top of a police

car and a siren sounded briefly. The Runt thumped her steering wheel in frustration, even though it was not to blame.

'Whoa,' she said bitterly and the car pulled obediently back into the side of the road. The police car stopped behind.

Without thinking about it the Runt checked her face in the driving mirror but then, as a policeman came up to her window, out of the corner of her eye she caught sight of the Diamond. It was sitting on the passenger seat, huge, naked and unmissable. And, she remembered with a powerful pang of the fear of being found out, it was stolen.

It takes only a moment to make the mistake of panicking and in that moment the Runt made it.

'Get going!' she said to the car. 'And for god's sake get a move on!' The car caught the sense of the Runt's panic and impressed itself by pulling away with a squealing of tyres.

'Wheelspin!' it chortled. 'Me! Wheelspin!' But it did not let itself get carried away with the magnificence of the moment. A high-speed car chase through rush hour traffic needs calculating precision and an icy nerve and the Runt was displaying neither. It was all down to the little car.

The police had not yet got going again, the car could see in its mirror, so it was in the lead for now but it had no illusions about staying there for long, even with only a panda car in pursuit. A quick sprint was all it was up to, and a quick sprint, it soon began to feel, was what it had already had.

Up ahead a lorry and a bus ahead were slowing and drawing together, preparing to stop at a red light. If it could get beyond those, reckoned the car, the police would be blind for a while. It could go where it wanted without being seen.

'Hold tight!' it muttered grimly, 'we're going through.'

The Runt stared unbelieving as she was carried into the narrowing gap between the two giants of the road. There

80

was not enough space. She stabbed at the brake but it did not work.

'Too late, we're committed,' grunted the car, 'don't look if you don't want to.'

The Runt shut her eyes.

'That's my girl. Leave it all to me.'

The little car flew. There was no shattering crash, no grinding of metal, no tearing pain and no final darkness. Which was a good thing, on the whole, thought the Runt, even though the simplicity of final darkness seemed pretty attractive right now.

She felt the car lurch to the left and again to the left and then stop. The engine switched itself off and there was silence. Somewhere, a short distance off, a police siren passed and faded and died. The Runt opened her eyes.

'Thank you,' she whispered, though she was not sure to whom.

'It was nothing,' said the car and although the Runt could not hear it she felt calmer. Beside her in the darkness the Diamond glowed with a subdued light. The Runt reached out and picked it up because now more than ever she wanted its warmth. But there was no warmth. The stone was cold.

The cellar door slammed and there was blackness. A key turned and heavy feet climbed a wooden stair and limped off along the hallway above.

'Beggars,' cursed Rudge. 'Slimy, crawling, cold-hearted bleedin' beggars.' As he spoke he was exploring his surroundings in the darkness but he was cut short as he fell over something like a man-trap. He yelped with pain.

'You've found that old coal bucket then,' said Dot, 'I don't know why I keep it now, with the central heating in and all. Anyway, just sit tight, eh? There's a light switch here somewhere.' There were shuffling noises as Dot felt her way cautiously along the wall and rattling noises as

Rudge struggled to free himself from the bucket. The rattling noises stopped suddenly.

'Frig it,' said Rudge. 'I've had about enough of this.'

'Of what?' said Dot slightly distractedly. 'Of chasing the diamond you mean?'

'Of the whole bleedin'...'

'Ah, here it is. Mind your eyes, it's a bit bright.' There was a click. Two hundred and fifty watts of unshaded light scorched the tiny, airless cellar.

'Bleedin' 'ell!' said Rudge. He was sitting on the floor with his foot in the coal bucket.

'Don't say I didn't warn you.'

Dot sat down on a rusting iron bedstead and looked at Rudge and Hubcaps.

'So. What now?' she said brightly and smiled.

Rudge disentangled himself from the coal bucket and shoved it rattling under the bed.

'What do you think?' he snarled. 'We grow wings and fly.'

'Oh. Sorry I asked, I'm sure,' said Dot. She turned to Hubcaps.

'You're very quiet.'

'What did you mean?' Hubcaps stood and towered over Rudge. 'About you've had enough of this?'

'Oh, I don't know,' said Rudge. He trailed his finger through the dust on the floor and did not look up. Hubcaps squatted in front of him.

'Well? Are you still after this diamond or aren't you?'

'I don't know,' said Rudge. 'I was thinking. We're getting no bleedin' where and...' And now he did look up. He stared coldly into the depths of Hubcaps's eyes. 'And so I was thinking I should stop messing about. I should just get on with it and finish what I was sent back for in the first place.'

The Diamond was cold. The Runt stared at it as if she was coming out of a dream. Of course it was cold. What else would it be? It was a lump of rock.

It had been warm once, she seemed to remember. And she... She paused as noxious black bubbles came boiling up at the front of her mind. They were not pretty, any of them.

She had been going to keep the Diamond. The silly idea made her smile and amusement lit her face as greed never would. What good the Diamond would have done her she failed to imagine. Could she have worn it? Did she know how to sell it? Or who to sell it to? Was it even hers?

She had driven without lights. An arrogant bastard had scared her. She had run away from the police and nearly been crushed between a bus and a lorry.

For heaven's sake, she had only had the thing for an hour or so. If she had it for a day she'd end up in prison. Or dead.

It had been madness. And madness was black bubbles. But now they had burst and she was sane again.

Aunty Dot had asked the Runt to hide the Diamond away for a while, until the fuss about its theft had died down. This was criminal, of course, but, although the Runt knew it, helping Aunty Dot could somehow never be a crime. Aunty Dot needed all the help she could get.

Besides, when Aunty Dot said she would sell the Diamond and use the money to make The Borough a cleaner, better place, the Runt believed her. So keeping the Diamond was better than giving it back to Harry Devine. It would do his bubbles no good at all.

With morality straightened out to her complete satisfaction the Runt backed out of the wine merchant's yard that she had not the faintest recollection of entering and went calmly on her way.

Hide the Diamond, that was the first thing. Then back to Aunty Dot's to let her know everything was all right. And then home.

A peaceful evening and an early bed were what was needed. It had been a very full day.

Hubcaps remained squatting in front of Rudge. He coughed nervously, glanced down at the floor and looked back up into Rudge's eyes but there was no comfort there at all.

'Say that again,' said Hubcaps. 'I want to be quite clear about it.'

'I was thinking I should just stop messing about and finish what I came for in the first place,' said Rudge.

'That's what I thought you said.' Hubcaps stood up. 'Look. You wanted me to find the old woman, right?'

'Yeah. Right. And the first thing you did was try to run out on me.'

'Well.' Hubcaps smiled ruefully. 'That is what I'm best at.' Rudge did not return the smile. 'Anyway. I did find the old woman for you. And she knew about the diamond. She even had it, which was a long shot in the first place. And it's not my fault she doesn't have it any more. Am I right?'

'Keep talking.'

'That was the deal. We shook on it.'

Rudge laughed.

'Right. We did. The Robbers' Code.'

Rudge stood and closed threateningly on Hubcaps.

'But like I said. You ran away.' He nodded in Dot's direction. 'Like her girl's gone and done to her.'

'We don't know that,' said Dot. 'She may be doing what I asked. Keeping it for me.'

Rudge sighed.

'Just like you'd have done eh? In her place.' He turned back to Hubcaps. 'So you see...'

Hubcaps struck. His hands flashed out and grabbed Rudge's neck. They squeezed and went on squeezing.

'Sorry,' said Hubcaps and he sounded truly regretful.

'Oh come on,' said Dot, 'that won't help, now will it?' But Rudge and Hubcaps had their attention fixed elsewhere.

Rudge was fighting for life but he was smaller than

Hubcaps and had a shorter reach. Dot watched as his struggles grew weaker. He was on his knees. There was a rattling in his throat.

'I may as well save my breath,' said Dot. She rose painfully to her feet, clutching at the bandages around her neck, and lowered herself stiffly to the floor. 'And me feeling like I've been through a mangle too,' she complained.

Carefully, Dot groped under the bed for the coal bucket. She grabbed its handle, dragged it out, stood, turned and, holding the bucket firmly in both hands, she raised it into the air. Hubcaps began to notice her.

'No,' he said as the bucket rose past his shoulders. He glanced desperately at Rudge. The little man's eyes were wide and staring and sightless but he was still alive. Still dangerous. Hubcaps focused again on the bucket.

'You wouldn't,' he said as it rose above his head.

'No!' he yelled letting go of Rudge but he was too late. Dot brought the bucket down solidly onto his wrists. There was a rattle as the handle bounced once.

'Jesus!' Hubcaps stuffed his hands into his armpits, spun round and sat heavily on the bed.

'Jesus H Christ.'

'Yes well,' said Dot. 'Let that be a lesson to you.' She looked at Rudge. He was bowed down on the floor and was clutching at his throat. Dot rattled the bucket at him.

'And I don't want any more nonsense from you, either. Got it?' Rudge could not speak but he nodded as eagerly as he could manage. Dot sat beside Hubcaps.

'Right then,' she said brightly, 'like I said before, what do we do now?'

Neither Rudge nor Hubcaps replied. Each was concerned with his own thoughts.

'Alright then,' Dot went on. 'I'll tell you what I'm going to do. I want that diamond, right? I want the money it will fetch because I can do good things with that money.'

'Who couldn't?' Rudge managed to croak.

'And you both want it too.'

'I don't,' murmured Hubcaps.

'Uhnng?' said Rudge.

'I don't want it,' said Hubcaps. 'Too much trouble. Not my kind of thing.'

'But...' Rudge managed to croak.

'It's alright dear,' Dot leant confidingly over him. 'It's just he hasn't seen it yet, and the poor boy's got no imagination. Which anyway leaves us splitting it just two ways, doesn't it?'

'But...'

'So that's settled then. The rest is easy. All we've got to do is go round to my niece and ask for it back.'

'Your niece?' Hubcaps was surprised, though he didn't know why. Why shouldn't the girl be Dot's niece?

'My niece.' Dot smiled at Hubcaps then went on outlining her thoughts to Rudge. 'She's not organised enough to have gone anywhere yet. So...'

'But...'

'It's alright, she won't make trouble. She's not the type.'

'But how...' said Rudge. He looked round at the cellar walls and the locked door.

'Oh that,' said Dot. 'There's always the coal chute.'

'Of course. But it's... it's locked. I already...' Rudge looked perplexedly at the stout steel shutter over the coal chute.

'Of course it's locked. This is The Borough. But that doesn't mean there isn't a key.' Dot rose stiffly to her feet.

'Stand up a moment, there's a love,' she said to Hubcaps.

Hubcaps stood and Dot lifted a corner of the bed. From out of its hollow leg a small, bright, brass key rattled to the floor.

Dot picked it up.

'I suppose you'll both be coming too?' she said.

The three escapees stood panting outside the house.

'So,' whispered Rudge, looking at the wrecked vehicles in the road. 'What now?'

'This way.' Dot scurried off towards the closed end of the street. She stopped and looked back. The others were watching and wondering where she was going.

'Don't worry, it's alright, there's a short cut past the sewage works.'

She disappeared into a narrow, unlit entrance and Hubcaps and Rudge set off in pursuit.

Headlamps swept the length of Dot's street as a car turned into the top of it. It has to be said that they were not the brightest headlamps in the world.

The Runt was feeling pleased with herself. She had been tested and not found wanting. It occurred to her, as she parked between the two newly stripped-out wrecks outside Dot's house, that it may have been her Aunt who was testing her.

Aunty was a cunning old woman and it was just as well not to under estimate her. But at least now they were still on the same side. And on the whole, thought the Runt, she preferred to stay on Aunty Dot's side with iffy business going on. She walked up the path and rang the doorbell.

'It's me, Aunty,' she called through the door as shuffling steps limped down the hallway. 'I'm back.'

Rupert was at twenty-five thousand feet in air-conditioned luxury. A glass of chilled champagne was at his elbow. A book was open on his lap. He had not read a word.

Rupert was scared of flying. Scared enough to be incapacitated. And there was nothing very much he could do about it. He had tried thinking about owning the Diamond and that had helped a bit.

Not that he intended to do anything about finding the Diamond himself. That was down to the Boss. He had the right sort of muscle while Rupert's contacts in London these days were more with informers than heavies overdosed on steroids. So no. The Boss could find it. And when he had it, Rupert would simply take it from him. Easy. A candy-from-a-baby-job.

Next, Rupert had tried gloating to take his mind off the flying. It was wrong, of course, to gloat. But since Rupert made a comfortable living out of things that were wrong, that made them right. It had been a good gloat too – picturing the Boss's face when he discovered that the Diamond had gone – but he couldn't gloat for ever. So finally he had tried champagne. It took his mind off... He closed his eyes and had a swift mouthful now of the pale golden bubbles. Off... He could scarcely bear to think the word. Off landing.

With a ding-dong like cheap doorbells lights came on

over Rupert's head indicating 'no smoking' and 'fasten seat belts'. Idiots. Catch him sitting in an aircraft with his seat belt undone. You never knew when you were going to need it.

The engines changed note. The nose of the aircraft pointed at the ground and the bottom of Rupert's world dropped away.

Landing.

It did not bear thinking about.

And it was impossible to think of anything else.

'So, what now?' said a rat-like voice.

'I don't know, you tell me,' said another rat-like voice. Among the remains of the Boss's boys only rat-voices were left and they all sounded much the same.

'Why ask me?' said another rat-voice. 'I got her address.'

'So?'

'And it was me remembered the old woman's name.' said yet another of the rat-voices. 'Remember? I've done my bit too.'

The chorus were leaderless, milling around under a lamp post avoiding each other's eyes. They had, to be fair, moved a good way down the High Street from the telephone box but, to be fair again, they had needed no leader to get them there. The policemen arriving to investigate the sudden rash of bodies and traffic accidents around the telephone box had had a magnetic effect on them – like poles repel – sending them briskly away.

'Just look at them now,' said a new rat-voice, 'silly beggars.'

No one knew whether he was talking about the police, the bodies or the small crowd that had gathered to watch but it did not matter. The chorus was only too happy to stop its milling and stand and watch as they put off the awful moment when someone would have to make a decision.

The street around the telephone box was well-lit and they

could see clearly as a woman came forward from the crowd and talked to a policeman. She pointed in the direction of the chorus. The policeman kept on questioning her as she grew increasingly irritated so that when he finally looked there was nothing left to see. The chorus had faded away.

The policeman turned back to the woman shaking his head. She protested. He patted her on the shoulder. She continued to protest. He propelled her back towards the crowd. She hit him with her handbag and was immediately bundled without ceremony into the back of a police van alongside two bodies in big, plastic bags. It is her last appearance in the story but undoubtedly no real harm came to her. If it had the chorus wouldn't have minded though. They didn't approve of being pointed out to policemen.

Out of sight around a convenient corner the chorus continued its debate.

'So. Anyone know where this place is, then?'

'Oh, come on, you've got to know where it is.'

'It's those tatty houses.'

'Down by the old gas-works.'

'Nah. It's by the sewage works.'

'Same thing. One each end of the street.'

Between them the boys knew their Borough.

'But that's bleedin' miles.'

'Maybe. But there's this shortcut, isn't there?'

'Oh yeah.' Light dawning. 'He's right.'

'Back of the sewage works.'

'That's it, this path...'

'Call that a path?'

'You can get through there anyway.'

'All right. Let's go then.' Carried away in the heat of the moment this was a voice too far.

'Yeah! Lead on!' came back the rest of the chorus like a flash. 'And if it all goes wrong it's down to you.'

''Sright.'

''Sright.'

''Sright.'

The single word skittered round the chorus as they all aired their relief at finding a leader. Here was someone who would carry the can.

'No... But... Hang about. I mean...' The rat-voice became squeaky and anxious, 'I didn't mean... I mean, what I meant was... Look, why don't we all decide together, eh?'

'Oh. Right. How?'

'Well, them who think we should go down the short cut say 'yes' and them who don't say 'no' and we do what comes out loudest. What do you think?'

'Sounds like bleedin' democracy to me.'

'What's that then? Democracy?'

'Voting.' Infinite scorn. 'Bleedin' voting.'

At the hospital a new admission was being tucked up in bed.

'Boys... back... should be back... Where are they?' The Boss sat bolt upright, sweating and panicky.

'There there.' A nurse pressed the Boss back down onto his bed. 'It's all going to be alright.' She looked at the doctor.

'There were some men with him earlier,' she explained, 'they were visiting.'

'Yes. Well,' said the doctor. He laid his hand on the Boss's forehead. 'He's had a lucky escape,' he added profoundly.

What other sorts of escape were there, the nurse wondered.

'It's shock,' went on the doctor. 'Not too serious though. The sedatives will get to work in about twenty minutes...'

'And he'll be right as rain in the morning,' chimed in the nurse in a sing-song voice.

'Nothing right about rain,' said the doctor tartly.

Unless you're a farmer, thought the nurse. Or a duck. Or

91

a goose. That was right. He was very like a goose, this doctor, all white-coated honking assertiveness with nothing behind it.

The doctor yawned.

'What I could really do with is some proper casualties, something to get my teeth into. Blood flowing. Broken bones, that sort of thing.' He yawned again, stretched, sighed and looked at his watch. 'God but it's going to be a long night.'

'Have some more of that tea and shut up your whining,' said the deadpan voice as he shuffled along the hallway towards Dot's front door.

'But I shouldn't be having tea,' said the light, boyish voice. 'You heard what the freelance said.'

'We're not going to hospital,' said the deadpan voice patiently, 'And that's that.' He opened the front door and took in the Runt at a glance. He smiled.

'Yes, my dear. What can I do for you?'

It was not so much the shuffling, limping footsteps that had told the Runt it was not Aunty Dot who was about to open the front door. It was the resonances of the approaching voice.

To begin with it wasn't Mad Harry Devine. The Runt had seen Harry not fifteen minutes ago when she went to hide the Diamond. He had been wandering round the hospital, still lost and still refusing to believe the signs. What he was doing with the signs instead was pulling down all he could lay his hands on. The Runt had mentioned this to the charge nurse in Casualty, on her way out.

And apart from Mad Harry there was no one else, at the moment, who the Runt was feeling frightened of. Which only went to show, she thought the moment the door opened, that she should use her imagination more.

The man at the door had a drawn face, dark stains all

down his coat and a ragged hole in the side of one shoe. And his voice, the Runt shuddered, an atheist answering the door to a posse of Jehovah's Witnesses would sound ecstatic by comparison. The Runt turned to run but she was slow, far too slow. A strong, bony hand gripped her upper arm.

'Not so fast, my dear,' said the deadpan voice and he was smiling now. 'Come inside, why don't you?'

The Runt immediately thought of a dozen good reasons why not and when she finished the front door slammed with her on the wrong side of it.

'Let me go at once,' she demanded. She stared straight into the deadpan voice's eyes and wished she didn't have to. 'I don't want to stay.'

'Maybe not,' said the deadpan voice, 'but I do want you to. You see. You're a nurse, aren't you?' The uniform was a dead give-away. 'And my foot hurts.'

The Runt looked down at the deadpan voice's foot.

'I'm not surprised it hurts. It looks a mess. Why don't you take it to hospital?'

'And my friend has hurt his arm.'

'He's no friend of mine,' came the light, boyish voice from the kitchen.

'Come on through,' said the deadpan voice to the Runt. 'See if you can help us.'

'Where's Aunty Dot?' said the Runt. She realised almost immediately that this was probably a mistake. 'I mean. Where's Mrs Coulson?'

'So the old woman's your aunt, is she?' The deadpan voice smiled. 'Interestinger and interestinger. Well your aunt's alright. Perfectly safe. You can see her in a while, if you like, and find out just how happy she is.'

Dot was, in fact, not at all happy. It was years since she had used the short-cut past the sewage works and things had changed considerably. It was not just that the path was

93

more broken and cluttered with scrap iron than before. Dot's ankles seemed less flexible than she remembered from the last time she walked over ground more uneven than a Borough pavement. And the short-cut was longer than she remembered. She sat down on a rusting oil drum, panting and exhausted. Though not, it has to be said, quite as panting and exhausted as she appeared to be.

'Hold on,' she called to the two dark shapes on the path ahead of her. 'I need a breather.'

Time passed and then Hubcaps loomed up out of the darkness.

'Are you alright?' he asked. He sounded genuinely concerned and Dot's heart warmed towards him. Maybe... Just maybe...

'Out of breath,' she gasped. 'Just out of breath, that's all.'

'I'm not surprised,' said Hubcaps sitting down beside her, 'the pace bloody Rudge is setting.' There was silence for a while.

'Bloody Rudge.' Dot laughed. 'I should have let you finish him while we had the chance.'

At this precise moment Rudge's footsteps became audible again. They were close enough for Dot to hear the accompanying breathing and they were coming closer still.

'Now there,' said Dot. 'Talk of the devil.'

'Ssh!' said Hubcaps. 'He's an impatient beggar at the best of times. You need to keep on the right side of him.' He stood but Dot caught at his sleeve.

'Was that right,' she whispered urgently, 'what you said earlier?'

'Eh?'

'About not wanting the diamond?'

Rudge's voice came to them out of the dark.

'Oi, you two, what the hell do you think you're playing at? I thought you were right behind me.'

'Oh we are, Mr Rudge, we are,' said Dot as she stood and moved towards him. 'We're behind you all the way.'

Suddenly Dot tripped on a cast-iron fire grate and stumbled, losing her balance. She hoped, as she nose-dived towards a dark heap of indescribable metal cast-offs, that Hubcaps was as quick as he looked. Strong arms caught her and she breathed a prayer of thanks. He was. Hubcaps lifted Dot up and set her back on her feet but, apparently still shaken, she clung to him for support. Her mouth was beside his ear.

'We still need to talk,' she said. There was no response and her urgency increased.

'We're not out of the woods yet. Neither of us.'

Rudge was now standing right beside them and, although Hubcaps said nothing, a gentle pressure on Dot's shoulder told her that he had at least heard.

In the living room of the Boss's house the telephone rang for the second time in ten minutes. Deirdre looked at the whisky bottle in her hand and decided to hold on to it for the time being. She did not want it getting away again.

She set off carefully across the room. Less furniture, that was what the Boss needed she thought as a small, green onyx-topped table fell with a heavy thud onto the thick-piled carpet. She kicked at it – bloody thing, right in the way-and mercifully she had drunk enough not to feel the pain in her toe.

Deirdre picked up the telephone. It was the hospital, she supposed, with more news of the Boss. Maybe he had gone and died. But then again maybe he hadn't. She had never been lucky and there was no good reason she could see for starting now.

''Ullo.'

'Hullo?'

'I already said that.'

'Who's this? I was wanting the Boss.'

'They all do dearie. They all do. No one wants me. Life's

a bitch like that.' Deirdre took a pull at the whisky bottle.
'A real bitch.'

'Er, is he in?'

Deirdre took another pull at the bottle. There was something about this voice on the phone that sounded vaguely
familiar. Something about it that... The bottle would help
her remember, she thought, even though usually it helped
her forget. Forget what? What a bitch life was, of course.
But this voice. It was making her heart go pitter-patter in
an unfamiliar, almost forgotten way. 'Rupert?' said
Deirdre, and the name sounded strange after all these
years.

'Rupert? Is that you?'

'Deirdre?'

The voice was disappointed now. But disappointment
was normal. It made her feel better.

'It is you isn't it, Rupert?'

'Deirdre. Hell. Where the devil did you spring from?'

'And I might ask you the same question. But I won't. I
won't. Look. He's out, Rupert. I don't know where, but
then, you know him. Come and go. Come and go.' She was
babbling. She slowed down.

'He'll be back later, though.' She lied convincingly, it was
one of the things she was good at. 'But not too late, I don't
think. You could come round and wait.'

He could come round and wait. With her. And the Boss
would never come.

'Would you like that?'

Maybe life wasn't such a bitch after all.

'This is bleedin' bloody!'

'Bleedin' right!'

'Yeah. Bleedin' path. Who said this was a path?'

'He did.'

'I never. I said 'Call that a bleedin' path?''

'I say we should go back and go round the long way. It'd

96

be quicker.'

'Me too.'

'So let's vote then.'

'We just voted.'

'So? Vote again.'

'We should vote whether we want to vote. Okay?'

'NO-YES-OO!'

The chorus were picking their way along the short-cut behind the sewage works. In their long, dark coats and industrial shoes they tiptoed daintily over battered galvanised watering-cans and through wire-lattice bed frames.

'Was that the vote we just had or was it voting for the vote?'

'It was the vote.'

'It was voting for a vote.'

'Don't look at me, I don't know.'

The chorus were scornful of the rat-voice who did not know.

'He doesn't know.' They jeered. 'You've got to know. People died for you to know.'

'Oh yeah? Like who?' asked the don't know rat-voice but no one paid him any attention. The founding father of democracy was speaking.

'Leave off him. It's alright. He's allowed not to know. We've got to have someone who doesn't know. It's on the telly. Don't knows, sixty per cent. They win all the time.'

'Well I want to be a don't know too then.'

'Me too.'

'That's the stuff.' The founding father sighed with satisfaction. 'Democracy in action.'

When democracy first arrived in the chorus it was greeted with scorn and derision. The idea that they could do anything by shouting 'yes' and 'no' had been perplexing and it had taken a while for the idea to sink in that that was not really the point.

The point was not so much getting things done as who

carried the can if nothing got done. After all, the Boss couldn't sack them all, could he? And another thing was, political theory aside, that the chorus was discovering that as a democratic brotherhood they were much happier than they had ever been as a band of ruthless brigands. And lastly, against all the odds, they were actually making progress. Real progress.

'This is great,' said a happy rat-voice, well, happily. 'We're really getting somewhere.'

'Yeah! Onwards lads, onwards!' cried newly evangelical democrats ready to convert the world.

'Onwards and upwards!'

Sourer rat-voices at the back snarled in response. Onwards and upwards was a silly slogan. And it wasn't even original. If they had to have a slogan, then they should have a slogan that real men could be proud up. They had a go at making one up.

'Inwards and outwards and upwards and downwards!' they began. 'Inwards and outwards and upwards and downwards!'

'Hey, that's a new slogan. We can't have that.'

'Why not? We like it.'

'Then we need to vote on it. Okay?'

'YE-NO-SS!'

'Then vote!'

'YE-NO-SS!'

'It's carried,' said a voice and the chorus passed on, all chanting their new slogan together.

'Inwards and outwards and upwards and downwards! Inwards and outwards and upwards and downwards! Take a vote! YE-NO-SS!'

'Brilliant. Absolutely brilliant.' The light, boyish voice did not approve of the deadpan voice's high-handed action in snatching a nurse without consulting him. 'We've got a

98

cellarful of them down below there and still you have to go and...'

But he got no further. The Runt had become interested and, when she was interested in a thing, nothing on earth could stop her from nosing in. Except perhaps a senior hospital consultant and they were in short supply in Dot's kitchen.

'A cellarful of who?' she asked.

'Never you mind,' said the deadpan voice. 'Have you got what you need yet?' The Runt shook her head.

'Well get a move on, I don't want to bleed to death.'

The Runt moved away, opening drawers in cabinets on the other side of the kitchen.

'There ought to be something here somewhere,' she said. 'She must mend things sometimes.'

'And as for you.' The deadpan voice looked at the light, boyish voice. 'Just shut up your whinging, okay? Just shut it up!'

The deadpan voice's irritation was not, in fact, caused either by his colleague's whinging or by the Runt's stubbornness but by the pain in his foot. It was beginning to be really bad and he shifted to try and make the foot more comfortable. There was a dull thump as the sub-machine gun bumped against the table. The light, boyish voice registered the sound. His face went still and he leant carefully back in his seat, but he was not relaxing.

Across the kitchen a drawer slammed and the Runt came back towards the two men.

'All I can find are these,' she said. She put a large darning needle and a reel of stout button-thread onto the table. The voices looked at the things in horror.

'But that needle's blunt,' said the light, boyish voice in horror. 'It's got a round end.'

The Runt nodded.

'So we'll need this.' She planted a large, full bottle of gin beside the needlework tools.

99

'Anaesthetic.' She rested her hand on the light, boyish voice's shoulder and smiled. 'But don't worry, it'll still hurt like hell.'

The light, boyish voice looked at the deadpan voice in a panic.

'We could buy some stuff, couldn't we?'

'Uh uh,' said the Runt, 'the shops are shut by now. The hospital's still open of course, and that,' she became as bossy as she could manage, 'is where you should both be.

'You need sterile equipment and antibiotics and someone who's properly qualified to do this job.' She looked at the deadpan voice. 'Especially you. There's next to nothing I can do for your foot with any of this.

'But.' She sighed. 'If you've really made up your minds then I shall just have to manage something, shan't I?'

There was a long silence. The voices stared at the gin bottle.

'Yeah. Well. That's all very well isn't it?' said the deadpan voice. 'But a knife wound and a gunshot wound, how much chance would we have going into hospital with them? We'd be nicked and you know it.'

'You want to know how much chance you've got if you don't go in?' said the Runt. She laughed. It was a knowledgeable laugh, the kind of laugh that experts use when non-experts are about to ignore their advice. 'Have you ever seen gangrene?' She looked serious and leant closer. 'Or smelt it?'

Leaving the voices to consider the question, the Runt went over to a cupboard and came back with a pair of large, pottery mugs. The only sound was the gurgling of gin as she filled the mugs to the brim.

'Okay then, drink!' She put a mug in front of each of the voices. They looked startled.

'But...'

'I'm not starting till you're both properly anaesthetised.' The Runt sat down at the table and crossed her arms.

100

'So go on. We haven't got all night.' She settled herself more comfortably in her chair and shut her eyes. 'That is, you haven't got all night. Either of you.'

The deadpan voice took a deep breath, reached out for his mug and drained it down.

'Good boy,' said the Runt. 'Now the rest of it.' She refilled his mug, but this time not to the top.

'Mustn't be greedy must we?' she said. 'We must leave some for your friend.'

The deadpan voice picked up his mug and looked across the top of it at the light, boyish voice.

'Drink!' he said. The light, boyish voice picked up his mug and sniffed at it, wrinkled his nose and sipped gingerly. He coughed.

'I don't think I like gin,' he said.

'Drink it like a man!'

The Runt leant across the table and rested her hand on the light, boyish voice's good arm.

'Yes, drink it up, there's a dear. It's not half so bad as what's coming.'

Cautiously the light, boyish voice swallowed a mouthful. He swallowed another and then another and finally he drained the mug to its dregs and wiped his mouth.

'It's not so bad, is it, once you get going?' he said.

The Runt emptied the gin bottle into his mug and smiled at the two men.

'Both together now then,' she said and she raised her hands slowly, palms upwards as the two men drained their second mugfuls of neat gin.

'Good. That's it. All gone?' She took the two mugs and looked inside them. 'Excellent. Well done,' she said and she took the mugs and the empty bottle across to the sink.

'Will half a bottle each be enough, eh?' said the deadpan voice. The Runt looked at the label on the bottle.

'Half a litre,' she said, 'well it's all we've got anyway but yes, I expect it will be enough.'

Two heavy heads hit the table simultaneously and the Runt smiled.

'I expect it will be quite enough.'

9

On the short-cut behind the sewage works Rudge's suspicions had been aroused enough by Hubcaps and Dot to keep him sticking close to them. Fairly close, anyway. But he was itching to press on and this urgency kept carrying him on ahead until, realising what he was doing, he had to hurry back to where Dot and Hubcaps were making slow but steady progress.

'Awfully nervy isn't he, your friend Rudge?' said Dot during one of Rudge's brief absences.

'He's no friend of mine,' Hubcaps replied. Rather sourly, thought Dot.

They picked their way in silence over a couple of bedsteads before Hubcaps spoke again.

'It's a bad idea, you see, having friends in this game.'

'Ah,' Dot said knowingly. 'The Robbers' Code.'

Hubcaps looked at her sharply but Dot only smiled.

'Like I said earlier,' she went on, 'I should just have let you finish him while we had the chance.'

Hubcaps shook his head.

'I'm glad you didn't. All that's not my style.' His hand rested briefly on Dot's shoulder and was gone as Rudge came back towards them through the dark.

'Can't you get a move on, you two? I'd like to get there sometime.'

From the far distances of the night a noise came faintly. It sounded, impossibly, like men chanting. The little party stopped without a word being said. They listened. The sound continued and now they could hear precisely what it was. It was, impossibly, men chanting. The voices came faint but clear on the dank, still air, repeating the same words over and over.

'Inwards and outwards and upwards and downwards!'

'Take a vote!'

'YE-NO-SS!'

'Inwards and outwards and upwards and downwards!'

'Take a vote!'

'YE-NO-SS!'

'What the hell's that?' said Rudge.

'Men. Chanting,' replied Dot.

Rudge turned savagely towards her. He was about to speak but Hubcaps got in first.

'Why don't you go and take a look?' he said innocently.

'Yes. Well. Right.' Rudge glanced anxiously over his shoulder then turned back again.

'It's alright.' Dot's voice was at its most persuasive. 'I'll make sure he doesn't go anywhere.'

'And I'll make sure she goes nowhere,' said Hubcaps.

'Yes. Well.' Rudge was deeply uncertain but there was one thing that he was certain of. There were more of those voices down there than there were people in his own party. And he didn't like the sound of them at all. He wanted to know who they were before they all met up.

'Make sure you do, then,' he said to no one in particular and faded away into the night. Dot let loose a pent-up sigh and behind her back she uncrossed her fingers.

'Robbers' Code applies,' she muttered. 'Robbers' Code applies.'

In Dot's kitchen the Runt watched the voices with a nagging doubt at the back of her mind. They were absolutely still with, and the doubt nagged more vigorously, the kind of stillness that said they were not playing games. She felt the pulse below the deadpan voice's jaw. He was alive, at least.

He should be alive of course. The question really was though, would he stay that way? She strained to remember everything she had learnt about alcohol, and not from the Perfect Bar Steward's Book Of Killer Cocktails either. What she could remember was not much but she had a reasonably confident feeling that half a litre of gin was not a fatal dose.

The Runt moved across and checked the light, boyish voice. Like the deadpan voice he was alive but his breathing was fast and shallow and his pulse was light and fluttery. The Runt frowned with concern and continued to stand with her hand on the light, boyish voice's neck for nearly a minute. There was no change to the feeling of the pulse and doubt continued to nag at her, louder and yet more loudly.

She had been kidnapped, that was beyond doubt. And so even if the light, boyish voice should die, he would deserve everything he got. Anyone in their right mind would agree. But how would the police see it, if it came to that? Or a jury? The Runt didn't know and she grew increasingly anxious as she stood thinking about it until, for the second time in the day, she panicked.

Luckily for the Runt panic suited her. Under its influence she did sensible things, like shutting her eyes to avoid witnessing her own death or rushing to the telephone and dialling nine, nine, nine. Right now she rushed to the telephone.

'Tell me.' Dot turned hurriedly to Hubcaps as soon as Rudge was decently out of ear shot. 'If you're not after the diamond, then what are you after?'

'Just what I've been after all day.'

'Which is what, exactly?'

'I've been trying to get away.'

'And that's all?'

'That's all.'

The chanting voices were becoming louder.

'Okay then. Well now's your chance.'

There were oil drums in the rubbish around them. Dot collected some and piled them in a pyramid beside the chain-link fence that separated the short-cut from the sewage works.

'It's a clear run over there. It used to be anyway. Up you get.'

'But...' Hubcaps looked assessingly about. Above the noise of the chanting he could hear someone making a hurried passage over metal refuse. 'What about you?'

Dot clucked impatiently, climbed on to the lower level of oil drums and pulled at Hubcaps arm.

'Come on,' she said, 'get on with it.'

Hubcaps stepped up and stood beside her.

'What about you?'

'Me? Well for starters I'll be happier without you around. You never know what Rudge'll be like when I get the Diamond. He's a dangerous man...

'Go on now, up you get. Right to the top.' Dot carried on talking as Hubcaps climbed the pyramid of oil drums.

'And secondly, if I get rid of you now, then you can't go changing your mind, can you? About not wanting the Diamond. I wouldn't want to have to sort you out too.'

Hubcaps was hanging now over the top of the fence. The wire peaks of it dug in under his ribcage and his legs hung down on the sewage works side. He reached down to Dot.

'Come on,' he said. 'I'll help you over.'

'But I don't want to go over there.'

'Leave Rudge behind, see your niece by yourself.' Hubcaps was urgent. 'Like you said, he's a dangerous man.' The approaching sounds were nearly on them. Dot laughed.

'Uh ah. I need Rudge. I've got work for him to do. And

besides, I could never get over this fence.'

'You should try at least!'

'I told you. I need Rudge. He's the pro'.'

Rudge's voice came to them out of the darkness.

'Go back. Go back! I think it's the boys.'

'You've got to try!'

'Okay. Alright. But shut up, eh?'

Cautiously Dot caught hold of Hubcaps's hand and he pulled her upwards until she was standing on the top oil drum. The voice of the chorus came loudly out of the night.

'Inwards and outwards and upwards and downwards!'

'Take a vote!'

'YE-NO-SS!'

Dot patted Hubcaps's hand with her free hand.

'Okay then,' she said. 'Ready?'

'Yes.' Hubcaps braced himself.

'Then for crying out loud, go!' Very deliberately Dot bit Hubcaps's hand where it clung on to her own. With a yell of pain Hubcaps let go and Dot shoved him hard so that he lost his balance and fell down into the sewage works. There was a single soft thud and then nothing. Silence.

The Runt hung up the telephone and felt better. She had done her duty by the two comatose voices. She had passed the problem on and she was no longer responsible. Aunty Dot was a different matter though.

As far as the Runt could see, she would always be responsible for Aunty Dot. Someone had to be. And maybe, she thought, that should have been an appalling thought. To many young women of her age it would have been. She had heard them say as much. But to the Runt it was a comfort. Aunty Dot was all she had. Pray god she still had her but, now that she had time to think about it, she began to be afraid that she might not.

'We've got a cellarful of them down below there,' the light, boyish voice had said. But he had not said what it was a cellarful of. For all the Runt knew, and this was the thought that was frightening her, it was a cellarful of corpses. The voices looked the type who might easily stockpile corpses.

The cellar stairs were steep and were lit only by what little light crept down from the hallway and out through cracks around the cellar door. The Runt went down carefully, not wishing either to kill herself falling or warn the occupants of her approach by being noisy. There was a cellarful of them, the Runt had to remember, and if not a cellarful of corpses, then perhaps a cellarful of dangerous and desperate men. Including Aunty Dot. She could be as dangerous and desperate as the best of them. So legend told.

Outside the cellar door the Runt stopped to listen but there were no sounds from within – none at all – and she was suddenly more frightened than ever – desperately and hideously frightened. Her caution was gone as she fumbled with the key in the lock. Please, she thought, not corpses. Please, please, please not corpses. She flung the door open.

A brilliant light flooded out from the cellar and swamped the dark stairway. The Runt blinked in the shattering brightness of it so that it was a few moments before she realised that the cellar was empty. Completely empty. Well, not empty exactly, it was more chock-a-block than empty, but it was chock-a-block with nothing that the Runt wanted, which came to the same thing.

Rudge came out of the dark and stood beside the oil drums, looking around in puzzlement. Out of the corner of his eyes he saw a pair of legs and he looked upwards.

'You!' He was blazingly angry but he reigned his voice in to a whisper. The chorus were very close. 'What are you doing up there?'

'Trying to stop the freelance from getting away.' Dot scowled convincingly. 'But he wriggled out of it, the beggar. Never mind though, eh? Who needs him. That's what I say.' She held her hand out to Rudge. 'Now. Are you helping me down or what?'

'Inwards and outwards and upwards and downwards!'

The chorus materialised around Rudge. He lost interest in Dot and turned to run but strong arms held him back.

'Hullo hullo hullo. So this is what's been running away from us, is it?' said a jovial rat-voice. A face peered into Rudge's face.

'Why. And if it isn't old Rudge.'

'I said it was, didn't I?' said a second rat-voice. 'I said I knew his voice.'

'So tell us. What've you been up to then, old lad?' said a third voice close by Rudge's ear. 'We'd all like to hear, I'm sure.'

'Just a minute,' said a fourth, 'there's someone with him.' More strong arms reached up and hoisted Dot to the ground.

'Gaah!' The voice was disgusted. 'Should have left her up there. It's only an old lady.'

'It's the old lady,' growled Rudge. Once again circumstances were forcing him to think fast. 'The one we're after. I was just bringing her back for the Boss.'

'Oh. And were you really?' said a rat-voice suspiciously. 'Well we don't think so, do we lads?'

'NO-YES-OO!'

'You see, Rudge old son, if it is the old lady, you were going in the wrong direction. Towards her house, not away from it.'

Strong arms pinioned Rudge.

'And we think that means only one thing. Don't we lads?'

'YE -NO -SS!'

'Oh yes?' Rudge's voice was as near a squeak as it ever could be. 'And what's that then?'

'You've gone freelance. That's what that is. And we don't like freelances, do we? Us pro's.'

Somewhere in the distance, a siren wailed.
'We don't like them at all.'

The siren in the street penetrated Dot's house and it gave
the Runt no time at all to consider the problem of the
empty cellar. She rushed up to the hallway and opened the
front door just as an ambulance man reached it.

'Thank god you're here,' she said opening the door wide
and standing back to let him in. 'They're in the kitchen.'
She followed as the ambulance man went purposefully
towards the door she had indicated. Standing in the
doorway she watched as he took in the scene.

'Alright then? I can leave you to it, can I?' She turned to
leave and the ambulance man was galvanised into activity.

'Hang about Miss. Not so fast.' He hurried after her and
caught her arm. 'There's things here we need to talk about.
To begin with.' He indicated the room with a sweep of his
arm and sighed patiently. 'Tell me you've called the police
about all this.'

'Called them about what?' said the Runt innocently.

'Ah, come on, that won't wash.' The ambulance man
looked up as the other member of his crew came into the
room.

'Here, Flo,' he said.

'Dave. If I've told you once, I've told you a thousand...'

'Florien then,' grumbled Dave. Florien looked surprised,
as if she didn't expect Dave to capitulate so easily. 'Have a
look at that will you.' He indicated the deadpan voice.
'And tell me what you make of it.'

Florien looked.

'Looks like a gunshot wound to me,' she said.

'There. You see?' The ambulance man looked triumphantly at the Runt. 'It's the hole in his boot, see. Like guns
make. And there's a gun lying on the floor there, too.'

'And this one's a knife wound,' said Florien, standing

beside the light, boyish voice. 'Has anyone called the police yet?'

Down behind the sewage works democracy was taking its slow but inevitable course. From his dark sanctuary on the safe side of the sewage works fence, Hubcaps listened. Being democratic the proceedings were somewhat confused and disorderly but one thing was rapidly becoming clear. Rudge was in trouble.

'Alright, so tell us again.'

'But I already told you all of it twice.'

'So? We want to hear it again.'

'Hang about. We need to vote on that. Do we want to hear it again?'

'YE-NO-SS!'

'Carried then. We want to hear it again.'

'So talk.' The strong arms that pinioned Rudge shook him vigorously. 'Tell us again.'

'Okay, okay. But take it easy, eh?' Rudge wriggled uncomfortably but the grip on him did not slacken.

'Like I said, there were five things the Boss said. Right? Five of them. 'I want to know who the old lady is.' Okay? 'Who she's working for.' Right? 'I want the Diamond,' and 'I want her dead.' And the last thing he said was...' Friskier elements of the chorus joined in.

''And someone see to that bastard back there!''

'Yeah, yeah. We all heard that,' said the glum, don't know rat-voices from the back but no one paid them any attention. Don't knows might be a necessary part of the democratic process, but that didn't mean people had to listen to them.

'So,' went on Rudge, 'since seeing to's my business, I goes back to see to him, don't I? And see to him is what I do.'

'So why's it take so long?'

'It takes so long...' Rudge sounded anxious. His brain was working overtime as he groped for verisimilitude and,

111

at the same time, tried to remember what he had already said.

'It takes so long because...' He relaxed slightly. He had it now. 'Because you know what the beggar's last request is?'

'Yeah,' said a glum rat-voice. 'Sprinkle me corpse on Hampstead Heath. Bleedin' romantic, eh. Poet is he, this freelance?'

'That's it. And it takes time, dragging him all the way out there. And to cut a long story short, he tells me...'

'But you've seen to him,' said a nasty rat-voice. 'So how's he tell you anything?'

'He tells me before I see to him, of course.' Rudge glowered at the questioner with bravado. 'And what he tells me is that he knows the old woman all along, she's his... his aunt or something, and he's been in on the deal from the start.'

'Deserves all he gets then, the bleeder.'

''Sright.'

'And to get me to let him go he tells me her address and I see to him anyway. And that's it. I come round and get the old woman and she doesn't talk so I walk her to get it out of her. The Boss should try it. It works like a dream, walking. Better than tickling any time.'

'So she's ready to give us the Diamond then, is she?'

'She's got to tell us who she's working for first. Remember?' objected a serious-minded rat voice. 'Point two that was.'

'Oh yeah. Point two.'

'So? Has she told us yet?'

'We was just getting there.' Rudge managed to sound aggrieved. 'When you lot come barging in.'

'So.' The inquisitor's rat-voice took on a nasty edge. 'She'd better start talking then, hadn't she? Fast. So's we can all hear.'

'Alright. Alright.' Dot too sounded aggrieved. 'Keep your hair on. I get the message.' She took a deep breath and began.

'Point one was my name, wasn't it? Well it's Dot Coulson. Point two is, I was working for Hubcaps rest his soul. Point three is you can't have it right now because I haven't got it with me and point four...' She smiled round at the rat voices. 'Why don't we give point four a miss?'

The rat-voices did not respond.

'For the time being anyway?'

Still no response.

'Maybe?'

A lone rat-voice broke the silence.

'What do we think then, boys?'

'Dunno.' This rat-voice was doubtful. 'Sounds dodgy to me.' There was an ugly silence.

'So how'd you work it, you and him?' enquired yet another rat-voice from near the back. 'You and the freelance, like? I mean...' The voice laughed. 'You and him against Axe and the Sailor?'

Dot heaved a sigh of relief. It was back to business.

'Well.' She sounded thoughtful. 'You see. We were lucky really. Hubcaps tells me when and where the hit is so I'm waiting, aren't I, when the boys come out the shop and just then this bomb goes off. Badoom! It lands them in hospital and saves me the trouble of tripping them up.' Dot paused for effect.

'You mean you were there?' The questioning voice was incredulous. 'With the bomb and all? But... But...' The voice remembered the image of the Boss's favourites unconscious in bed in the hospital.

'Oh, I had my good stocking on of course.'

And that was it. All that was necessary. Any woman who trusted to the quality of her stockings to defeat the Axe and the Sailor was all right by the chorus. They would follow her to the ends of the earth. Most of them. Just one suspicious rat-voice had one last try.

'So why were you climbing the fence then? We all saw

you.'

'Gaah shut up.'

'No. 'Sright. We did.'

'To hide from you lot of course.' Dot was indignant. 'Who wouldn't? I mean. Just look at you. The lot of you.'

There was a silence broken only by the shuffling of industrial quality footware amongst scrap metal.

'And now,' she went on briskly, 'what we all need is a nice cup of tea. My house is only down there. Just round the corner.'

'We know.'

'So. What are we waiting for then?'

In Dot's kitchen there was a longish silence after Florien's question about the police.

'You see.' Dave put on a patient voice, the one he reserved for pensioners, children and idiots. 'We get back to Casualty with a pair like this and people are going to want to know, aren't they? "Have you called the police?" they'll ask. And they'll want to know. You're a nurse,' he concluded, reasonably enough. 'You'd want to know.'

'Well... But couldn't we... Er... Just this once?'

'No. We couldn't.' Florien was adamant. 'Not even just this once.'

'I see.'

'Well then.' The Runt shrugged and managed to look pathetic. 'I'd better just call the police then.' She moved to go back into the hall.

'Oh no you don't,' said Dave, who was still holding the Runt's arm. 'You stay here. I'll call the police. On the radio. Flo, you look after her eh. Oh. And Flo...'

'My name is not Flo.'

'Be careful.'

As Dave went, Florien moved towards the Runt, reaching out for the arm that Dave had just let go.

'Look please...' said the Runt. She held up her hands and backed off slightly. But Florien shook her head and smiled sympathetically as she gripped the Runt's arm.

'Sorry,' she said. 'But you do see how it is, don't you?'

'Oh yes,' said the Runt. 'Of course. And I'm sorry too. Believe me.'

Florien looked puzzled.

'What are you sorry for?' she said.

'This,' said the Runt and with her free hand, she hit the point of Florien's chin with all the force she could muster.

Down behind the sewage works democracy was dying. Faced with a leader like Dot and the prospect of a nice cup of tea it never stood a chance.

It was not, however, giving up entirely without a struggle.

'What about the Diamond then?' said one of the glum rat-voices at the back. 'Not that I don't fancy a cup of tea, mind,' he added quickly, feeling all eyes upon him. 'It's just that she's never said anything about the Diamond.'

'She did. She said she hadn't got it.'

'So why are we going with her then?'

'Because she's promised to get it for us.'

'Oh. Is that right? I must have missed that.' The glum rat-voice subsided into silence. He may never have approved of democracy, but it still seemed fair enough to want to know where he was being lead. Not that he was going to be too picky. Anywhere except up the garden path was fine by him.

'We should hang on to that bleeder though,' he said. 'Old Rudge. Just in case.'

'Yeah, okay, well that's what we're doing, isn't it?'

It was indeed. The chorus's advance along the rubbish-strewn short-cut had slowed to a crawl because of Rudge.

'In case of what?' piped up the inquisitive rat-voice.

'Eh?'

'In case of what?'

'Oh. Just in case. I think.'

'Come on now, boys,' Dot shouted suddenly. 'You've all gone quiet on me. What happened to that thing you were shouting earlier on? How'd it go? Upwards and onwards was it?'

'Er, no. It was...'

'Well whatever it was, let's liven up the party a bit. One! Two! Three! Go!'

'Inwards and outwards and upwards and downwards. Take a vote.'

'Ye-no-ss.' The chorus was embarrassed by the memory of its earlier enthusiasm.

'That's pathetic. Louder!

'Inwards. And outwards. And upwards. And downwards. Take a vote!'

'Ye-no-ss.'

'And louder!'

'Inwards! And outwards! And upwards! And downwards! Take a vote!'

'YE-NO-SS!'

'That's it. Now keep it going!'

'Inwards! And outwards! And upwards! And downwards! Take a vote!'

'YE-NO-SS!'

Under cover of the chorus's newly restored confidence Dot sidled up alongside Rudge.

'Right oh, bright eyes,' she said. 'We're going in the safe direction now, okay? Away from the Runt.'

'Away from the what?'

'My niece. And I've tamed these boys of yours as much as they're going to be tamed. So what I'm saying is, I reckon I've done my bit. And since you got us into this mess, it's up to you, now.'

'Up to me to what?'

'To get us out of it of course. You're the pro' after all.

116

You can surely manage a little thing like that?'

'Oh yeah. Right. No problem,' muttered Rudge morose-ly. 'Abra-ca-bleedin'-dabra.'

The Runt stood beside the fallen ambulance woman, looking around the kitchen and nursing the hand she had used to hit her.

'Right. Now.' Beside the sink was Rudge's knife. 'I'll take that.' She stepped carefully over Florien's recumbent body and picked it up. 'And the gun.' The Runt wanted to leave as little as possible behind to incriminate Aunty Dot.

When she was ready to go the Runt stood once more in the kitchen doorway and had a last look round. Satisfied she turned and hurried away down the hallway.

'Look out Aunty, here I come,' she said under her breath.

Dave was halfway up Dot's path when the Runt erupted out of the house.

'Oi!' said Dave. 'Where are you off to?'

The Runt made no reply but carried on straight towards him.

'Right you,' said Dave. 'I've had about enough of you.' He steadied himself and shut his eyes, ready to take the impact of the Runt at full tilt. Nothing happened. He opened his eyes. The Runt was standing calmly in front of him.

'Out of the way,' she said in an impressive impersonation of the deadpan voice.

'Or what?'

'Or this!'

Dot's front garden was lit by the violent release of half a magazine of sub-machine gun ammunition into the night sky.

When the noise and fire ceased the path in front of the Runt was clear. Without hesitating she ran for her car, tore open the door threw her armaments into the back, leapt in and started the engine. Then she paused before pulling

117

away because the brilliant muzzle flash of the gun was still dancing in her eyes.

'Gosh,' she said, 'did I really do that?'

'Yes,' said a voice from out of the darkness, 'Yes. I'm afraid that you did.'

10

The doorbell rang. Deirdre hurried to answer it. She was out of breath though and it rang twice more before she finally reached the front door.

'Hold on, hold on,' she called anxiously, 'I'm coming.' Rupert was easier to startle than a fawn, she had been telling herself ever since speaking to him on the telephone, and she did not want him to take fright at being kept waiting and run away.

Deirdre straightened her skirt, a clean one that she had just put on, and patted at her hair, which she had just brushed. She glanced back over her shoulder at the living room, which she had just tidied, and caught sight of the whisky bottle, which she had just stoppered up, on the sideboard, which she had just dusted and rearranged. Finally happy that everything was in order she unchained the door and swung it wide, stepping back as she did so. The high, pointed heel of her shoe caught in the thick pile of the hall carpet and she stumbled backwards, twisting her ankle as she fell. She screamed.

Rupert walked in.

'Deirdre?' he said cautiously.

'Oh Rupert.' She burst into tears. 'I've hurt my ankle.'

Where the Diamond was it was warm and dark and lovely and its eventful day was drawing to a mercifully uneventful conclusion.

119

The Diamond was not, in the normal way of things, averse to a bit of eventfulness but then eventfulness did not usually take the form of people making attempts on its life, as Mad Harry had done, or rejecting its allure, as the Runt had done. What with one thing and another it was a day to forget and the Diamond set about forgetting it.

It lay on its back, in a manner of speaking, and stared up at the ceiling and tried to forget. But it could not.

It rolled over on its side and curled up in a ball and tried to forget. And could not. It got up and went to the lavatory and drank a glass of water, all in a manner of speaking, and still it could not forget. So finally it put on its lamb's fleece slippers and its brown check dressing gown with the cord of slippery rope that never stayed tied up and it sat on the edge of the bed and had a good think instead. All in a manner of speaking.

The manner of speaking behind this imagined behaviour was not the manner of speaking of anyone who had owned the Diamond. The Diamond's owners had silk dressing gowns and Morocco slippers. But the Diamond had a theory that to really understand the finer things of life then the grubbier things must be tasted to provide a basis for comparison and sharpen the appreciation. So occasionally it went slumming, in its mind. It was slumming now.

It shifted its imaginary bottom on the edge of its imaginary, lumpy bed and considered its situation. This revolved, for the time being, around Mad Harry Devine.

Mad Harry was not the complicated character that people imagined. He was, instead, a simple man. He was quite simply terribly mad and, because of a simple little misunderstanding, terribly, terribly dangerous.

The misunderstanding began with Harry's ability to read the Diamond's mind, which was just Nature's way of telling him that it had screwed up the wiring in his brain (though there are other causes of such extreme telepathic skill). Because he could read its mind, Harry believed that he understood the Diamond (in much the same way that people who read the Bible believe they understand god). And what Harry saw in the Diamond was nothing less than the end of the world. To him, the chunky lump of carbon was evil incarnate, an impersonal and devilish force that played with people like toys and wished to destroy them all.

To the Diamond, Harry's ideas were laughable. Of course it played with people. What else were toys for? But destroy them all? That was madness piled on madness! What would there be to play with then?

What was worse, Harry was not only dangerous, he was inconvenient. The Diamond didn't merely play. It lived to play. There was nothing else to do. And for as long as Harry was about, it could not play at all. To play, it needed to make telepathic transmissions and if it made them now, then Harry would home in on them. He was a thoroughly relentless man.

So, as the Diamond had said earlier, Harry had to die. It shifted on its uncomfortable bed, in a manner of speaking and considered the next question. How?

Well, there were severe practical difficulties. The Diamond could not kill anybody. It could not do anything at all, which was why it took such pleasure in its imagining doing things. Usually, when it wanted someone dead, it allowed them to own it and then let events take their course. But to be owned again by Mad Harry would be suicide. It was a tough problem, but there had to be a solution.

Rupert looked down at Deirdre lying on the sofa in the Boss's sitting room. Her ankle was hurt, yes, but not as badly as she was making out. She was faking and he was letting her get away with it.

What had not been not faking, though, was the desperation with which she had clung to him as he carried her in from the hall. And Rupert had been touched. For all he had thought about her in the last fifteen years Deirdre might as well have been dead. Perhaps he had even hoped she was. Was that putting it too strongly? But now, as he stood gazing down at the wreck of a woman, now when...

He needed a drink.

He went across to the sideboard, noticed the nearly empty whisky bottle and picked up a full bottle of vodka.

'One for you?' he said, turning back to Deirdre. He was not only unsurprised but glad that her eyes were still fixed on him. She shook her head.

'Not on the wagon are you?'

'No. I've just had enough. For now at least.'

For now, thought Rupert. How long was that? Till she felt thirsty? Till her confidence waned? Or her hope? Whatever that was.

No. It wasn't so easy. He couldn't duck out of it like that. He was her hope. Quite suddenly, out of the blue, it was him, whether he wanted it or not. The realisation brought a responsibility with it and it was not a responsibility that Rupert could ignore for, contrary to popular opinion, he was not a greedy, insensitive man. He was merely a greedy one.

The Runt froze. She stared straight ahead. She listened. Apart from the uneven tick-over of the car, there was nothing, not a sound. So perhaps there had been nothing before. She was overwrought after all. Too much excitement. She tried again, tentatively.

'Gosh,' she said, 'did I really do that?'

'Yes,' said the voice out of the darkness, 'still no change I'm afraid. And what a show, eh? You should have seen old Dave there jump.'

The Runt turned to look at the man beside her but he was only a darker shape in the darkness of the night.

'Dave? The ambulance man? You know him?'

The voice laughed.

'No. Never met him.'

'But...'

'Listening at doors. I suppose I ought to apologise. It's a dreadful habit. Your aunt sends her love by the way.'

The Runt reached up and switched on the car's weak interior light. She stared into Hubcaps's face.

'Aunty Dot?'

'Is that her name?' Hubcaps tried it for size. 'Dot. Yes, it suits her. Aunty Dot.'

'Good of you to say so.' The Runt turned away and stared out through the windscreen. 'Whoever you are.'

Hubcaps turned too to peer out through the back window of the car. By the light from the open doorway of Dot's house he could see Dave the ambulance man cautiously climbing to his feet from out of a flower bed. In the street shadowy figures were gathering round the ambulance making trial assaults against it with spanners and, distant in the night, there was the sound of approaching sirens.

Hubcaps turned back to the Runt.

'I think,' he said, 'that it's time we were going.'

The Runt sat motionless and made no reply. Her stillness was echoed by the car which chose that moment to stall its engine. It might have many differences of opinion with the Runt, but she was still all it had.

'Look,' said Hubcaps, 'I can't blame you if...'

'I'm not going anywhere with you.' The Runt was blazingly angry, her eyes flashed and her mouth was set in thin straight line. 'Not till you tell me where Aunty is.'

Hubcaps looked again out of the back of the car. Dave had successfully chased away the lurking do-it-yourselfers and was now looking thoughtfully at the Runt's car. He started walking towards it.

'Alright,' said Hubcaps, 'they've taken her to hospital.'

'To hospital?'

'Yes.'

'Why should I believe you?'

'Look. We really haven't got time for all this. Just start

the car, eh.' Hubcaps glanced behind again. Dave was only a few paces away.

'Start the car!'

The Runt continued to sit obstinately still. Hubcaps leant across and twisted the ignition key. Much against the little car's will the warm engine started first time.

'You beauty,' murmured Hubcaps under his breath. 'You little beauty.' The Runt remained motionless as Hubcaps began pleading with her, inches from her face. 'Just go, eh? For Pete's sake go. We can sort all this out later, we really can, but for now...'

Then to Hubcaps's surprise the car set off all by itself. The Runt never moved.

'He called me a beauty,' buzzed the little car as it set off down the road. 'Darling man. He actually called me a beauty.' Which only goes to show that while loyalty is all very well, flattery will move mountains. Or battered little cars, anyway.

The car rounded the corner at the top of the street on two wheels and gave its customary skip of pleasure at yet again escaping the depredations of the do-it-yourselfers. The Runt angrily took control. She shook the steering wheel violently and the little car swerved hazardously across the road only narrowly missing a police car which was travelling the opposite way with its blue light flashing.

Rupert held out a packet of cigarettes to Deirdre. She took one and looked up at him.

'Thanks,' she said. 'You're a dar...'

'Ssh!' Rupert held a hand softly over Deirdre's mouth. 'Not so much. Not so fast.' He sat in an armchair at a safe distance.

'So then,' he said. 'Tell me how you are.'

Deirdre's hand shook as she reached out for the pink marble lighter on the green onyx table beside her.

'How am I?' She took a long drag at her cigarette, sucked

the smoke down greedily and blew it out through her nose. 'So much, eh? So fast?' Smoke continued to curl slowly out of her mouth as she spoke and her voice grew harsh and grating. 'Long time no see, Deirdre. It's lovely to see you Deirdre. Let's screw, Deirdre.' She stopped talking, looked hastily away then back again.

'Sorry.' She was shaking her head. 'I'm sorry, I'm sorry, I'm sorry.' She looked up again and away as Rupert remained silent.

'Look, it's going to be a while before he gets back. Our precious Boss. We should play a game or something. Pass the time. You used to enjoy games.'

Deirdre waited for Rupert to respond then waved vaguely in the direction of a walnut chest of drawers.

'They used to be in there, middle drawer, I expect they still are. Choose something eh? Whatever you want.'

When Rupert still did not respond Deirdre sat up angrily.

'For god's sake, we can't just sit here, can we? Staring at each other all night and not saying anything.'

Rupert put his drink down carefully.

'No,' he said, 'I suppose not.' He went across the room, opened the middle drawer, carefully considered its contents and turned back to Deirdre holding a box in either hand.

'Monopoly do you think?' he said, holding up the familiar red box. 'Or,' and his eyes lit up savagely, 'are you feeling up to chess?'

The Diamond had a plan. In its mind it ran over the important points of it.

Point one, it did not know precisely where it was. An acute sense of self preservation had stopped it from reading the Runt's mind as she hid it. And what it did not know, Mad Harry could not read.

Point two, even if Mad Harry tried to home in once the Diamond started transmitting, the madness of the hospital corridors would head him off and stop him from getting anywhere.

Point three. When it really came down to it, the Diamond was cleverer than Mad Harry. And more experienced. The outcome was a foregone conclusion.

Point four. The plan was still risky though. Complacency was out, but, and the Diamond smiled, it was going to be a lot of fun

And now, it was time. The air hummed and vibrated as the Diamond sent out a narrow but powerful telepathic search beam to find Mad Harry.

'A penny for them,' said a voice in the Diamond's ear.

'Eh?' said the Diamond. Its search beam stuttered and died as it tried to find out who had interrupted it.

'I said, 'A penny for them.'' said the voice again.

'I know that,' said the Diamond, 'I heard first time.'

'Well really!' said the voice. 'Then why say "eh", eh? Rude, I call it, when I was only trying to be civil.'

'I'm sorry,' said the Diamond, 'if I was uncivil but...'

'If he was uncivil, he says,' said the voice on a rising sharp note. 'If he was uncivil. He was either uncivil or he wasn't. There's no "if" about it.' Voices from all around the Diamond muttered agreement with the aggrieved voice.

'Look!' said the Diamond loudly. 'I was uncivil. I'm sorry. And now, if you'll excuse me, I'm busy.'

'Oh,' said the aggrieved voice, 'so he's busy. And wouldn't we all like that, to be busy? I mean, look at me, a perfectly good powder puff.' The surrounding voices murmured assent. 'Nothing wrong with me. But am I busy? Since she decided all she wanted was "the natural look". Hah! And what's so natural about soap and water anyway? That's what I'd like to know.

'Grease, that's natural. Blackheads, they're natural. But clean?' The voice of the powder puff shuddered. 'Ugh!'

'It's nothing a good bit of foundation wouldn't cure, though,' said a mascara placatingly. 'Excuse my friend,' it went on, 'but we've all been a bit on edge in here since...'

'And don't you go apologising for me neither,' shrieked the powder puff in a sudden ecstasy of outrage. 'We're all in the same boat here so it's no good you putting on your airs and graces. Mascara indeed!'

'""In here", eh?' said a voice that the Diamond knew at once was vastly more disturbed than mere neurotic cosmetics. The voice laughed.

'That's right, it's me. I got your little flash just now. So tell me, where might "here" be then?'

The Runt's car was rapidly approaching a junction where Hubcaps and the Runt would need to turn into the High Street.

'We could stop here if you like,' said Hubcaps, 'we should be safe enough now.' The Runt did not reply. She kept her foot firmly pressed down on the accelerator.

'We'd better not go into the High Street,' said Hubcaps, 'we might be too conspicuous.'

Still the Runt did not respond.

Hubcaps sighed deeply, looked up at the ceiling and said, 'Stop will you my beauty? Just here on the left will be fine.'

The car started indicating left and pulled up smoothly under a lamp post. The Runt kicked at the accelerator and everything else in sight but there was no response from the car.

'Thank you,' murmured Hubcaps softly. He turned to the Runt. 'Good little car you've got here,' he said, 'I hope you appreciate it properly.' There was a noise like sardonic laughter until the car's engine cut out and then there was silence.

'We were meant to be going to the hospital,' said the Runt through clenched teeth.

Hubcaps shook his head.

'No point. Your aunt's not there.'

'But you said...'

'I lied.'

'I see.' The Runt pursed her lips. 'So where is she then? What have you done with her?'

'Me?' Hubcaps sounded incredulous. 'What have I done with her? This is your aunt we're talking about.' He leant back, exasperated. 'Last I saw of her she was taking charge of a gang of thugs and, as far as I could tell, was on her way back home to sort out a couple of other thugs who thought they had her locked in the cellar.'

'Why should I believe you? You've already lied once.'

Hubcaps shrugged.

'Who'd make it up? It's too improbable.'

Like so many people before him, Hubcaps was finding the Runt infuriating. But she was lovely with it too he thought, now that he came to look more closely. His voice softened.

'Look. Look at it this way. There you were, right, with machine guns and ambulance men and police screaming around all over the place and who got you out of it? Me. And all I want now is to get you and your Aunt back together and out of trouble.'

'Why?'

'Because I owe her a favour.'

'And you expect me to believe that?' said the Runt. 'What do you want really? And what are you going to do with me? You've already got my car working for you.'

Hubcaps sighed again.

'Can't you just trust me?'

The Runt did not reply.

'Look. Would it help if I said that I know you've got the Diamond and that I'm not interested in it?'

'Ah! You see? You're after the Diamond.'

'I am not after the Diamond.'

'Well "Hah!" to that. You're just a crook. One of them.'

'For heaven's sake!' Hubcaps stared moodily out of his

window, breathing deeply. How on earth was he going to...

Hubcaps's thoughts were interrupted by something small and hard nudging gently into his side. He froze. Oh no. Oh dear no. Oh please, please no. Very, very slowly he turned his head to look at the Runt. She was smiling pleasantly and in her hands was the deadpan voice's sub-machine gun.

'Go to jail, go directly to jail, do not pass "Go" do not collect two hundred pounds.' Deirdre smiled at Rupert. 'Off you go then,' she said.

'How long before the Boss gets back did you say?' said Rupert but Deirdre ignored him.

'Go to jail,' she said. 'Come on, off you go.' She put the pink card back at the bottom of its pile, picked up the little top hat that was Rupert's token and put it in jail.

'There,' she said. She paused and looked directly at Rupert.

'About the Boss. You didn't say what you wanted him for. Wasn't he meant to be going to stay with you tomorrow anyway?'

Rupert looked at his watch.

'Yeah,' he said, 'it still is tomorrow. God but it's been a long day.'

Deirdre picked up the dice and passed them to Rupert.

'It's your go again, you threw doubles.'

Rupert took the dice and dropped them lethargically onto the board.

'Double four,' said Deirdre, 'You're out again. Easy eh?'

Rupert moved his token eight spaces.

'And that's mine,' said Deirdre, 'Rent please.' She fumbled through the pile of cards at her elbow. 'Marlborough Street, with a hotel, nine hundred and fifty pounds.'

Rupert picked up his last two toy pound notes and dropped them on Deirdre's side of the board.

'That's it,' he said, 'I'm done. You've won.' He looked up and met Deirdre's eyes for the first time since they had started playing the game. He had forgotten how powerful those eyes were. They could get right to you, if you let them. Those eyes.

And the tragic thing about Deirdre was that in all her life she had never won. Not a thing.

Those eyes.

First she had had him and then she had had the Boss. She was a two-time loser in spades.

Those eyes.

And none of it was her fault. Not really. Not at all.

He was responsible.

Without thinking what he was doing Rupert reached across the Monopoly board, caught hold of Deirdre's hands and, cradling them in his own, he blurted out,

'For god's sake, Deirdre, what are we doing sitting here, playing games, wasting time. He'll be back any time now. We need to talk.'

The Diamond listened to Mad Harry's voice and felt anxious. It wondered why. But, with Harry inside its head again, thinking was difficult.

'Yes, it's an interesting question,' said the invasive voice. 'Why are you anxious? I assumed you wanted to talk to me.'

'I did.'

'But?'

'I thought someone was going to tell me where I was.'

'Yes, handy that. Not knowing. But you needn't worry. They already have.'

'Well I don't know where I am, I'm sure.'

'Then think about it.'

The Diamond thought about it with the nervy clumsiness of a skilled driver being watched by an advanced driving instructor.

'Got anywhere yet? A powder puff. Mascara? Where the hell do you think you are?'

130

'In a make-up bag?'

'I'd say so, wouldn't you?' The Diamond made no reply. Cold shivers were running up and down its spine and its bowels had turned to water, in a manner of speaking.

'And where do you suppose the old woman keeps her make-up bag?'

Inside the Diamond's head the thought was out without thinking. Harry pounced.

'Ah! But not the old woman at all. A girl.'

'Young woman,' corrected the Diamond sadly.

'Whatever you say.' Mad Harry was thoughtful as he riffled through the Diamond's mind. 'Good looking girl too, isn't she? By normal standards.'

The Diamond tried desperately to shut down and lock Mad Harry out again. The powder puff had thrown it off balance. It needed a second chance. But the great drawback to telepathy is that once a two-way link is established it needs the agreement of both parties to break it. Mad Harry laughed at the Diamond's efforts. Then. 'Well, well,' he said. 'She seems familiar. This young woman. Do I know her?'

'How would I know?'

'Yes. Yes. I think I do. I've seen that face before. But where, eh? That's the question. Where?' Once again the Diamond was unable to keep the answer back.

'Of course, she's a nurse, the nurse, the one I saw...' Mad Harry's voice shifted from pleasure to pain.

'First left, second left, first left, first left, second left and it's second on the right. Not far. Well I'd certainly like to meet her again.' Harry paused to recover control of himself. 'And where do you suppose a nurse might keep her make-up bag?'

'Don't know.' The Diamond felt it had given away quite enough already. And it was worried.

'At home?'

'Search me.'

'In her locker in the staff room? Do they have one of those? Somewhere to tart themselves up when they come off duty?'

'Look, Harry.' The Diamond was practically pleading. 'Is all this really necessary? Shouldn't we work it out peacefully? Couldn't we talk?'

Parked in the Runt's car with the sub-machine gun poking into his ribs, Hubcaps grasped firmly at all the non-chalance he could muster but most of it slipped through his fingers.

'Great,' he said, 'really helpful. So what are you going to do now?'

'Shut up!' The Runt jabbed Hubcaps with the gun. 'I need to think.'

Hubcaps smiled winningly.

'I said shut up!' The Runt jabbed Hubcaps again.

'Yes,' said Hubcaps, 'I heard. You need to think.' Very slowly he turned to look ahead.

'And that's fine with me. Take all the time you like. Personally though...' Hubcaps spoke with tremendous care. 'I think we should talk.'

11

'And abra-ca-bleedin'-dabra to you and all.' Dot was
hissing at Rudge under cover of the chorus's chanting. 'It's
not abra-ca-bleedin'-dabra I want. It's for you to start...'
Suddenly Dot stopped walking and stiffened. Her head was
cocked to one side, listening. Rudge was carried away
ahead of her into the night and a large body cannoned into
her from behind.

'Look out eh?' grunted a rat-voice. 'What the hell do
you... Oh. Sorry Mrs Coulson.'

'Miss it is. But call me Dot. Everyone does.' Dot patted
the rat-voice's arm. 'And keep up the chanting, eh. We
don't want spirits flagging do we?' She hurried on from the
now bewildered rat-voice and called out to the chorus in a
voice that she was trying to keep anxiety out of.

'That's it lads! Keep up the good work! Inwards and
outwards and upwards and downwards, take a vote!'

'YE-NO-SS!'

Dot may have been merely a little, old woman. But, like
a spur on the flanks of a war-horse, she was plenty big
enough to keep the Boss's boys stirred up. They attacked
their chanting with renewed vigour and Dot went surging
on through the throng till she was again alongside Rudge.

'Did you hear that?' she hissed at him. He looked round,
startled.

'Oh, it's you. Don't keep doing that.'

'Did you hear it?'

'Hear what?'

'Just then. A machine gun. A long burst.'

'No. Never heard a thing. You're sure, are you?'

A peevish expression was a waste of time, under the circumstances, so Dot settled instead for 'I'm sure.' Rudge didn't hear anyway. He was again dragged on ahead of her. She hurried for a dozen paces, trying to get back beside him but before she reached him a new noise came through the night and this time it made itself clearly heard, not by rising above the chanting of the chorus but by slicing clean through it.

Dot reached Rudge and gripped his arm, what she could reach of it round the twining arms of the rat-voices.

'You can hear them I suppose? Those sirens.'

'Yes.' Rudge was peevish.

'And do you want to guess where they're going?'

'I can imagine where they're going. But if you think I... Urrggh!' Rudge just managed to stifle the cry of pain that was caused by Dot's fingernails suddenly digging into his arm and Dot gave him no time for further complaint. She was all at once urgent and decisive.

'I've had an idea,' she hissed. 'Just follow my lead. Right?'

'But...'

'No time for questions. Think on your feet. And if we play our cards right, we can ditch the lot of them.'

'But...'

'That is what we need to do, isn't it?' urged Dot. Then she was gone, elbowing her way towards the front of the crowd.

'Shut up a moment!' she yelled at the chorus swarming round her. 'Shut up, eh!' But the chorus did not hear and it continued its inexorable march.

Ahead of them a small, dim patch of yellow light was growing larger moment by moment. It was the end of the short cut, where it met Dot's street.

'Lads! Lads!' yelled Dot but she was unable to make herself heard. And the noise of the sirens was louder now. Soon it would all be too late. In a moment of decision Dot span round and kicked the nearest rat-voice hard on the shin.

'Shut up!' she yelled full into his face and now he got the message. Dot lashed out again with her foot and connected with a knee cap. 'Look, shut up, eh.' Gradually she brought the whole chorus to a halt.

'Er, what's up?' said a rat-voice. 'I thought we was going...'

'Where we were going,' said Dot sharply, 'is just down there.' She pointed in the direction of the light at the end of the short cut. 'But right now "down there" is trouble.'

'And how do you know?'

'Listen to her lads.' It was Rudge's voice, cutting through the disbelief. 'She knows what she's on about.'

Well done Rudge, thought Dot.

The chorus grumblingly fell silent. Following Dot was all very well, since no one else was leading them anywhere, but Rudge was a different matter. Dot continued.

'You hear the sirens down there? Well I think they mean something, don't you?'

There were murmurs of agreement.

'And what I think they mean is that the police have been getting themselves together a little party. Quite a little party. And, though this is only a guess mind, I'd say they're having their party round my house.'

Dot paused to let the chorus digest this.

'Round your house?'

'Bang goes our tea then. I was looking forward to a nice cup of tea.'

'But why your house?'

'Why my house?' Dot laughed. 'Why my house?' She sighed deeply. It sounded like exasperation, but it was satisfaction. The chorus were so predictable.

'Because they're on to her of course.' Rudge put in quickly. He had half guessed what Dot was about. He hoped he was right. 'Good Mr Rudge. Very good,' said Dot. He was catching on fast. She decided to see if he was with her all the way.

'But that's not the half of the problem, is it?" she said.

'No,' agreed Rudge, 'it's not. The real thing is whether or not the police get the Diamond before we do.'

Dot heaved a sigh of relief. Rudge really was good. He was so very good.

'Eh?' said a rat-voice. 'You mean the jewel's in the house? With the police?'

'Not for long it's not,' said Rudge getting into his stride. 'Pretty soon it'll be down the nick. Gone for ever.'

'He's right,' said Dot brightly.

'So what do we do?' said a rat-voice nervously. Where the police were involved, the chorus's instinct was to run a mile.

'Oh, there's any number of things we could do,' said Dot airily. 'Isn't that right Mr Rudge?' She could trust him now. They were working together.

'Oh yeah,' said Rudge obligingly. 'Any number of things.'

'Like what?' said a grumpy voice.

'Doesn't matter,' said Rudge, 'because we're not doing any of them. We're going to turn round, leave them to it and tell the Boss that we tried but we just couldn't get it back.'

Dot was horror struck. Just when things were going so well, just when it looked like Rudge was right there with her, he had turned against her.

The chorus's stunned silence was broken by a peevish rat-voice.

'Says who?'

Oh Mister Rudge, I am sorry, thought Dot at the sound of that voice.

'Yeah! 'Sright. Says who?'

Sorry I doubted you.

'He's gone freelance. Remember?'

Even for a moment.

'Can't do what he says.'

'Vote on it?' suggested Dot. She gave the words just the right touch of hesitation. There were murmurs of approval.

'The motion is,' said Dot becoming much more authoritative, 'that we don't do what Rudge suggests. One, two, three. Vote!'

'YEESS!'

'That's unanimous then, is it, then?'

'Yeah!'

'Right. Then quiet. This is what we'll do instead.'

Down in Dot's street the atmosphere had become extremely tense. A bull-like police inspector wearing overalls, body armour, gun belt and visored helmet was towering over Dave the ambulance man and gripping him by the shoulders.

'So. Take it steady, right? How many hostages? How many hostage takers? What room were they in when you last saw them? How many rooms?'

'Look, I think there must be some...' but Dave was not allowed to finish. The inspector went on unregarding.

'And doors. How many? Open or shut? Are the hostages standing or sitting? Are they under restraint? And what about supplies and services? Food? Water? Sewers? For god's sake man I need answers!'

In his excitement the inspector was shaking Dave backwards and forwards but, suddenly, he froze, an anxious expression crept over his face and he looked slowly round.

The street was brilliantly flood lit. The wrecks of the white minibus and Hubcaps's car had been dragged to the end of the street and Dave's ambulance had been parked beside them to give a clear field of view to the wide arc of police cars and vans that was facing Dot's house. From behind each vehicle policemen trained guns on the old woman's front door and from out of the shadows hungry eyes gazed assessingly at the shiny ambulance and police cars. Now that the inspector had stopped shaking Dave, the whole street was motionless. Standing in that empty space in front of the police cordon Dave felt exposed and suddenly frightened. Apparently the inspector felt the same for he abruptly folded Dave under his arm and sprinted towards the police cars.

'For god's sake man,' he shouted as he ran, 'what were you thinking of? Standing out there like a drip in a drought.' With a loud cry of 'Take cover!' he took a flying leap and landed heavily behind a police van with Dave underneath him. Then, gripping Dave to his chest in a massive bear hug, the inspector rolled sideways ten yards, coming to rest on top of the unfortunate and, by now, unconscious ambulance man. He raised his head and looked around.

'Okay then.' The inspector was panting loudly. 'We're safe enough here.' He rolled off Dave, gripped him by the front of his jersey and stabbed a finger against his chest.

'Right, sonny, it's time for some answers. And I don't want...' But there was something about Dave that gave the inspector pause for thought.

'Sonny?' He shook Dave. It was his first remotely gentle gesture but it came too late. Dave wasn't listening. The inspector dropped him, wiped his hands as though to eradicate contamination and bellowed out to no one in particular, 'Fetch me another witness! This one's broken!' Quizzical glances and shrugs passed rapidly along the police cordon but no one replied.

'I said...' bellowed the inspector but he was cut short by a cheerful voice.

'There aren't no more witnesses sir!' The inspector rose to his knees to see who had spoken but all his men were absolutely still.

'Only the one!' came the cheerful voice again.

Cheeky beggar. The inspector's cheeks were burning. How dare he be amused? And there was tittering. He was sure there was tittering.

'Are you sure there aren't any more?'

'Quite sure sir.'

There was tittering. Well. If that was the way they wanted to play things, they were playing them with the wrong man. He would show them. Throwing caution to the winds the inspector stood and strode out into the empty space in front of Dot's garden.

'Okay lads,' he shouted, 'then there's only thing for it. We can't take risks with people's lives, can we?'

'But sir...'

The inspector scrutinised his men carefully but it was impossible, with the shadows, the armour and the visors, to see who was talking.

'Sir. That ambulance man said...'

'Beggar what he said. Unreliable witness. Look at him now, asleep for god's sake.'

Tittering.

The inspector scowled. He would give them tittering. He turned to face Dot's house, drew his pistol, held it high in the air and cocked it.

'Alright lads. We're going in. On the count of three. One. Two...'

In a narrow back alley behind Dot's house the chorus waited in a sweaty, breathy silence.

For Dot it had been hard work. She had first persuaded the chorus to her plan, then pushed them along into the back alley, showed them the house and finally then sorted into order for going in. She wanted no confusion over going in because – she thought of the key under its stone by the back door – the sooner they were in, the sooner she could stop then coming out. She swallowed nervously.

139

'Right then,' she whispered, 'one, two...'

'Looks bleedin' quiet to me,' said a nervous rat-voice.

'Yeah,' sighed Dot, 'cunning bleeders. Now, if you're quite ready, we'll try again. One, two,...'

'What about Rudge?' said another voice. 'Freelance. I don't trust him.'

'We agreed about Rudge.' Dot sighed. 'We voted. Remember? I look after him here till you get back with the Diamond.'

'Oh yeah.'

'Right then. Anyone else got anything to say?' Dot allowed a note of peevishness to creep into her voice. 'No? Okay then. When I say "three". One. Two...'

Behind the inspector a knowing wink and a smile were running along the police cordon.

'Posey beggar,' said the wink.

'Sit tight,' replied the smile. 'There's nothing in there any-way.'

'THREE!' The inspector sprinted for Dot's house with never a backward glance.

'THREE!' yelled Dot at the top of her voice. Instantly a company of tough men in dark, flowing coats was hurtling down her back yard and into the quiet silence of her house. She found the spectacle surprisingly moving and exhilarating. But there was no time to watch for long. Dot followed the chorus and, as soon as the last man was in, she slammed the back door and locked it.

'Time to go, I think,' she said. 'The Runt won't hang about for ever.'

'No,' agreed Rudge right behind her. 'Not if she's half as smart as her aunt.'

The police cordon was more or less expecting to see their inspector again fairly soon. What was surprising was to see him unconscious and rolling like a football out of Dot's house in front of a hoard of men in dark, flowing coats.

The hoard of men were surprised too. They had screwed their nerves to such a pitch of tension for their uncharacteristic confrontation with the police that, when they met no more resistance than one, agitated inspector, the force of their charge carried them right through the house, down the garden and into the street beyond. And now there was this white line of police cars with a darker line of rifles drawn around it. They came shuddering to a halt. The darker rim of rifles rattled slightly as butts were drawn more tightly into shoulders.

Time stood still.

Then, suddenly, 'Don't shoot,' yelled an urgent voice from the police line. 'They're not armed.'

The chorus studied their hands as if they were surprised to find that what had been shouted was true. There was a thoughtful pause.

'So it's just a bundle then, is it?' enquired another police voice.

'Yeah. Looks like it.'

'Good idea.'

'Right then, a bundle it is,' said an authoritative voice. 'Rifles in the trucks lads.'

In general, British bobbies don't like shooting people. But a good, vigorous bundle, that's a different matter. A good, vigorous bundle is what keeping the peace is all about. The Boss's boys waited patiently as the cordon dissolved into a milling chaos of dark blue overalls depositing fire arms, armour and helmets safely in the back of transit vans.

The police gathered again in front of the chorus. They looked vastly more cheerful,

'Okay then. Alright,' said the authoritative voice and a doughty police sergeant stepped forward to confront the chorus. 'You lot ready, are you?'

'Um, I'm not sure,' said the rat-voice who had ended up

at the front. 'We'll need to take a vote.' He turned to his colleagues.

'What about it then? The motion is, are we ready? One, two, three...'

'YEESS!' Adrenaline was flowing freely through the chorus's veins. It is a foolish drug.

The rat-voice turned back to the police spokesman.

'Unanimous,' He smiled nervously and shrugged. 'Well that's democracy for you.'

'Humpph.' The sergeant did not smile. 'There's none of that where I come from.' He turned to the serried ranks of blue behind him. 'Bundle it is lads,' he called. Then, turning back to face the chorus, he raised his right arm high in the air, like a general at Waterloo, and brought it down with a magnificent flourish. In a shout that rent the night the policemen gave voice to their immortal battle cry, 'Oi, oi, oi oi, oi. You're NICKED!' and as a single man they rushed down on the steadfast ranks of the Boss's bravest and best.

12

Far away, in the living room of the lonely villa on its empty stretch of Spanish coast, Poppy was deep in thought. And that in itself, she reflected, would be enough to make Rupert smile. It was not Poppy's business to think. She frowned and raised a hand to wipe at an itchy smear of grease on her forehead. Like her hands and the overalls she was still wearing, her face was well covered in grease. And so, now, was the ostentatious, white leather sofa on which she was lying. She wasn't at ease, though. This was an act of revolt and revolutions are not restful.

Poppy hated the sofa. It represented Rupert's worst side, his love of things. He surrounded himself with things. They were beautiful, in their way, Poppy supposed, but they were so ... take this sofa for example ... so bossy. They demanded infinite caution and care. And got them.

Even now, they got them.

Poppy stood up, not knowing quite why, and looked at the grime she had smeared over the pristine leather. Without her doing anything about it her head became filled with thoughts of methylated spirits and Swarfega. It was as if the sofa was... But now she was being silly. The sofa was not to blame for Rupert's faults. The sofa just was what it was. It could not be anything else.

'How kind of you to think so.'

Poppy was startled. It was enough to drive anyone crazy, being alone in this place all the time, but voices in her head were something new. She was worried.

'There's really no need to worry.'

Poppy looked hastily around. The voice sounded terribly real.

'Though I would too, I suppose, in your shoes.'

Poppy turned her back to the sofa and stood, brave and challenging, prepared to face the worst.

'Where... Where are you?' Her voice was tentative at first but it became more confident as the sound of it gave her reassurance. 'Who are you?'

'I could well ask you the same question,' said the voice. 'But the answer would be too shocking.'

'What...' Poppy's confidence was shaken. 'What do you mean?'

'That's for me to know.' The voice was indifferent. 'And for you to find out.' It paused. 'I'm behind you, by the way.'

Poppy spun round, wide eyed and staring. Beyond the sofa there was no one, only empty parquet, a rough-textured, white wall and an unframed Expressionist painting. Beside the picture a tall, blank, black window reached from ceiling to floor. Poppy rushed round the sofa and drew the drapes, hanging in desperation onto the cord in case they should fly open and reveal...

'There's no one out there,' said the voice. 'You're quite safe. I'm over here.'

Poppy looked up, frightened. There was the sofa again, and more empty parquet and the living room door. It was open. She fled across the room, slammed the door and leant against it, panting and panicky.

'Look,' said the voice gently. 'Use your eyes. I'm right here in front of you.'

All that was there was the sofa, rock-solid and real, unbearably real, more real than it had ever been.

'But...' Poppy felt weak. 'But you're a sofa.'

'You're finally there. And it wasn't so difficult, was it?'

144

'But... A sofa.'

'Well there's nothing wrong with being a sofa. Like you said, it's the mould I was cast in, the way I was wrought. I couldn't be anything else.'

'But... But...'

'But I'm a thing. I can't talk. Is that what you're going to say?'

'Yes.'

'You can talk,' said the sofa in a very reasonable voice.

'But I'm not a thing.'

'You're talking to me.'

In the hospital the sleepers continued to sleep but they were less unconscious than they had been. They stirred in their beds and uttered noises that sounded like words but were not words. Coloured with sounds from the waking world, their dreams were becoming increasingly vivid.

Not that there were many sounds. The hospital was quiet, unnervingly quiet, and there were rumours going about of a madman on the loose. Being cautious people, the hospital staff were going around in pairs as they made their evening rounds. In the sleepers' ward a doctor and a nurse patrolled in silence. Well, silence? Not quite.

To the Sailor the slight sound of their rubber-soled shoes was the tacky, pulsating whisper that fills the cold, dank spaces at the after end of submarines. There, in brilliantly lit whiteness, the propeller shafts lazily rotate, round and round and round and round in beds of sticky grease.

To the Axe the sound was whispered messages passing through prison darkness.

To the Boss the sound was the soft creaking of rope when a victim has finished talking. He hangs, swinging gently, and hopes, but never expects, that now the pain will go away.

To Vernon the whispering was more than shoes. It was voices. They stopped by his bed.

'God, what a night. Have you ever known anything like it?'

'No, I never have. It's never been so quiet. Which means, doesn't it...' A chair creaked as someone sat in it. 'That we can afford to take a rest.'

'I suppose so.' A bedside locker bumped against the wall as a heavy body leant on it.

'Nice though, isn't it?' In the world beyond Vernon's dreams a nurse turned contentedly towards a doctor who looked anxiously at his watch.

'No it bloody isn't. If I've got to hang around all night, I'd prefer to be doing something useful.'

The nurse sighed.

'They sent an ambulance out earlier on,' she said. 'So I heard.'

'Yes, but it hasn't come back yet, has it?' The doctor sighed too and looked again at his watch. The nurse watched, thoughtfully.

'That's the second time you've done that in a minute.'

'Yes. Well. Have you got any idea what time it is?'

'No.'

'Not half as late as it feels.'

The doctor clasped his hands and unclasped them, folded his arms and unfolded them, thrust his hands into the pockets of his white coat then took them out and finally studied his fingernails. The nurse reached out and touched his hand.

'Relax, eh?'

'I can't relax.' He looked once more at his watch then stood up and moved away.

'Are you coming?'

The nurse sighed.

Vernon half-opened one eye and watched the backs of the doctor and the nurse as they dwindled down the length of the ward. He smiled. They were wraiths, these white figures in the warm gloom. They were ghosts. They were – the

146

thought was shocking – intruders in his bedroom. He sat up, wide eyed and staring. He didn't have a bedroom. He hadn't had a bedroom for a long time. So where the hell was he? And what was going on?

'But...' Poppy was having a tough time. She understood all right what the sofa was telling her - her agile brain had won her first class honours in electronic engineering at Aston-in-Birmingham - but her problem was that she didn't want to believe it.

'But all these things...' she said. 'You, the swimming pool, the Franz Marc, the Ferrari, the villa...'

'And you.' The sofa was persistent, patient and persistent. 'Don't forget you.'

'But I am not a thing. I keep on telling you.'

'What are you then?'

'I'm... I'm...' Poppy knew perfectly well what she was. She had always known what she was. But in front of a sofa she didn't like to say. She ducked the issue again.

'Whatever I am, I'm not part of this competition of yours. I don't care which of you gets the most admiration, attention, whatever it is you're after.

'I mean. For heaven's sake. I clean the swimming pool. I dust the picture. I fix the car.'

'And you cover me in grease. I do hope you'll be good and clean me up before Rupert gets back. I'd hate him to see me looking like this.'

Poppy looked down and shuffled her feet uncomfortably.

'Yes, well, I'm sorry about that. I mean, I didn't know that...'

'No need to apologise. And why don't you sit down? You look so uncomfortable.'

Poppy lowered herself gracefully to sit cross-legged on the floor.

'Oh, really. Now I'm terribly hurt. Aren't I more comfortable than parquet?'

147

Poppy laughed.

'It's no laughing matter,' said the sofa stiffly.

'Sorry, it's just, I couldn't possibly sit on you and talk to you at the same time.'

'Whatever you like. Only don't say I never offered.'

There was a long pause and Poppy began to feel ridiculous. She stared hard at a dint in the parquet to hide the smile that she could not keep back. Then, making a great effort to keep a straight face she looked up and politely enquired,

'So. What's it like? Being a sofa?'

In The Borough night an ambulance siren fell suddenly silent.

'That's better,' grunted Florien the ambulance woman. She leaned forward with her head in her hands. 'Oh god. My head.'

'Some punch, it must have been,' said Dave with a slight laugh. A spasm of pain cut him short and he winced.

'It's not funny, you silly beggar,' said Florien. She was angry.

But then, she was often angry, thought Dave.

'She was a nurse for god's sake,' Florien went on.

And peevish.

'Nurses are meant to be sweet and nice.'

Dave snorted. It was easier than laughing.

'Oh yeah? None I ever met.'

They drove on in silence for a while.

'Anyway,' said Dave, 'you can thank your lucky stars that it wasn't you being landed on by bloody great policemen.' He tried to breath in deeply but the pain in his ribs stopped him.

'And shouldn't you be back with those two.' He gestured over his shoulder. 'What if they start vomiting or something?'

Florien rested her head in her hands again and groaned.

'I'm not up to it. They'll just have to manage by themselves. And anyway, they're bloody lucky we got them out at all. If that riot hadn't rolled off up the street...'

'Which reminds me,' said Dave, 'we should be lining up more blood wagons. Lots of them. A whole bleedin' convoy.' He reached out for the radio handset but winced as the pain stabbed him in the chest again so that he had to withdraw his hand.

'You do it, eh.'

Florien picked up the hand set.

'And make sure that...'

'Alright. Alright. I know what I'm doing.'

'That's good then,' he said, letting go of the steering wheel with one hand to explore what felt like a broken rib. 'So you'll know how to leave us out of it, won't you?'

'Oh for god's sake!' said the sofa.

'Whoever he is, 'said Poppy.

'You see? There you go again. Changing the subject. Can't you just stick to the point?'

'Alright.' Poppy stood up and leant over the sofa. 'The point. I am not a thing. Whatever you say. I am not a part of your silly competition and I don't give a damn which of you Rupert prefers. Pictures, pools, cars, furniture. Whatever. And now, if you'll excuse me, I have better things to spend my time on than talking to mere sofas.'

'Unfair!' For a moment the sofa sounded really hurt and Poppy felt a pang of remorse. But then it went on with acid in its voice. 'I never said you were a mere doll.'

Poppy froze. She glared at the sofa and her head was filled with thoughts of destruction.

'Yes. Well. No need to be like that.' The sofa sounded contrite. 'It wouldn't be true anyway, would it?'

Poppy remained frozen.

'You're not merely a doll. You are one hell of a doll.' They were Rupert's words. Words he used often.

'You bastard,' breathed Poppy.

'Metaphor.' The sofa's contrition was gone. 'Euphemism. Poetic licence. How hard you all do work, persuading yourselves that what you hear is not the literal truth.'

'Damn you!' Poppy turned abruptly and walked to the door.

'So you don't mind then?' the sofa called after her as she disappeared into the hallway. Poppy came back and leant with her arms folded against the door frame. It did not shimmer.

'Mind what?'

'That Rupert prefers me to you.'

'He doesn't!' The reaction was instant. Poppy was out-raged. 'He can't! How do you...' And then she realised what the sofa had done.

'No,' she gasped.

'Yes,' said the sofa.

Poppy slid down to the floor.

'No, no, no, no, no.'

'Can I do it to you?' said Poppy some time later.

'What's that?' said the sofa.

'Read your mind. That's how you talk, isn't it? You things. With telepathy.' She paused. 'We things.'

'Yes,' said the sofa. 'With practice, I suppose. If I'm not trying to keep you out. Dolls are often very good at it.'

Poppy hung her head and caught sight of herself. She was still wearing the grease-covered overalls.

'I don't look much of a doll at the moment.'

'Ah, but you've got a day off.' Acid returned to the sofa's voice. 'So lucky you. I never get a day off being a sofa.'

13

In the Runt's car, Hubcaps continued to look straight ahead with a frozen stare. Eventually he blinked.

'Go on then,' said the Runt, 'what are you waiting for? I thought you said we should talk.'

In its warm but compromised hiding place in the Runt's make-up bag the Diamond was trying to work out how best to make its proposal to Mad Harry.

'However you like,' said Marry Harry inside the Diamond's mind. 'Come on, why hesitate? It was you who wanted to talk.'

'Rupert!' said Deirdre, but her protest was not strong. She was enjoying too much the sensation of Rupert's hands under her skirt and inside her blouse. 'I thought we were meant to be talking.'

'Yes,' said Rupert thoughtfully. He was still for a moment, kneeling beside the sofa. 'We were meant to be, weren't we?' He leant forward and gently kissed Deirdre's mouth. 'After all.' He kissed her again. 'You're the last person I expected to see.' And another kiss. And not so gentle. 'That needs some explaining.'

'Come on then.' (Jab.) 'Talk.' Much to Hubcaps's discomfort the Runt was punctuating her remarks with good hard jabs of the gun into his side. 'You got into my car.'

151

(Jab.) 'You made it drive off.' (Jab.) 'You stole my aunt.'
(Jab.) 'So talk.' (Jab, jab.)

'I wish you'd stop doing that,' said Hubcaps with infinite
care. 'It might go off.'

On The Borough's telepathic wave bands there was
silence. Impatience thrummed through it.

'Well? I'm waiting.'

'I know you are,' said the Diamond.

'I know you...'

'It's just... Well. You're such a difficult man to talk to.'

'Difficult!' roared Mad Harry. 'For crying out loud. Me?
Difficult?'

In the Boss's living room, the conversation, as such, did
not last long. There continued to be vocalisations though.
They went like this.

'Aaah, Deirdre.'

'Rupert.'

'It's been so long.'

'Ohhhh. Forever.'

'Aaaguunghh.'

'Rupert! That hurt.'

'Damn! Damn! Oh damn!'

'What's the matter?'

'Cramp.'

'Cramp?'

'Yes! My leg.'

'Let me see. Oh yes. There. There. There.'

The silence of skilled massage.

'Better?'

'Yes. But...'

'More better?'

'Oh yes.'

'Should we go somewhere comfy, then?'

'Ohhhh. Yes.'

'Calling me "difficult".' Mad Harry was incensed. 'I know what all this is about. You're buying time. You've got nothing to say.'

'Oh yes I have.'

'Oh no you... Shut up! Stop that! I think I'll just have a look.'

The Diamond felt Harry's fingers riffle down through the layers of its consciousness. It was an unpleasant experience but, even if it could not lock Harry out, it could perhaps do something about it. Something savage.

Mad Harry screamed. There was the sound of sore fingers being sucked.

'What do you want to do that for?'

'Now,' said the Diamond primly, 'are you listening?'

'Ungmm,' said Harry in the voice of a man with a mouthful of fingers.

'Good. Then first of all, a question.' The Diamond took a deep breath. 'How do you fancy ruling the world?'

'You know, when you come to think about it...' Hubcaps was sitting extremely still. The Runt's gun was still pressing into his side. 'What's the point?'

'Eh?'

'In me talking.'

'I don't...' The Runt looked puzzled for a moment and then suddenly she brightened.

'Ah,' she said.

'Exactly,' said Hubcaps.

'You'd like to talk, of course...'

'Love to. But then...'

'How can I be expected to believe...'

'A crook like me.'

Hubcaps laughed and turned to look at the Runt. She really was very good looking, he thought.

'We did that well together, didn't we?' he said.

153

'Maybe.' (Jab.) 'But it still doesn't let you off the hook.'

'Oh, I don't know.' Hubcaps felt a resurgence of non-chalance. He had just a seen a way to get rid of the gun in his side. 'I can respect your feelings there. The Robber's Code and all that.'

'Eh?' said the Runt.

'The Robbers' Code,' said Hubcaps. He sounded surprised, as though the Runt must surely know all about the Robbers' Code. The Runt looked blank.

'Don't tell me you haven't heard of it.'

'Of course I haven't.' (Jab.) 'What do you take me for?'

'Well...' Hubcaps raised an eyebrow suggestively.

'Nerve!' (Jab.) 'Calling me a robber.'

'But aren't you one?'

'No!' (A strong tone of protest but no jab.)

'Not even when you and your aunt just stole the biggest diamond in England?'

'No!' (Jab, but only a weak one.)

Silence. The pressure on Hubcaps's side eased slightly.

'So you handed it in to the police then, did you?' said Hubcaps gently.

The pressure eased some more.

'Or anyway. You're going to?'

'Not exactly,' said the Runt sullenly. Hubcaps had given her food for thought. She laid the gun across her lap, folded her arms and pouted. Very slowly and carefully Hubcaps reached out. The Runt caught his eye and he froze. He smiled, nodding slightly at the gun.

'Only for safety, you understand,' he said calmly.

'Oh, take it. Take it.' The Runt flapped her hand at him. 'After all, we're all robbers together now, aren't we?'

Mad Harry had a terrible laugh. A truly terrible laugh. And it did not make it any better, from the Diamond's point of view, that no one else could hear it.

Eventually the laugh subsided.

'Have you finished now?' said the Diamond.

'Rule the world. Me. Yes well.' Mad Harry finally recovered his composure. 'Full marks for trying, anyway.'

'What's the matter?' The Diamond managed to sound hurt. 'Don't you think you're up to it?'

Silence.

'I said...'

'I heard!'

More silence.

'Well?'

There was no reply, only more silence. Then more but now the voltage of it was rising fast. It crackled, it sparked and then it exploded into a blaze of white-hot anger that came lancing through the air, bounced off the Diamond and incinerated the powder puff next to it.

'And that's just a taste of what's coming,' snarled Mad Harry. 'So get ready. I'm on my way.'

'Not so fast, Harry. Not so fast,' The Diamond was badly shaken. 'Of course I think you're up to it. I just needed to know if you thought...'

A snarling noise filled the wavebands.

'Yes, well, anyway. And then there's another question, isn't there? How will you find me in this?' The Diamond projected an image of the hospital corridors. Well, it was an image of corridors anyway. They were worming through ten dimensional space. And battalions of monkeys were perpetually trying and failing to write Hamlet. (Though why they should bother was a question that always defeated the Diamond. Hamlet was already written. They would have been better off writing original work.) And...

'Enough,' said Harry meekly. 'Please.' Which was pretty mild really. Anyone else would have been in a strait jacket. The corridors disappeared.

The Diamond felt more confident now that it had fought back. And besides, what it was offering was more than just a little thing. It was asking Harry if he wanted to rule the world or remain an abject failure all his life.

'Oh come on,' said Harry plaintively. 'Abject failure's a bit strong, isn't it?'

'Is it? Really?' The Diamond adopted a more distant voice.

'So I suppose you go round making offers like this to all the abject failures,' said Harry.

'Of course not.' The Diamond was angry now. 'I usually only work with the highest quality material.'

'So why me?'

'Because you want to kill me. This is the only way out I can think of.'

'Well that sounds honest anyway.'

'It is. But then, we need to be, don't we? It's the only way we're going to get anywhere.'

'Shouldn't you be smoking a cigarette or something?'

Rupert looked quizzically at Deirdre.

'Why?'

'Well... Because.'

'The post-coital cigarette, huh?'

'Yes.'

'I don't smoke.'

'Oh.' Deirdre looked lost.

'I never did.'

'A drink then?'

Rupert shook his head. Deirdre looked away. She seemed to shrink.

'Hey. Hey. Come here.' Rupert leant across and put his arm around Deirdre's shoulders. They were cold.

'I didn't mean...' He was lost for words. 'It's just...'

Deirdre patted his hand.

'I know,' she said. 'It's been a long time.' She swung her legs out of the enormous bed that dominated the Boss's bedroom. 'Well if you don't need a drink, I do.' She stood and headed for the door to the sitting room pulling down

156

the hem of her skirt and buttoning her blouse as she went. Rupert watched her. She was thin and unsteady now in the cold of afterwards, altogether a pitiful sight. And, watching her go, unshed tears seared the corners of his eyes. If only, fifteen years ago he had... If only. If only. If only.

In the living room Deirdre held a glass under the mouth of the nearly empty whisky bottle. She did not hear Rupert come up behind her. But she saw his hand close over the top of her glass, she watched his arm steal around her and she felt the warm length of his naked body pressing against her from behind. She felt it and she felt the guilt and it irritated her.

'Forgive me,' Rupert whispered and that irritated her too. 'Forgive me. I've been such a fool. Marry me, Deirdre. Marry me.'

'Marry you?' She did not turn her head to look at him. 'Really?'

'Yes. Really.'

'Hadn't you better tell me about Poppy first?'

Rupert looked stunned. As if in a trance he disengaged himself from Deirdre and sat on the sofa.

'But... But how...' His puzzlement was genuine. Which made it worse.

'How do I know about Poppy?'

'Yes.'

'Oh. She's just a name you came out with. Just now.'

'We got off to a bit of a bad start there, didn't we?' said Hubcaps as he worked at the gun on his lap, making it safe. He sounded rueful.

'As far as I'm concerned,' said the Runt, 'you've still got a lot of ground to make up.'

'Well how am I supposed to begin,' said Hubcaps, 'when you won't believe me anyway?' The Runt looked at him with her lips pursed and then she made a decision.

'Okay then,' she said. 'Practicalities. You're a robber.

157

Right?'

'Sort of,' agreed Hubcaps. He turned to look at the Runt.

'So tell me. I've got... My aunt's got this diamond.'

'Uh ah,' said Hubcaps. 'You've got the Diamond. Your aunt gave it to you to hide and now she thinks... She's worried that you've decided to keep it for yourself.'

'Bally cheek!'

'Well she would have kept it. She said as much. But you never gave it a thought, I suppose.'

A guilty expression crept across the Runt's face.

'We've got this diamond. So what do we do now? What do people do with a thing like that?'

Hubcaps shook his head.

'Search me,' He looked again out of his window. 'Transport's my line, not fencing.' He turned to the Runt, suddenly anxious.

'You have hidden it haven't you? You haven't got it on you?'

The Runt laughed teasingly.

'And what does that matter to you? You're not interested in it. Remember?'

'No but... It's just...' Hubcaps was unsure why he had asked. 'There's a lot of people out looking for it, that's all.' It sounded lame to him. 'A lot of heavy people,' he added, looking straight into the Runt's eyes.

'Oh dear,' said the Runt. 'And me only a poor helpless woman.'

'Well I feel I got you into this mess, you and your aunt.' Hubcaps looked away. 'That's all.' There was a longish silence.

'I wasn't going to keep it you know,' said the Runt. She didn't know why, but she felt the urge to explain. 'Have you seen it? The Diamond.' Hubcaps shook his head.

'I'm really not interested. I'm just the driver. I do the job. I get paid. I like it.'

'You!' The Runt started to giggle. She tried to smother it.

'That was you! The get away driver!'

Hubcaps reddened.

'Yeah well.' He shrugged. There was another longish silence. The Runt broke it.

'So. What now?'

Hubcaps turned to her and gazed into her eyes. Eventually he spoke.

'We say "good bye".' he said. He opened the door beside him and got out of the car.

'It's been a pleasure meeting you.' He laid the gun on the passenger seat. 'And you'd better keep this. You may be needing it.'

'What... What are you doing?'

'Just what I've been trying to do all day. Article one of the Robber's Code. Look after number one.' He slammed the car door and walked away in the direction of the High Street. The Runt leant across, wound down the passenger window and called out after him.

'So tell me, since I'm in the trade now, what's article number two?' Hubcaps stopped and turned to face her.

'There is no article two.'

'Sounds beastly to me then.'

'It is.' Hubcaps turned again and walked on. 'Believe me,' he muttered to himself. 'It is.'

'Well?' said the Diamond. 'Yes or no? Do you want to rule the world or don't you?'

'It's quite a big job, isn't it?' said Mad Harry tentatively.

'It's just a job like any other. You need to delegate a lot, that's all.' Harry did not respond. The Diamond sighed impatiently and tried a new tack.

'You know the trouble with losers?' it said challengingly. 'They lose because that's what they really want. Let them win once in a while and they come completely unstuck.'

'Maybe. But still...' The Diamond sent Harry some pictures to help him make up his mind.

'Yeah well. That's all very well,' said Harry. 'While omnipotence may be...'

More pictures flashed through the air.

'And of course unlimited wealth has its attractions but...'

The Diamond really needed to persuade Harry. It had to succeed because if Harry could not be persuaded to back off then its immortality was nearly certainly at an end. With some difficulty it restrained a cynical laugh. The situation was ludicrous.

Behind the Diamond lay millions of years of awareness and knowledge, millions of years of consciousness such as no living creature could imagine. And now what it all came down to was winning the heart of a madman lost in hospital corridors because he would not trust the signs. What there were left of them. The Diamond sighed. However ludicrous the situation was, it was still deadly serious. But the Diamond knew Harry well and it knew what to do. In its mind it summoned a picture, a picture more powerful than any picture that was ever dreamed of. In it there were lonely bunkers filled with paranoid mistrust. In it there were shattered armies retreating over winter plains. In it were apocalyptic fears and torments magnified through the agony of numberless human hearts and, the concluding touch of genius this, right on the edge, clear to see but not dominating the scene, was the end of the world.

The picture was ready. It gathered itself. It leapt and it hit Mad Harry's mind in a cataclysm of blinding revelation. A loud cry came back. A cry of ecstasy, a cry of pain, a cry of expanded horizons and a new vision. Mad Harry was on his knees, not in anguish but in heaven. A red tiled corridor had become his road to Tarsus.

'That's It Harry! Rule!' The Diamond's voice had grown. This was no mere crystal talking. 'Rule The World. And Then When You Screw Up, You Can Screw Up REAL BIG.'

The situation in the Boss's sitting room had regained a veneer of normality. Rupert was dressed and Deirdre's clothes were straight again, though still crumpled to look at, and they both had drinks. Fresh ones.

'So you've come back for a divorce? I thought that must have happened years ago.'

Deirdre shook her head.

'No. He's always been so old fashioned about it.'

'And he doesn't even know you're here yet?'

'I kept my key. He should have known to change the locks really. In his business.'

'So why now? Why come back now?'

'Why now?' Deirdre swirled the whisky in her glass and took a mouthful. 'Why now? When he's held on to me for fifteen years like...' She drank again. 'Like I was some kind of possession.'

Deirdre looked up then, straight at Rupert.

'What's Poppy like?' she asked.

'Well, she's... She's...' Rupert fumbled for words and looked away.

'She's young then, is she? And beautiful too, I suppose? Everything I'm not. Everything except available. Christ!' She flung her head back and looked at the ceiling. 'If he'd only let me go I'd have been...' She bowed her head over her glass and took a sip. 'He's held me back, all this time. I mean, just look at me. The state of me. Which was why I came back. Time to take charge of myself, I said. Time to get a grip.' She looked up again. 'And for once I turned out lucky, eh?' She toasted Rupert and drank.

'Look. Deirdre. I didn't know... I didn't mean...'

'I know you didn't know. I know you didn't mean. And I only hoped for a moment. Really. Only for a moment. I shouldn't have expected anything. Like I said, I'd already decided. So it's all down to me now.' She stood and crossed to the drinks. 'Another one for you, too?'

Ruminating on the abundant blessings of life, Hubcaps missed the sound of a car approaching him from behind. It was the Runt. She stopped beside him and, looking too late, Hubcaps saw that she was once again pointing the sub-machine gun at him.

'Get in!' said the Runt in a cold, distant voice. 'You're not going anywhere yet.'

Hubcaps looked at her in disbelief.

'Don't mess about!' she said. 'I'm not joking. Get in or I shoot.'

Hubcaps looked back down the street but it was deserted.

'I shall count to three,' said the Runt. 'One.'

Hubcaps looked towards the High Street but there was no help there either.

'Two.'

Hubcaps considered the distance to the street corner and wondered whether he could reach it before the Runt could draw a steady aim.

'Three.' There was a long, long, still moment and then, very slowly, Hubcaps reached for the car door handle. He opened the door and climbed in.

'What now?' he said.

'Robber's Code, article one,' said the Runt. 'We look after number one. And until I say otherwise, I am Number One.'

14

Down the short cut behind the sewage works Rudge was setting a cracking pace in the direction of the High Street. The sounds of conflict in Dot's street had faded to silence as he and Dot put distance between themselves and the battle between the police and the boys, and Rudge was doing some thinking about the facts of life.

The facts were these. Once upon a time there had been a freelance in this little gang but now the freelance was gone. Next there had been a whole bunch of the Boss's boys and now they were gone too. And it wasn't him, Rudge, who had caused any of these things to happen. A sneaking respect crept over him at this point in his thoughts. The old woman wasn't bad. She wasn't bad at all. For an amateur.

If Rudge had been less involved with his thoughts and more aware, instead, of what was going on around him then he would have noticed that Dot's footsteps were closer behind him than they had been. But he didn't notice.

The clunk that Dot delivered with a rusty iron bar to the back of Rudge's head was beautifully judged. It didn't kill him, which it certainly could have done. It didn't even knock him unconscious. It simply deprived him of the use of his legs. One moment he had a perfectly functional set of pins, and the next moment he had a pair of flimsy, India rubber sticks which buckled under their own weight.

Dot leant over Rudge to make sure he was all right. He was groaning and muttering and, instead of hurrying away immediately, she stopped instead to listen.

'But why?' he was saying. 'Why now? Why not just leave me back there with the boys?'

'What, throw you to the wolves, Mr Rudge?' Dot chucked away the thin iron bar she had used as a club and it fell to the ground with a clatter. 'I couldn't have done that. You see, I like you.'

'Oh. Good,' said Rudge weakly. 'Bleedin' good. But what about our deal? We had a deal.'

'Ah yes, but we never shook I'm afraid.' Dot's voice was coming to Rudge weak and faint. 'We never shook. So the Robbers' Code applies.'

'I thought we were getting on rather well just now.' Hubcaps was in the driving seat of the Runt's car and the Runt was in the passenger seat beside him. The muzzle of the machine gun was renewing its acquaintance with his side. 'Yes, I thought we were getting on well.' Hubcaps nodded at the gun and raised a quizzical eyebrow. 'So why...'

'Don't talk.' The Runt was really getting into her role of armed desperado. She was talking out of the side of her mouth. Hubcaps sighed. In the robbery business that was always a danger sign.

'Just drive,' he mouthed silently.

'Just drive,' grated the Runt.

And was that really an American accent?

'Right oh. I'll drive.' Hubcaps fastened his seat belt and nodded at the Runt's. 'Will you...'

Without taking her eyes from her prisoner the Runt reached up and pulled the down the seat belt behind her. There was a momentary difficulty as she struggled to plug the buckle home while still keeping the gun trained on Hubcaps, but eventually she managed it.

'Now drive.'

'Right oh.' Hubcaps started the car, adjusted the driving

mirror, indicated right, selected first gear and looked at the Runt. 'How fast?'

'Just don't attract attention. We're going to the hospital.'

Eat your heart out Edward G Robinson, thought Hubcaps. He pulled sedately out from the kerb and approached the junction with the High Street.

'You do realise don't you?' said Hubcaps, 'that your aunt isn't at the hospital? I know I said she was. But I was lying. I did mention it.'

'My aunt,' growled the Runt, 'is not what we're going to the hospital for.' She peered nervously out through her window. 'And can't you manage a bit more style? "Don't attract attention" I said. And here you are driving like a granny.'

'But...'

'In The Borough no one drives like a granny.'

'Not even the grannies?'

'Specially not the grannies.'

'Okay,' said Hubcaps as his right foot hit the floor. 'Hold on tight then.'

In Dot's street there was, once again, very little movement. Occasionally among the litter of fallen bodies there was one body that stirred as it struggled against unconsciousness but most were content just to lie still. In the deep shadows cast by the temporary floodlighting the do it yourselfers continued to loiter. They would stay hidden for as long as any of the combatants were still standing. And two were still standing, the last of the police and the last of the Boss's boys.

'We won,' said the last of the policemen. His fist swung in a long, slow, painful arc through the air and missed the point of the boy's chin by a mile.

'No.' The boy raised his fist to strike. 'We won.' The fist shot out straight in a jab and fell to the boy's side. He was too weak to support the weight of his arm.

Both men wobbled dangerously, their balance disastrously upset by the shifting weight of their limbs. They swung forwards. They recovered. They swung backwards. And recovered. Then slowly they swung forwards again. Further and further they swung until, finally losing their grip on perpendicularity, they fell and their heads came together like the clash of mountain goats. Then there was silence.

Slowly, like ghosts out of the shadows, the do-it-yourselfers drew forward. Their faces were drawn and hungry and their dead eyes lingered lovingly on the shiny paint work of the ranks of police cars. The silence was broken by a hubcap falling to the ground just as, distant over the dark Borough, sirens came once again. They were ambulances, scores of them, screaming towards the street. Without haste but deftly the do-it-yourselfers set to work to finish before they should be disturbed.

Hubcaps and the Runt shot out into the High Street and were narrowly missed by an ambulance surging into the street they had just left.

'We got out of there just in time then,' said Hubcaps merrily.

'Just shut up and drive.' The Runt's finger twitched over the trigger of the gun. She was not amused and her attitude was hurtful to Hubcaps.

'It was you asked for style, don't forget,' he said. 'And when I'm asked for style, then I deliver it.' He flicked the steering wheel lightly as a second ambulance passed only inches away from them.

'What's going on?' demanded the Runt, looking at the stream of ambulances rushing towards them. 'There's millions of them.'

'Don't know,' said Hubcaps. He watched in his mirror as the ambulances all took the turning towards Dot's house.

'But I'd bet money that it's something to do with your aunt.'

At the wheel of his ambulance Dave was powerfully moved by the sight of the mercy convoy as it came screaming past him along the High Street.

'Quick response that eh?' he said to Florien beside him. 'Bleedin' marvellous I call it.'

A convoy ambulance approached with a roar and Dave greeted it by turning on his own siren, flashing his headlights and sounding his horn.

'That's the stuff lads,' he yelled leaning out of his window. 'Go fetch 'em in, stupid beggars!'

'For god's sake Dave,' snarled Florien, 'can't you just watch where you're going?'

Dave was steering with one hand now and waving with the other and as a result he was weaving all over the road.

'Gah! Shut up Flo. After what we've been through it's as good as a tonic, all this.' His face twisted in ecstasy. 'I mean. Listen to the those sirens, eh. That's music to my ears.'

Dave waved wildly as another ambulance approached and he careered across the road towards it. The approaching ambulance flashed its lights onto full beam and the driver made a stiff-fingered gesture at Dave as he roared past.

'Yeah, that's the stuff.' Dave leant out of his window to watch the ambulance disappear down the road behind him. 'Just what you need.' The ambulance heeled over dramatically as it took the corner towards Dot's street. 'Adrenaline!'

Dot came out of the short-cut past the sewage works and up into the High Street feeling very old indeed. She was faint and weary, and her neck was terribly sore. She dabbed at it with her fingers, it was sticky and, in the yellow flare

167

of the sodium street lamps, her fingers looked black. The cut was bleeding again. And then, while she was in the mood for self examination, there were her feet.

Dot was carrying her shoes. And she was not carrying them to cosset them. They were the kind of sensible, low-heeled walking shoes that stay comfortable and serv- iceable under all foreseeable conditions of use without cosseting. But unfortunately one of the conditions of use that had not been foreseen was the short cut down the back of the sewage works and the shoes had suffered. One of the sensible, low heels had been torn off and, in the interests of symmetry and balance, Dot had been forced to finish her journey in stockinged feet. So thank god for stockings, she thought. They had suffered too, but not so much.

Certain breeds of stocking makers have an endless fascination with indestructibility and they sell their heavy-weight goods mostly to old ladies who treasure them dearly. No old lady anywhere had ever treasured her stockings as much as Dot did right now. Her feet were bruised to be sure, and she had stubbed her toes several times, but the indestructible stockings had kept out all those terrible, ragged, tearing edges of rusting metal.

In her weakened state Dot was quite suddenly very frightened. Things were getting out of hand. She wanted to stop... She wanted someone else to take over...

There was an immense wailing noise. The world began pulsating with a hellish blue light. And all of Dot's weakness and fear became focused on the shoes in her hand. She was overwhelmed by the futility of carrying this pair of useless shoes. Drawing her arm back she flung them away from her as far and hard as she could.

Looking ahead again Dave wondered why his view was filled with a pair of flying shoes. Strange shoes too, he thought in that long, long moment before violence. One of them had something missing...

168

'Jesus!' screamed Florien. 'What the he...' Working automatically and without direct communication with his brain Dave's foot stood heavily on the brake pedal. Since Florien was not wearing a seat belt her shout was cut short as she was flung forward into the windscreen.

'Aaagh!' shouted Dave. Holding one-handed onto the steering wheel the full force of the braking passed straight through to his injured ribs. They were just not up to carrying the weight and Dave felt a hot, searing pain burn right across his chest. Like Florien, Dave was not wearing a seat belt and so he was not conscious of the pain for long.

The ambulance was still moving briskly and now, suddenly driverless and with all four wheels locked, it slewed sideways and was only saved from rolling over by a conveniently positioned lamp post. The ambulance stopped. Everything was still. Including the battered little car that skidded into it from behind.

The sound of a violent crash brought Dot back to her senses. Her head cleared and she began to watch with interest the scene on the other side of the road.

Very cautiously Hubcaps got out of the Runt's car and started poking around at the front end of it where it was embedded in the ambulance. Clouds of steam filled the air.

As the Runt also emerged into the night Dot was pleased to see that Hubcaps's caution had less to do with injuries sustained in the crash than the fact that the Runt had a machine gun trained on his back.

Hubcaps turned to look at the Runt and shook his head. The Runt said something angry. Hubcaps shook his head again, laughed and went to peer in at the front of the ambulance. The Runt went round to the back and opened the doors.

Into the brighter night of the High Street Rudge emerged from the short cut past the sewage works rubbing at his sore head. The night was filled with a hellish wailing and a pulsating blue light. In front of him a stream of ambulances was flashing past. He looked around and saw Dot. He looked in the direction she was looking in and saw the freelance and the old woman's niece. They were pushing the wreck of the girl's car away from an ambulance which was leaning heavily against a lamp post. Hubcaps was working hard. The girl was working hard too but she was hindered by the gun which she was trying to keep trained on Hubcaps.

Rudge snarled. Amateurs, he thought, bleedin' freelancers and amateurs. Well, now that he had them all together they were going to be a push over. The whole lot of them.

'Okay, that's enough.' Hubcaps wiped his hands on his trousers. 'It's time to get those two out of there now.' He nodded in the direction of the ambulance cab. 'And you're sure about the men in the back are you? The same as in your aunt's house?'

'Yes.' The Runt nodded. 'They're the same. And fast asleep still.' She smiled.

'Right then,' said Hubcaps. He opened Florien's door and caught her limp body as it rolled sideways out of the seat. Still keeping the gun pointed at Hubcaps, the Runt examined Florien's face. There was a lump the size of an egg on her forehead and a dark, swollen bruise on her jaw.

'That looks really nasty,' said Hubcaps looking at the bruise.

'Oh that,' said the Runt philosophically. 'That's the least of her problems. I did that.'

The problem for Dot was how to cross the road with the constant stream of ambulances rushing past. She looked around. Hubcaps and the Runt had nearly finished moving the two crew from the front to the back of the crashed ambulance and if she did not get over there in a couple of minutes they would be gone without her. The chase would still be on and the way Dot's feet were feeling they were not up to chasing anything.

Fifty yards away down the road was a pedestrian crossing. Dot tcched. She should have seen it before and she felt cross with herself as she hobbled off towards it. She wished too, on the whole, that she had held on to her shoes. She could have balanced them up by knocking the second heel off and they would have been better on this hard pavement than nothing. On the other hand though, she sighed, she should be grateful for small mercies. The shoes had at least got her a ride. If she could reach it in time.

Hubcaps settled himself into the driver's seat of the ambulance and fastened the seat belt.

'You brought the knife in from your car as well did you?' he said glancing at the gun poking into his ribs. 'It would make people ask questions if they found something like that in your car.'

'I said I did once already,' replied the Runt. 'It's in the back.'

'And they're all alright are they, back there?'

The Runt sighed.

'I said that too. As alright as can be expected. Considering.' She jabbed the gun roughly into Hubcaps's side. 'Now can we get on?'

'Yes. Of course.' Hubcaps turned the ignition key and the ambulance sprang to life.

'I think,' said the Runt, 'that we can dispense with the siren, don't you?'

'Oh.' Hubcaps sounded disappointed. 'But...'

'We've made enough of a spectacle of ourselves already without going on a screamer through the whole Borough.'

'Yes.' Hubcaps was disappointed. 'But still, you see, I've always wanted...'

171

The Runt sighed. This was not what life as a robber was meant to be like.

'Well keep the blue light on then, if you must.'

'Thanks,' said Hubcaps with a broad smile. He blew the Runt a kiss. 'You're a real sport.'

Dot hurried along the pavement towards the ambulance. It seemed like a minute or so since Hubcaps and the Runt had finally closed it up and climbed into the cab and she was worried that at any moment they would drive off leaving her behind. But, worried or not, there was only so fast that her feet would carry her.

The ambulance engine fired up and the air was full of the sound of its siren. Dot's heart leapt. She had missed it now, sure as eggs. She stopped and watched in anguish, waiting for Hub caps to roar away but he did not go. He was having difficulty separating the ambulance from the lamp post, even after so short an acquaintance, and the ambulance was moving only in short, spasmodic jerks. First it moved backwards. Dot pressed on again. Then forwards. Dot pressed on harder. Then it moved backwards once more and finally it was free. Dot began running and caught hold of the back door handles as the ambulance started to pull away from her. She was nearly dragged off her feet but just when it seemed certain that she would fall, she managed to gain a footing on the little step beneath the doors. Grunting with exertion she pulled herself up and clung on tight as the ambulance bumped off the pavement, onto the road and away down the High Street.

15

Poppy was ready to go. She put her suitcase in the hall
and went into the sitting room. The air was heavy with the
reek of petrol and an empty twenty litre petrol can lay on
its side in one corner.

'You're ready then?' said the sofa. 'Well you look very
pretty, if I may say so. Rupert will approve.'

'Damn Rupert.' Poppy was fumbling in her handbag, her
hands were shaking.

'Tut tut.'

'And damn you too.'

Poppy found what she was looking for. A matchbox. She
took it out, opened it and took out a match.

'And away you go then, in a blaze of glory,' said the sofa.

Poppy stood with the match poised to strike.

'I am going to do it you know.'

'I do know, yes,' said the sofa. 'You said you would and
I believe you.'

'So aren't you going to try and stop me?'

The sofa thought about this.

'No,' it said. 'No, I'm not. Because to tell the truth I can't
say I blame you.'

'Oh, come on.'

'No, really. I understand perfectly. I mean, it's the way
we are, isn't it? Do you think that I wouldn't burn that
beastly picture over there if I could? Or smash the car? Or
destroy the swimming pool? Just let me at them. Then

173

you'd see.'

Poppy was silent. Her face was a mask but it is useless hiding behind a mask in a conversation with a telepath.

'Ah,' said the sofa, 'now you're angry with me. But there's really no need to descend to that level, is there? Just light the match and have done with it.' Its voice was persuasive, cajoling.

Poppy started to laugh. She paddled forward through the puddles of petrol on the floor, fell into the comfortable, wide spaces of the sofa and abandoned herself to full-blown hysteria.

'And what's so funny?' The sofa's acid tone cut straight through Poppy's comforting abandonment. She stopped laughing and became petulant.

'You know already so why ask?' she said.

'Because telepathic conversation is still conversation,' said the sofa primly. 'It's rude to take too much for granted. And petulance is all wrong, you know. It's just not you.'

Poppy sat hesitantly on the sofa, undecided about what to do next.

'The answer to your question, by the way,' she said, 'is that I was laughing at your cleverness. Somehow I don't expect sofas to be clever.'

'I don't know what you mean, I'm sure.'

'Yes you do.'

'So you can read my mind now, can you?'

'Occasionally, yes, when you don't concentrate properly.'

'Then you're a fast learner,' said the sofa. Poppy nodded.

'Yes,' she said. 'For instance, what you were thinking just now was this. You tell me that by burning you I'm doing what you'd do yourself. And since you know that I don't want to be like you...'

'Charmed I'm sure.' said the sofa. It sounded offhand but it was not feeling offhand. What it was feeling was relief that Poppy had not probed more deeply into its mind.

'But I don't want to be like you, do I? I don't want to be

174

a thing.' Poppy's voice dropped a note lower. 'I want to be a person.'

'Then why burn us at all?'

'Why? Why? Oh! You wouldn't understand.'

'I think I might. If you tried explaining it to yourself.' Those were the sofa's words. And they sounded kind. But they masked the real meaning. 'Concentrate on your own mind, Poppy not on mine.' That was what the sofa was saying. 'Your mind, not mine.'

'Well it's because...' Poppy found her ideas floundering. 'I need... a... a fresh start, a clean break...'

'Leaving nothing of the old life behind you.'

'Yes.' Then much more brightly. 'Yes!' She was seeing her way clear before her again.

'You see, I do understand,' the sofa went on. 'And what's more, I think you've got nothing to worry about. Burning us only makes you the same as us if you do it for the same reasons.'

Poppy felt a great weight lift from her mind. She tightened her grip on the match and matchbox.

'And...' She hesitated to ask the question. 'And you're really sure that you don't mind?'

'You know I don't,' said the sofa. 'You just read it. In fact...' It hesitated modestly. 'I'd be proud to burn in such a good cause.'

'Well that's very...' began Poppy but she could find nothing more to say.

'And you should get on with it straight away, I think. Before you change your mind.' The sofa's voice was changing. 'So do it, Poppy.' It was becoming rich and full and persuasive. 'Do it now.'

Maybe it was the petrol fumes that filled the room or maybe it was the relief of reaching such a satisfactory conclusion with the sofa but Poppy suddenly felt lightheaded. She sensed a change in the atmosphere and where before she had been alone with the sofa, her head was now full of voices.

'Do it Poppy.' That voice was high and nervy, the voice of the Expressionist picture.

'Do it now.' A voice of flowing power, the car.

'Now Poppy.' An unending liquid trill, the swimming pool.

'Now Poppy, now,' chorused Rupert's possessions. 'Do it now!'

'It's for the best,' said the sofa and all the voices fell silent leaving a tremor of expectation.

In a daze Poppy raised the match and set its head against the striker on the side of the matchbox.

The expectation mounted.

The match began to move slowly along the side of the matchbox and the expectation turned to glee.

'Any moment now,' the voices seemed to be saying to each other, though not to Poppy. 'Any moment now.' But Poppy heard them too. In their anxiety for her to strike the match, the things had dropped their guard and Poppy suddenly saw their minds falling open like books. They were short books with no small print and only one word. And the word was written in capitals. Red capitals. Capitals of blood and fire.

'HATE.'

She froze. All around her was the hollow noise of minds slamming hastily shut but the word was not gone, it persisted in her own mind, seared in by the heat of as yet unlit flames.

Very slowly Poppy put down the match and matchbox and rose to her feet. She needed to be so very careful. One spark was all it would take. And that was what the things wanted. The things that hated her so much they were prepared themselves to burn in the heat of the inferno that would consume her. They had alien minds, these things. Poppy shuddered. They were creatures of a different kind.

Carefully Poppy moved round the sofa and across

176

towards the window. Waves of petrol fumes parted before her face. In this room one spark would ignite not just a gentle fire to be run away from and forgotten but a searing, exploding fireball from which she would never emerge.

'HATE.'

With extreme caution Poppy opened the window, sliding it away to one side. Warm untainted air burst into the room like a flood of sanity and from round the front of the villa a car horn sounded impatiently. Poppy looked at her watch. It was almost exactly midnight. She must hurry if she was to catch the jet on which she had managed to hitch a ride to London. She ran. It was the best thing she had done in her life.

Inside the living room a sharp click announced that the security system had automatically switched the house lights off. There was sparking in the switch, there always is, and, slight though it was, it was enough to ignite the fume laden atmosphere. There was a furious, full-throated roar and the back of Rupert's villa fell away from the main building into a boiling pit of fire.

The driver of the hired limousine gave Poppy a slightly curious look as she climbed into the front of the car beside him. She turned on him aggressively.

'Well? What's the matter? What are you waiting for?'

The driver's face was lit by the living red light from the villa and his nose twitched at the reek of petrol that clung to Poppy's clothes but he managed to refrain from comment. Almost.

'So madam is going to London,' he paused disdainfully, 'with no luggage then, is she?'

'Oh Deirdre.' Rupert was striding around the sitting room. 'I can't tell you how bad I feel about all this. The things you've had to put up with.'

'Rupert, for heaven's sake sit down.' Deirdre made her request sound like it was for Rupert's benefit but the truth

177

was that watching him going round and round and up and down was making the room spin unpleasantly.

'Deirdre!' Rupert knelt beside her in a fit of passion and caught impetuously at her hand. 'I know we can't be married, that was a stupid thought.' Deirdre's hand went stiff in his. 'It wouldn't be right for you,' he added quickly. 'Not after... After everything that's happened.'

Nothing much ever had happened, thought Deirdre. Wasn't that the point? A brief, hot fling all those years ago. And now this evening. Nothing to write home about.

'There, there,' she muttered inconsequentially and patted Rupert's hand.

'But Deirdre!' Rupert looked up aghast. 'I betrayed you.'

'I suppose. If you say so.'

'And now... When I look at you now...'

Deirdre felt this was all getting way beyond her. It wasn't his fault, what she was. Was it? She took a quick, sustaining gulp of whisky. Everything was getting beyond her.

'I want to help you.'

'Very nice too.' Deirdre emptied her glass. 'So help me to another of those. That'll do for now.'

Rupert stood up and took Deirdre's glass. He couldn't very well say 'no'. But...

'I don't think you're taking this seriously, Deirdre.' He sounded hurt. And in a moment of stunning clarity Deirdre saw that, yes, she wasn't taking this seriously. And she should be. She watched Rupert's back as he poured the drink. The man was crawling to her and whether or not that was right, it must be worth something. It might even be worth quite a lot. She reached eagerly for her drink as Rupert came back with it. She needed it now. She needed to be able to think straight.

'Of course, it's not just me,' Rupert was saying. 'It's him too.' His expressive gesture took in the whole flat. Everything that was the Boss's. 'Both of us. It's up to us to see you alright. And I'll make sure he does his bit, Deirdre.

178

Whatever he's done up to now.' Rupert liked that thought. 'Oh yes. I'll make sure he does.' He looked at his watch. 'What time did you say he'd be back, by the way?'

16

At the hospital things were much as they had been earlier. The atmosphere remained calm, on the surface, and for some time there had been no further reports of the roving madman. The staff were feeling more comfortable and, in the canteen, the doctor and nurse were almost amicable as they drank tepid coffee from plastic mugs. But below the surface changes were afoot. There was a trembling, like a curtain with a burglar behind it, and fear was gathering, for fear feeds on peace.

In his bed, newly awake, Vernon felt the trembling. It seemed an interesting sort of trembling, threatening, strangely seductive and full of meaning but he shouldn't be listening to it. It distracted him from remembering why he was there.

The Axe, the Sailor and the Boss also sensed the trembling. Contrary to the doctor's prognosis they had already moved half way from sleeping to waking and out of this dreamy state the trembling roused them fully.

The Boss sat up and looked around. His eyes were gleaming. To him the trembling seemed a portent. Something wonderful. He felt excitement and he wanted to share it. In the bed beside the Boss the Sailor sat up too and beyond the Sailor, the Axe. The Sailor's eyes were clouded and fearful. The Axe was keenly alert.

'It's here,' said the Boss. 'The Diamond, it's here.' He swung his legs out of bed and stood up. He sniffed the air and listened. 'It's gone now,' he said, 'but I heard it, clear as clear. It has to be here.'

The Axe too swung out of bed.

'I don't what you heard Boss but I just had this, like, dream. I was in this...'

The Boss stiffened, quivering.

'There. It's coming again,' he said. 'And it's louder now, too.'

'I don't hear nothing Boss,' said the Axe stolidly.

The Sailor's eyes rolled up, he gave a low moan and hid shivering under his bedclothes.

'And what's eating him?' said the Axe.

The Boss went over and peeled back the Sailor's bed-clothes.

'Sailor,' he said softly, shaking the Sailor's shoulder. 'Sailor. It's alright. You hear me? You're safe. It's just...' The Boss stopped talking and listened again. His eyes closed in ecstasy and he uttered a low moan.

'It's calling,' he said. 'It's calling me.' In a trance he left the Sailor's bedside and started walking towards the door of the ward. His bare feet slapped on the cold, tiled floor.

'But Boss...' The Axe made a move towards him then glanced at the Sailor who was still curled up in a tight, fearful ball. The Axe made an impatient sound, hurried back across to the Sailor's bed, grabbed the huge man's arm and dragged at him.

'Get up,' he said. 'Get up!' The Sailor rose but seemed unable to move. He stood abjectly with his head bowed, his shoulders hunched and his arms folded tightly across his chest.

'Ah, come on.' The Axe punched the Sailor sympatheti-cally on the shoulder. 'It's not so bad as all that.'

A sympathetic punch from the Axe could break a brick yet the Sailor did not shift a millimetre.

'The Boss is on to something. Trouble, maybe,' said the Axe. He looked into the Sailor's face. 'The Boss,' he said again, loudly and slowly.

At the sound of the Boss's name the Sailor half raised his head and looked wildly round but the Boss had gone. He uttered a loud, wordless cry and, desperate but still shambling, he crossed to the doorway and looked out, up and down the corridor. There was no one in sight. He uttered a second cry, piteous and frightened.

The Axe ran to the door and looked out for himself. He grabbed the Sailor's arm.

'Come on,' he said, 'we must go.' The Sailor looked pathetically at the Axe. He was full of doubt and hesitation. But the Axe wasn't the man to hesitate when there was work to do.

'The Boss needs us,' he said. He grabbed the Sailor's arm and dragged him out of the door.

Vernon Carpenter watched them go and then climbed hurriedly out of bed. However interesting the trembling was, with all its hidden meanings, he had other things to attend to. And maybe the two big men could help him attend to them. He had seen them before, with their backs to a fireball. And, he suddenly remembered, there had been a little old lady too. And then finally he remembered, surprisingly since he had been unconscious at the time, lying on top of the little old woman and feeling her experience a moment of great joy. It must have been a fierce joy, passionate almost beyond belief, that could communicate itself by touch to an unconscious man. He wondered what had caused it.

Instead of sorting things out, this jumble of half-memories made Vernon feel confused – he hated confusion – and it occurred to him that a simple answer to his confusion might be to follow the two big men. Perhaps they would lead him to some answers. Or back to simplicity. Or somewhere. And wherever they led him, Vernon felt, it would be a better place than his hospital bed with its crumpled sheets. He hurried out into the corridor. Behind him the doors swung shut and the ward was still again. Except for the trembling. But then, that was everywhere.

The Diamond was pleased with itself. It had done a good job on Mad Harry and now it could afford to relax a little. It lay back in the softness of the make-up bag and smoked a cigarette, in a manner of speaking.

Somewhere out in the infinite reaches of the hospital corridors Mad Harry sat, tucked into a corner with his back to a wall. He was not relaxing. He was keyed up and full of energy and through his head was passing a series of pictures of his glorious future. The pictures formed slowly in Harry's mind, each one emerging like a butterfly from the chrysalis of its predecessor and remaining in focus just long enough for Harry to gain an impression of its novelty and beauty without becoming tired of it.

In a leisurely way that was in tune with its own mood the Diamond was showing Harry what the future held in store for him. The Diamond was also keeping Harry busy. It needed to get on with some quiet thinking on its own account without having Harry poking his nose in.

Turning Harry into a paranoid megalomaniac with dominion over a wide expanse of the globe was simple enough for the Diamond since Harry was an ideal subject to work with. He was, for example, better by far than Napoleon. It had been real hard work, driving him mad. And the political circumstances were also favourable. Ever since Hitler, the Diamond had been put off playing at global politics by the nuclear deterrent – it had no wish to fry or be buried for eternity. But now that the West had achieved the collapse of the East, the threat of nuclear war had receded far enough to allow for a little harmless tinkering.

So no, the Diamond paused in its thoughts to compile and transmit a new picture to Mad Harry, the problem was no longer what to do with Harry. The problem was what to do with itself. Where should it go while it was winning and losing Harry's empire? Who should it set up house with?

Of course Mad Harry would expect the Diamond to live with him. But that would not be a good idea. It would make the Diamond a hostage to its own fortune. But who else was there? The Diamond considered its options.

It could stay with the Runt, perhaps. That might be fun. She had rejected the Diamond's allure and so it would be a real challenge, to conquer her.

And then there was the Boss, the man who had tried to steal the Diamond today. He would value the Diamond. He would brood over it and hoard it and flatter its vanity. Which would be pleasant for a while.

And there was Dot. Dot the proletarian. Life with her would be slumming it of course, the Diamond paused again in its thoughts to send Harry a fresh picture, but it might be interesting too. A new experience. The Diamond had never lived with anyone for whom sophistication was a shag pile carpet and excitement was threepence off a tin of beans.

Had she even begun to think about it, Dot would have thought that threepence off a tin of beans was a level of excitement that she could cope with very well right now. But, hanging for dear life onto the back of Hubcaps's speeding ambulance, the only food on Dot's mind was minced beef. She glanced down at the road racing past inches below her feet. If she fell on to it at this speed then minced beef would be all that was left.

Hubcaps was enjoying himself. He loved vehicles – cars, lorries, buses, vehicles of any kind – and he liked to find out all about them. Right now he was finding out exactly what an ambulance could do.

An ambulance could go on two wheels – it could really go on two wheels. Either side, equally well – and that was amazing. Most vehicles were easier to drive tipped over to the right.

184

And an ambulance was fast – fifty in third gear – and nippy too. Hubcaps swung past an articulated lorry and dodged an oncoming taxi with only inches to spare.

And an ambulance could... Hubcaps glanced sidelong at the Runt. An ambulance could go WOOooo WWOOOoooo WWWOOOOOooo.

'Weeee!' yelled Hubcaps.

'Turn it off!' snapped the Runt and Hubcaps obeyed. There was no gainsaying the Runt, not when she still had the sub-machine gun.

'I thought told you not to do that,' she said.

'True, oh Queen!' said Hubcaps grinning unashamedly. He was enjoying himself for the first time in the day.

'Well don't do it again, then.' The Runt pursed her lips. 'Or you'll be turning off the light as well.' Her tone was sharp but Hubcaps's spirits were ballooning high, safely out of reach.

On the back of the ambulance Dot let go with one hand to rub at ears savaged by the siren. Her timing was poor. The ambulance suddenly gathered speed and rocked violently to the right. Hubcaps was just checking that there really was no difference between driving on the right or the left wheels. There ought to be, he felt. There really ought to be.

Dot screamed as her feet left their small platform. With one hand she hung on desperately as pain tore through her shoulder and her feet dragged along the ground. Poor feet. They felt like they were burning. In fact, though, they were not. The indestructible stockings were giving the performance of their life. But even they could not last for ever, dragging over tarmac at speed.

Dot struggled for a better hold on the door handles. She could not hold on much longer. Any moment now she was going to fall.

The ambulance rocked upright. Dot's free hand caught

hold. One frantically paddling foot found the door step. She was almost upright and secure when the ambulance lurched over again, to the left this time, and again she lost her footing.

'For god's sake,' she moaned as she hung on for dear life. 'Somebody help me.'

Vernon stood outside the Burns and General Surgery Ward and looked up and down the corridor. There was no one in sight. He listened, hoping to hear the dwindling sounds of the Axe and the Sailor in pursuit of the Boss, but although he listened hard there was nothing to hear. Nothing, that is, but the trembling.

That trembling. Vernon was fascinated by it. He felt sure that it was a code but, much as he would have loved to learn its secrets, for now he had other problems and no time to spend on breaking it.

The immediate problem was which way to go. Had the big, confident man and the big, frightened man seen the Boss before going off in pursuit? He thought not. But in that case, which way had they gone?

He looked up and down the corridor. Which way? If he had had a coin he would have tossed it and trusted to luck. Vernon was very much given to trusting to luck. He had done it for most of his life. It saved him from thinking and from having to go wherever thought might lead him.

But just now Vernon had no coin. And if he did not act quickly then he might never find the Boss and his men since there was something about this corridor that suggested it could lose people easily. So, much against his better judgement, Vernon thought. He shut his eyes and pictured the scene as the confident man and the frightened man left the ward.

The confident one had grabbed the frightened one's arm. Sailor, that was his name. It had been the Sailor's right arm. Vernon mimed the action and moved away, pulling in

186

the most natural direction. He moved to the right. So to the right thought was leading him. He shut his eyes briefly as the trembling started up again but, alas, there was still no time.

'No time, no time Mrs Tittlemouse,' he muttered, misquoting a half-remembered story from his youth. 'Never no time,' he added regretfully. With a deep sigh he set off down the corridor at a brisk pace and, turning right again at the end, he disappeared.

In the hospital canteen the stillness was broken by the sound of the bleeper in the doctor's pocket.

'Time to go,' he said. 'Thank god.' And he went.

'Of course,' said the nurse. 'Just when we were getting on so well.' She drank her last mouthful of coffee and followed the doctor, but at a leisurely pace. 'Wouldn't you know it?'

'Damn!' said Hubcaps. The noise inside the cab of the ambulance diminished as his foot eased back on the accelerator and there was a jolt as the ambulance rocked back onto four wheels and slowed to a crawl.

'Just look at it! At this time of night, too.' He thumped the steering wheel in frustration and indicated the road ahead. It was chock-a-block with the red tail lights of cars all heading towards the hospital. From out of every side road more cars were coming, and more and more and all of them were in a hurry, swerving and weaving back and forth across the road, clogging it up entirely.

Hubcaps glanced across at the Runt. She was smiling and waving at someone in the car beside them.

'Friends of yours, are they?' said Hubcaps sourly. He stared gloomily ahead again. 'I might have known.'

'Friends?' said the Runt. 'Not really. They're off-duty staff from the hospital, going our way.' She waved excitedly as another car crawled past on her side. 'It looks like an emergency call out. Something to do with that convoy, I suppose.'

'You don't say?' said Hubcaps but the Runt was impervious to his sarcasm. Even in the street darkness he could see that her eyes were sparkling.

'It's going to be quite a night,' she said. 'With all this.'

'Yeah, great. And it's so lovely being stuck at the back of it, too.'

'Oh come on. Look on the bright side, eh. The hospital will be so busy that nobody will notice us. No one will be suspicious.'

'Alright,' said Hubcaps, 'I'll look on the bright side.' He sighed. 'And I'll just hope that it doesn't blind me.'

At the back of the ambulance Dot could see the bright side perfectly. She was back on the step of the ambulance and holding on without strain.

'Coo!' she said, 'that was a close one, girl.' She looked down at the road passing beneath her feet. It looked kinder than it had before.

'You could almost jump down and walk,' she told herself. 'It'd be quicker.' But she had no intention of walking. She shifted her weight on the step, settling herself more comfortably, and as she did so she accidentally pushed up on one of the door handles. It moved.

'Well,' she said. She looked thoughtful and moved the handle up as far as it could go. The door gave slightly under her grasp and she cautiously eased it towards her, trying to avoid knocking herself off the step. 'You might be more comfortable in here, anyway.' She raised a foot into the inky blackness of the back of the ambulance and trod on a body on the floor.

'Oops, sorry love,' she said. She felt sideways with her foot and trod on a second body. As gently as she could Dot found where the two bodies met and she wriggled her foot down between them. Leaning heavily on the door which threatened to swing dangerously back and drop her onto the road, she carefully levered herself up into the back of the ambulance and, precariously balanced, she leant out to shut the door.

'Right then,' she said. 'Where now?'

'Well I don't recommend the stretchers, Miss Coulson.' A voice like tide-washed gravel came soughing out of the darkness. 'They're all full.'

At the entrance to the hospital's Casualty Department the doctor and nurse stood with clipboards and pens noting the arrival of the emergency staff as they poured in. The doctor was breathless. The nurse less so. But then he had run all the way from the Canteen. It was a long way. Or at least, the corridors made it feel like that. But in spite of his being breathless, the doctor's eyes were sparkling.

'Come on in, come on in,' he was saying brightly as, with the authority vested in him by the clipboard, he officiously pushed incoming staff members away down the entrance hall. 'Plenty of room for everyone.' He turned to the nurse. 'Isn't there, eh?' She sighed windily and avoided meeting his eye.

'And plenty of work too.' The doctor looked out of the door as the stream of arrivals began to thin and, away in the distance beyond the hospital gates, he saw the flash of a blue light. 'Or there will be soon.'

Behind him, further up the hallway, two distinct flows of humanity were struggling with each other to make progress. The newest arrivals, still in their street clothes, were ignoring the reception committee and rushing to offices and staff rooms to get changed. Those who had arrived earlier were rushing in the opposite direction, struggling into white coats or buckling uniform belts as they went.

'Come on,' shouted the duty doctor. 'Hurry up! The first ambulance is arriving now.'

The doctor's words galvanised the room into frantically chaotic motion so that no one could go anywhere and when Hubcaps's ambulance pulled up outside there was only the duty doctor and his nurse to meet it.

'Alright, alright!' the doctor yelled up at Hubcaps in the driver's seat. 'Let the cat see the mouse.' Behind him the nurse lowered her eyes to cover her embarrassment. 'Open up the back and show us what you've got.' Hubcaps gave the doctor a long hard stare and the doctor responded by puffing himself up to an inch above his full height.

'I'd give a hand myself of course,' he said holding up the clipboard as if it was permanently fixed to his arm. 'Only...' He waved the board. 'You know how it is.'

'Yeah, of course,' grunted Hubcaps. He swung down from the ambulance and slammed the door. The Runt came and stood at his side. 'But then I expect you'll excuse me too, won't you?' He took hold of the Runt's arm and began to steer her away. 'Only, places to go, you see. People to meet. I expect you know how it is.'

Lost for words, the doctor took a sharp pace backwards out of Hubcaps's way. He almost collided with the nurse who was now having trouble suppressing her giggles. Hubcaps and the Runt had almost disappeared.

'Stand back!' said a voice from behind the doctor. 'And let the workers at it!' The doctor moved back just in time to avoid being trampled by the cloud of white coats and blue frocks that was descending on the ambulance. He looked at the nurse standing patiently beside him.

'Oh dear,' he said. 'Dear oh dear. Things seem to be getting out of hand, don't they?'

'Quick!' said Rudge as the back doors of the ambulance began to open. 'Out the front.' He pointed his knife threateningly at Dot. 'And don't hang about.' He kicked open the passenger door and briskly shoved Dot into the night. 'And catch this eh! We may be needing it. 'A heavy metal object landed awkwardly in Dot's arms. It was the sub-machine gun.

'Hey! You two!' came a voice from the back of ambulance. Rudge looked, saw a heavyweight nursing orderly, and set off running into the night.

'Hang about! I want to talk to you!' The orderly jumped down from the ambulance and was about to set off in pursuit when he landed flat on his face. Dot surreptitiously withdrew her outstretched foot.

'What the hell...' began the orderly but he got no further.

'Oh, you mustn't chase him you know,' began Dot. 'My friend. He's frightened of hospitals. Gets terribly violent. It was all I could do to get him into the ambulance with me. You see...' But she interrupted herself by staggering and falling heavily against the orderly who had just managed to get to his feet and was again about to give chase.

'Oh dear, there's me at it again. It's my legs. They keep going all weak on me.' She took a couple of shuffling paces forward to demonstrate the weakness. 'I don't know what it is, I'm sure....' Which was inaccurate. It was the machine gun she was holding between her knees. 'But the doctor will know, won't he. You couldn't just...' She leant heavily on the orderly's shoulder. '...give me a hand, could you? Casualty's this way, isn't it?'

'Are you alright back there?' The headphones in Poppy's flying helmet came to life. 'Only, you've been pretty quiet for a while and...'

Poppy laughed.

'Oh, don't worry. I'm fine.' She rested her heavy flying helmet back against the hard seat and looked up through the canopy at the stars above. It was hard work doing even that. The tight harness that held her in her seat, the weight of the helmet and the constriction of the oxygen mask made her feel almost incapable of movement. 'I was just thinking, that's all.'

'Ah,' said the pilot's voice in her headphones. 'Thinking.' It made the word sound like it came from a foreign language. 'That's alright then.'

And then there was another voice. It giggled.

'Pervert,' it said. 'Thinking. Up here it's all reactions.'

'Ah yes,' replied Poppy, 'maybe. But then I'm not in the driving seat, am I?' Earlier in the day the voice would have frightened her. But now she was beginning to be used to her new status as a thing. She was even beginning to enjoy it. In a way.

'Er?' said the pilot's voice. His even, unhurried monotone was not quite as calm as it had been. 'What was that?'

'It was nothing,' said Poppy smoothly. 'Forget I spoke.'

The giggly voice giggled again.

'Shut up!' thought Poppy without moving her lips.

'Alright,' said the giggly voice, sounding hurt. 'I will then.'

And now Poppy felt bad.

'I didn't mean...' she began but her thought was interrupted by the pilot.

'So. What were you thinking about?'

Poppy reddened under her mask.

'Oh, nothing.' Her voice was tight.

The giggly voice laughed.

'Nothing's nothing.'

Inside her flying helmet Poppy blushed.

'As it happens,' she said, 'I was thinking about sex and flying,'

'Aaah.' The pilot sounded interested. 'Real thinking.'

'About how I was frightened of one and tired of the other.'

'Tired of flying?' The pilot was amazed.

'No.'

The pilot laughed.

'That's all right then. I can help you with both.'

And now Poppy laughed.

'What, even up here?'

'Up here, Poppy my love, they're the same thing. If you've got the right aircraft. And believe me, we have. Hold on tight and I'll show you.' There was a slight jolt. 'Taking manual control now.'

The giggly voice giggled.

'He thinks,' it said.

'So that's it then, is it?' The voice in the duty doctor's ear was aggrieved and in that respect it represented all the other voices clustering around him.

'You're telling us that's it? One mouldy ambulance, two little RTAs and two others so drunk we won't be able to operate for a fortnight.' The aggrieved voice was standing, arms akimbo, nose to nose with the duty doctor. 'Some emergency that is.' The voice turned to the rest of the emergency staff clustering on the gravel outside the Casualty Department doors.

'Some emergency that is, eh?'

There was an ugly chorus of agreement.

'They'll be here.' The doctor waved his arms about in a way that was supposed to suppress panic and discord. It failed.

'Yeah? When then? I don't hear nothing.'

'Yeah,' chorused the voices. 'When? We don't hear nothing.'

'Well if you'd all be quiet a moment, then perhaps we might hear something,' said the doctor petulantly.

'Alright,' said the voice sneeringly. 'Quiet everyone. Let's see if he's right, eh?'

'Now just a minute you,' said the doctor, 'there's no need for...'

'I thought we was being quiet, eh.'

The doctor subsided , embarrassed.

Absolute silence descended on the crowd. Not a foot scrunched the gravel. Not a single cough took to the air. No one found some compelling reason to whisper to a neighbour. It was a rare moment. Civilisation was reasserting itself. But not for long.

'See?' The voice broke the silence. 'Nothing. Not a dick-ey bird. So. I've got better things to do, I have. Even if you haven't.' The voice turned away from the doctor amidst an accompanying chorus of 'Yeah' and 'Me too.'

The doctor was flabbergasted. 'But... but... but...' But there was no one to flabber at. The crowd had dissolved.

'Alright then,' called the doctor. 'Alright! Emergency team stand down!' He turned back towards the Casualty department. 'And see if I care.'

The ambulance convoy had finally reached Dot's street but where there should have been the bustle of skilled aid

194

being administered to stricken casualties, there was only stillness and silence.

'Look at it. I mean, just look at it!' The driver of the first ambulance made a violent, unhappy gesture that comprehensively embraced the street, the casualties that littered it from end to end stopping the ambulances getting in and her contempt for inefficiency generally.

'And have you seen it back there? Bumper to bumper, all the way up to the High Street. Can't move forward. Can't move back. Can't move any bleedin' where. And then there's these wrecks too.' She indicated the remains of the police cars and vans that the do-it-yourselfers had left behind. 'They're not going to make things any easier, are they? And where the hell are the police?'

'Er...' said the first ambulance driver's crewmate. He was kneeling on the ground beside one of the casualties.

'I mean I ask you. I thought they were meant to be here.'

'Er...'

'But are they? Are they hell. Never around when you want them.'

'Er.' The crewmate indicated the prostrate figure in front of him. 'They are here look. It's just...'

The driver leant over her partner's casualty. It was dressed in blue police overalls.

'Oh,' she said. 'I see. But surely they can't all be...' She looked confused. 'They were down here in strength. That's what they told us. In strength. So you're never telling me...'

The crewmate nodded.

'What? All of them?'

The crewmate nodded again.

'Yeah!' There was awe in his voice. 'Every last one.'

'Oh damn,' said the driver. 'Well you can't rely on anyone these days, can you?' She began rolling her sleeves up to her elbows.

'Yes, well that's all very well, that is, saying that.' The crewmate was a good older than his driver, and a great deal more experienced. 'But the question is...' His expression was strained. 'The question is...' He looked up from patiently plodding through his thoughts and found that his driver was gone. He shook his head. She was like that, impatient. It never did no good in the end though. He shrugged and turned back to his work, loosening the collar around the casualty's neck, checking for a free airway and moving the stricken man into the recovery position.

'I don't expect you care what the question is though, do you?' the crewmate asked conversationally. 'Which is just as well really.' He rose stiffly and moved away to the next prone figure. 'Because I'm beggared if I know.'

Dot did not sit for long in Casualty after the harassed orderly left her there. She went to sit instead behind a locked door in the ladies' lavatory while she had a good think.

Dot was normally optimistic. Well I mean, she would say, you have to be, don't you? But right now she was not optimistic. Not optimistic at all. She could cope with the fact that her arms felt like they were dropping off. That was just life, human frailty and all that. And she could cope with the fact that she had lost her shoes. Shoes were just shoes, when all was said and done. And she could even, she thought, cope with the fact that there was a ladder in her stockings, she examined them regretfully, her best stockings. But it was the Runt she was finding hard to swallow. And Hubcaps. He'd seemed such a nice boy, Hubcaps.

And it was no use telling herself that she'd have done the same thing, in the Runt's place. That didn't work, not after seeing it like that, right in front of her own eyes. It didn't stop the hurt.

There were some consolations in the situation though. She knew the Runt, for one, and she knew the hospital too so she had a good idea where the Diamond would be hidden. And then there was her little friend here – she patted the sub-machine gun lying across her lap – she had met sub-machine guns before. And although this one was not a model she knew, they were all be pretty much the same, weren't they?

They all had this little lever on the side anyway, and once you'd twiddled that, you pointed the gun and squeezed the trigger and you either got one bullet or you got lots. Unless there were no bullets left. In that case all you had, Dot hefted the gun in her hand, was a clumsy sort of club. But then again, Dot smiled at the thought, who asks how many bullets a gun has got when the gun is pointing at them? It only needs one, after all.

The world was a shattered ruin and astride it stood Mad Harry, a colossus of failure. Around Mad Harry's feet the disenchanted ranks of humanity stood, abusing and vilifying him. All in all it was a very attractive picture. For Harry. It needed to be if the Diamond wanted to keep Mad Harry occupied while it got on with considering its own future.

It would have been sensible, under the circumstances, for the Diamond to have taken a peek into Harry's mind from time to time to make sure that its pictures were having the desired effect. But the Diamond did not think to do this. As far as it was concerned, Mad Harry was at the pictures. And because it could do nothing itself, it did not consider that Mad Harry could do more than one thing at a time.

In fact at that moment Harry was doing three things. He was indeed gloating over the glories of his future. But he was also moving steadily down the Diamond's telepathic beams, using them as a homing signal. And finally, because he was now angry with the corridors, he was breaking holes through walls to avoid them altogether. This was less difficult than it might have been, since most of the hospital's interior walls were little more than cardboard partitions.

Harry was set on getting hold of the Diamond as soon as

possible. He liked what the Diamond was showing him and he wanted to have it now. And also, if the Diamond did not keep its promises, he wanted to be able to do something about it. He punched his fist straight through a wall. Something that the Diamond would not like.

The doctor and nurse came round a corner a short way off from Harry. They were pushing trolleys with bodies on them. Harry was so busy with his destruction that he did not notice them. And they didn't stop long to see if he would.

The Boss wandered along the corridors in a trance. He paid no attention to where he was going. He scarcely noticed the trembling in the air. His head was filled with a succession of pictures and each one was like a promise.

To his delight the Boss had discovered that if he moved in one direction then the pictures grew better, brighter, more highly coloured. If he moved in other directions then the pictures lost their lustre. Oblivious of his surroundings he scuttled along, making rapid progress here, losing the scent there and casting around like a bloodhound until he was back on the trail. He stood still for a moment. A new picture was arriving and his whole body trembled in ecstasy.

'Aaah,' he sighed, 'more, more more.'

Poppy sat back in her seat in wonder. This flying was like no other flying she had ever known.

'Rolling out of the loop now.' The pilot's monotone was calm and reassuring. 'Straight and level.' The gravity metre on the control panel in front of Poppy registered a rare, brief zero. 'And climbing.'

The aircraft lifted abruptly to a vertical attitude and Poppy's thighs and calves were squeezed momentarily by her G-suit to stop the blood from collecting in her legs and, more importantly, to keep some of it in her brain.

'Twenty thousand feet.' The pilot counted off the height

as they soared starwards. 'Twenty five thousand. Thirty thousand.'

After twelve minutes of violent aerobatics Poppy did not know whether she was coming or going. Up was down, down was up, but, immensely reassuring, wherever the thundering jet pointed its nose, it felt like that was where it was meant to going.

'Of course,' said the giggly voice in her head. 'No room for doubt up here.'

The voice was, Poppy noticed, not all that giggly any more. It sounded like it was concentrating hard. The voice laughed.

'Concentrating yes. Wouldn't you be? But hard? Not yet. We haven't even begun yet.'

'Forty thousand feet. Rolling out to the right,' intoned the pilot.

Poppy's legs were clamped by the G-suit.

'You want to really see something?' said the aircraft. 'Watch this.'

'And diving,' went on the pilot.

'And how,' added the jet. There was no giggle in its voice at all now. It was hard edged and shiny and incredibly sharp and it sliced deep into the blackest part of Poppy's mind. Fascinated she looked into it. And there, just there, there was something, if only she could... She looked more closely and went straight towards it. Like she was meant to be going there.

'Rate of descent, two thousand feet per second.' That was the pilot's voice but Poppy ignored it because now she was right inside the aircraft's mind and suddenly it was hostile. It didn't like it.

'Get out of here!' it shrieked at her. 'How the hell can I concentrate?' But Poppy could not get out. She did not know how.

'Rate of descent two thousand two hundred.'

'Jesus wept,' moaned the aircraft. It began to spin lazily

on its axis.

'Two thousand five hundred,' said the pilot. And now he was worried. 'I think I'm losing it.'

'He's losing it!' shrieked the plane. And then it was no longer flying. It was falling. End over end. Round and round. Fluttering almost. Ever downwards. Like a wind-born sweet paper.

'Poppy,' the pilot's voice was faint. 'I'm sorry. I...'

Around Poppy the world exploded in a roar of sound, it bucked, it twisted, it danced and her G-suit clamped her tight. It was no longer reassuring. It hurt. It hurt like... She screamed. Her helmet went heavy. The bones of her legs were being squeezed to...

'Straight and level.' The pilot's voice crackled in Poppy's headphones. 'Five hundred feet. And climbing.' The aircraft tilted gently upwards. 'Rate of climb, two hundred feet per second.'

Poppy said nothing.

'Poppy, are you alright?'

'Yes.' She was groggy. 'What happened?'

'I got a bit carried away. Something went wrong. And how we...' He stopped. Frightened to go on. 'We were lucky, I guess.'

'Yes.' Poppy was thoughtful. 'I suppose.' But she was not concentrating any more on the pilot. She was thinking about something else.

'Well,' said the plane. Its voice was not giggly. It was tense and cross. 'That was quite some performance. And I'm not talking about myself. Did you know what you were doing?'

'No, you see I...'

'Then I think,' said the aircraft firmly, 'that we should talk, don't you? Before you get yourself hurt.'

200

18

Dot leant against a wall and peered around a corner. That is to say, the machine gun peered around the corner for her. The black hole of the gun's muzzle stared silently down the empty length of the brightly lit and equally silent corridor. Slowly, very slowly, Dot's head came out behind the gun to share its view. The corridor was empty.

This was a ridiculous way to walk around a hospital in the middle of the night. Dot knew it. In her bones, even, she knew it. And yet...

The fast jet plane landed on the broad, brightly lit sweep of the runway and taxied rapidly into a dark corner of the airfield. The canopy lifted high with a sigh of hydraulics and the pilot unplugged his helmet and stood up in the front of the cockpit. He raised his visor.

'Right. Out you get, quick, before anyone sees us.'

Poppy unplugged her connections to the navigator's seat at the back of the cockpit and climbed out onto the wing.

'And...' the pilot hesitated, 'I'm sorry. About...'

Poppy turned back to him.

'We made it,' she said. 'That's all that matters.'

'Yes. Well.' The pilot was shamefaced. 'I don't know how.'

Poppy kissed her fingers and lightly touched his cheek.

'Sssh. It's been... fascinating. And thanks. Thanks a million.'

The pilot laughed.

'Don't mention it. It's what brothers-in-law are for. Trespass on air force property. Illegal immigration. Trying to kill you. Little things like that.'

Poppy jumped down from the wing.

'There's a hole in the fence by that landing light over there,' the pilot called after her. 'At least, there was one last week. Leave your flying kit by it. I'll pick it up later.'

'Right.' Poppy looked back, blew the pilot a kiss and disappeared into the night.

'Go safe, then,' said a voice in her head. It was the aircraft.

'Stay safe,' thought Poppy in reply.

A giggle came from the direction of the runway.

'Stay safe? Who? Me?' Behind Poppy the night was split by the fire and thunder of jet engines on afterburn. 'That's not what I was made for.'

As Poppy stood stripping off her flying suit by the perimeter fence of the airport she ran through in her head the conversation she was going to have with Rupert.

To begin with she would be firm. Extremely firm. She rolled up the flying suit and stuffed it inside her helmet. After all, what had Rupert ever done for her? She could feel her indignation rising as she asked the question. He had turned her into a toy, that's what he had done for her.

The G-suit fell to the ground. She stood the helmet on top of it. And now as well as indignation there was anger too. And what good was being a toy supposed to be? Without a backward glance she found the pilot's hole in the fence, climbed through it and began hitching along the main road that ran beside the airfield.

He was a bad beggar. Rupert. He had taken her whole and given her nothing in return. Hell! He had never even asked her to marry him. A midnight black Porsche squealed to a halt twenty yards down the road and Poppy ran towards it. He might at least have asked.

The Porsche's passenger door swung open.

'London?' smiled a voice from out of the dark.

'London,' agreed Poppy as she climbed in. 'And do you mind if we don't talk?' she added as she adjusted her seat belt. 'I've got a lot on my mind.'

'Sure,' said the voice complacently. 'Just hold on tight while I bring you new meaning to the word 'drive'.'

'Okay.' Poppy smiled sweetly. She doubted very much that he could. But she was happy to let him try.

In Burns and General Surgery the doctor was considering the situation. The nurse stood cool and collected beside him, waiting for him to make a decision.

'Over there I think.' The doctor pointed towards two empty beds side by side at the far end of ward. 'You take him.' He nodded in the direction of a trolley bearing the recumbent form of the light, boyish voice. 'And I'll take this one.' He caught hold of a second trolley bearing the slighter frame of the deadpan voice and began to push it across the ward. 'And don't hang about eh? We haven't got all night.'

The stillness woke Dave the ambulance driver. And the silence. And the trembling. They made an atmosphere laden with threat.

He opened his eyes and it was like looking down a tunnel. The tunnel had no walls. It was bordered with darkness. And Dave lay staring at the... what was it? Right at the end? A ceiling. It must be. The ceiling of... of he did not know where and that was threatening too.

The ceiling was white – no clues in that – and there were cracks running through the whiteness. There were wide, black cracks and thin, hair-line cracks and they all came together to make a picture. At least, they suggested a picture. Or anyway, they hinted that a picture was lurking there, somewhere.

Dave shut his eyes and opened them again and still the picture was only the ghost of a thing – vague, shifting, uncertain – and, for some reason that was entirely beyond him, he desperately wanted to know what it was. Maybe it was because, at that moment, it was all he had.

He sighed. All he had apart from the pain of course, the sharpness in his chest that had been there before.

Before what? He did not know. He knew so little. He sighed again, deeply, and this time the pain was really bad. He screamed.

'Right then, ready?' In Burns and General Surgery the doctor and nurse braced themselves ready to lift the deadpan voice from off his trolley onto a freshly made-up bed. The nurse nodded.

'So. One, two, three...' said the doctor and the nurse began taking up the deadpan voice's weight.

'No. Wait. Hang about.' The doctor released his hold on the deadpan voice and straightened up, listening intently. 'There it is again,' he said.

'There what is again?' said the nurse, tartly

'Ssh!' The doctor flapped his hand at her. 'Can't you feel it?'

And now that her attention had been drawn to it, the nurse could feel it. It was a trembling, no more. But it suggested the calm before all hell breaks loose.

'Er...' she began.

'Ssh!' The doctor flapped again.

'Couldn't we just get on with this?' The nurse nodded at the deadpan voice. 'I'd quite like to get finished up, I think.'

It was the screaming that woke Florien, Dave's ambulance crewmate. She opened her eyes and found herself in a place she knew well but had never before visited as a

204

customer. And if she was in hospital, then there must be a reason for it. What was it?

Gingerly she moved her feet. They seemed to work all right. There was no pain anyway. And legs? Okay too. Abdomen? Yes. Chest? Ditto. And arms. And neck. And... There. Pain there. But not a lot. Nothing too bad.

There was a small mirror on the wall. Florien sat up and turned to it to examine her face where it hurt. Her nose was bigger than its usual size. And flatter. And there was a dark bruise right across her swollen forehead. Nothing to worry about though, if only because there was nothing to be done about it.

Gently, but urgently because the screaming was still going on and there were no sounds of running feet, Florien stood. She did not fall. The effects of concussion may come later but for now she was all right. She left the small Casualty Department cubicle where she had been deposited and pulled back the curtain of the cubicle next door. Dave lay on the narrow examination couch inside. He turned his head at the sound of the curtain and saw her.

'Flo?'

'My name's not Flo.'

Dave gasped, short of breath and screamed again, briefly. Florien smacked him and he stopped.

'And don't do that again either or I'm off,' she said.

Dave caught at her hand.

'Sorry!' he said. 'But stay, eh. It's been awful.'

Florien sat on the chair at the bedside and Dave's head turned as his eyes followed her down.

'So,' she said. 'What's been awful?'

Dave's eyes widened.

'Can't you feel it?' he said urgently. 'In the air?'

And now that he had mentioned it, Florien could feel it, in the air. And she felt that she didn't like it. And that she didn't want to be alone with it. But also she saw that Dave needed help.

205

'I've got to get someone to see to you,' she said. 'You're in a bad way.'

Dave's grip tightened on her hand.

'No,' he said. 'Stay.' And then, because he was near to panic, 'Or take me with you if you must go. This thing's got wheels, hasn't it? Push me.'

Florien sighed.

'Alright,' she said, 'I suppose I could manage that. Only no more screaming. Right?'

A midnight-black Porsche skidded to a halt in a small side street near Trafalgar Square. The headlights dimmed to nothing. The tinny sound of the engine fell silent. Inside, the air reeked of self-satisfaction.

'So,' said the smug voice of the driver, 'what did you think, eh?'

Poppy opened her eyes in a leisurely fashion and turned languidly towards him.

'Had it long have you?'

'No, it's new.' Pride dripped from every syllable. Then there was the small sound of a balloon being punctured. A very soft balloon. 'But... Er... What makes you ask?'

'Well,' said Poppy thoughtfully with her hand on the door latch, 'you're not bad really. But you've still got a lot to learn.' She opened the door. 'If you live long enough.'

Anger blossomed, fiery and red and lit the inside of the car. The driver reached out across Poppy and pulled her door shut.

'Oh yeah?' His face was an inch from hers. 'So what do you know?'

'You did ask,' said Poppy. 'And that's my opinion.'

'Yeah. Right. For what it's worth.' The driver flung himself back in his seat and thumped the steering wheel with both hands. He sat sulking for a few moments. Then.

'Got far to go have you?' he said challengingly.

'South of the river, just,' replied Poppy.

206

'Right. Okay.' The driver turned towards her with a wicked smile. 'Then if you're so good, you show me. Know the way, do you?' Poppy nodded.

'Then drive.' The driver climbed out of the car and walked round the back. Poppy clambered over into his seat and shut the door. She felt the weight of the steering, adjusted the seat and checked the rear-view mirror.

'Okay,' she said to the car as she fired up the engine, 'be a lamb eh, and show me what you can do.'

With a squeal of tyres the car leapt forward and disappeared round a corner, trailing smoke. The driver stood on the pavement, reaching out to where the door handle had been.

'Oh beggar it!' he said. 'Now what?' He did not wait long for an answer. There was a roar and a squeal of tyres as his car drew up behind him. The passenger door swung open.

'Okay,' said Poppy's voice. 'Hop in! I think I've got the feel of it.'

In Dot's street the driver of the first ambulance was getting things organised. Her crewmate watched with a sort of bewitched fascination. She was always rushing about, that one, he thought, and here she was, at it again, doing what was none of her business, by rights.

It never did no good in the end neither, the crewmate told himself again. But expect her to listen to reason? You might just as well expect a broken leg to mend itself.

Though of course, he conceded, they did mend themselves didn't they, legs, but that was only natural. All this rushing about though... well, that wasn't natural. It wasn't natural at all.

The first ambulance driver was moving down the convoy from the rear, getting the ambulances to back up and pull into the side of the road so as to leave a clear path out for any that managed to get loaded. She was directing one of them now, standing behind it and waving and shouting as it inched perilously towards her in the dark.

'Oi, oi, oi, oi. Whoa!' she yelled and banged on the rear doors. 'That's it, lovely, just wait there for now.

'And you!' She went round and banged on the crewmate's door. 'Hop out, eh, and help with getting the casualties sorted.'

The crewmate slowly opened his door and climbed out to join the steady stream of crewmates from the ambulances at the back as they trudged towards Dot's street. The air was filled with the low mutter of complaining voices and dark glances were cast at the first ambulance driver as the shadowy figures passed her but she did not notice them. She was already at work on the next ambulance.

'Oi, oi, oi, oi,' she shouted as she directed it back in against the kerb. Then suddenly the ambulance gave a great leap backwards and nearly landed on her foot.

'Whoa! Watch out! You nearly had me there!' yelled the first ambulance driver crossly.

'Not bleedin' nearly enough,' growled a dark shadow from close by her.

You had to hand it to her though, thought the first ambulance crewmate. He had finished tending his quota of casualties and was leaning on a wall, watching from the end of Dot's street. Yes, you had to hand it to her, the hide of a rhinoceros she had, and the tackle of a stallion. At this rate she'd have the job done by, oooh, he looked at his watch and his brain hummed with complex calculations, well by breakfast at the very latest.

It would still never do no good in the end though. Start doing the police's job for them and who could say where you'd end up? Except that it wouldn't be comfortable. Once things started changing then the first thing to go was comfort. He sighed. Any fool could make themselves uncomfortable. But comfort, that needed working at. And patience. Lots and lots of patience.

In a side street off The Borough High Street a midnight-black Porsche skidded to a halt. The headlights dimmed to nothing. The tinny sound of the engine fell silent. Inside, the air was heavy with a quiet triumph.

'So,' said Poppy in a calm voice, 'what do you think?'

'Er...' whimpered the driver.

'That's alright then,' said Poppy. 'And thanks for the lift.' She opened her door, climbed out and patted the car on its roof.

'And thank you too,' she thought quietly.

'Don't mention it,' said a tinny voice inside her head. 'It's always a pleasure, working with people who know what they're doing.'

The Porsche drew sedately away from the kerb and pottered up towards the junction with the High Street. An indicator blinked right, brake lights showed briefly, there was a subdued 'Vroom!' and then silence.

Poppy reached into a pocket and took out Rupert's address book. She opened it at 'B' for Boss. Yes, she had found the right street and, unless she was very much mistaken, the Boss's place must be in those flats, she looked up, over there. And that was where Rupert would be. She was sure of it.

She stepped into the road and then drew swiftly back. The main door of the flats was opening, someone was coming out and it was Rupert. There was a woman with him, a middle-aged and drink-ravaged woman she was but Poppy knew, even at this distance and in the dark, that she had once been beautiful, almost as beautiful as Poppy herself.

Instantly Poppy was jealous. It was absurd. She was giving up competing for Rupert's admiration. She was about to walk out on him for heaven's sake. But still she was jealous. She wanted to know who this woman was, who seemed so familiar with Rupert. And she wanted to know where they were going. And why.

Rupert and the woman reached the junction with the

High Street, turned left and disappeared. Poppy took a deep breath. Well. If she wanted to know then there was only one way to find out. She followed.

19

For nearly a minute now the hospital had been perfectly
still. The trembling had ceased.

'Hey? What have you stopped for?' Mad Harry's voice
came lancing across the telepathic wavebands in a single,
intense burst of puzzled anger. A lesser thing than the
Diamond, something soft and fluffy and highly inflamma-
ble – a powder-puff, say – might have expired in a flurry
of spontaneous combustion on receiving such a message.
But not the Diamond. The Diamond was made of sterner
stuff.

'What?' it said.

'The pictures.'

'Pictures?'

'Yes. Pictures. You stopped.'

'Oh. Yes. Right. Pictures.' The Diamond was feeling
disorientated. It had been thinking about its future and had
reached no conclusions. And now that it had been dragged
back into contact with the outside world, it found that the
outside world had changed. Changed a lot.

'That's it. Pictures.'

For one thing, Mad Harry was much closer than he had
been. He had moved.

'What about them, eh?'

He had been homing in on the pictures. And he had been
breaking down walls. But there was something else too.
The Diamond sniffed the air and risked a quick, telepathic

sweep of the hospital. There were a lot more people about and with them there was, it sniffed again and smiled, there was the smell of fear. It affected the Diamond like burnt cordite affects a soldier. It quickened the pulse. In a manner of speaking.

The Diamond decided to try a second sweep to see who these people were, who were so fearful. And maybe see why they were fearful too. It was a risk. These powerful search sweeps gave Harry further opportunities for homing in. But what the hell? In for a penny, in for a pound and knowledge was power. Who knew what benefits it might yield in the end?

As the Diamond's search beam streamed out again there was a cry of pain. It was Harry. The Diamond stopped searching to investigate.

'What's up Harry?' it said.

'Bricks,' said Harry in a broken voice. 'Bleedin' bricks.'

The significance of bricks was not immediately obvious so the Diamond had a quick rummage in Harry's mind. And then it laughed.

Harry stood facing a blank, white wall in a long, straight corridor somewhere in the hospital. Behind him a ragged hole gave a clear view into the senior administrator's office.

Harry's hands were bleeding – even thin, partition walls are tough to pull down bare-handed – and to extend their working life he had improvised a wall-borer out of the leg of a chair. He had been using it on the wall in front of him but had succeeded only in chipping away plaster to reveal solid-looking brickwork underneath.

And although th e chair leg had its limitations when confronted with a brick wall, its effects were like a sledge-hammer when compared with Harry's head.

'It's not funny!' he sobbed as he beat it against the wall. 'It's not funny. It's not funny. It's not funny.'

He banged his head once more and then turned and slid down to the floor. He dropped the chair leg, stuck his elbows against the inside of his knees and rested his head on his hands. All in all it had been a long, difficult and dispiriting day.

'And it's not fair neither,' he muttered.

Abruptly the telepathic laughter stopped. Harry glanced over his shoulder at the wall through which powerful, confident search beams had once more begun to stream.

'It's bleedin' well not fair!'

Dot continued to be cautious as she moved along the corridors but there was a difference now from her earlier caution. Now she no longer felt that it was ridiculous. To begin with she was lost - on account of the signs all being to blazes - and, what with that and the trembling and the stillness and the screaming she had heard, she had no doubts at all about caution being precisely the right note to strike. A door came up on her left and, as she had done with other doors before it, she swung it open. Sooner or later she would come across a place she knew.

'Get her!' yelled a voice from the room beyond. A dead-pan voice.

Strong hands gripped Dot's arms on either side.

'Oh,' said Dot. 'Hullo. Haven't we met before?'

In Burns and General Surgery, just a few moments earlier, the doctor and the nurse had been bracing themselves once again to lift the deadpan voice from off his trolley onto a freshly made bed.

'One, two, three...' murmured the doctor. He was feeling cowed by the atmosphere of the hospital and was not speaking very clearly. '...and... Lift!'

'Sorry?' said the nurse. 'I didn't hear.'

'I said 'Lift!'' said the doctor but by then it was too late. Left unexpectedly alone with the full weight of the deadpan voice, he fumbled it. With an awkward movement the limp

213

body rolled from off the trolley and fell to the floor with a bone-shaking crunch.

If the deadpan voice had been conscious then his fall would probably have knocked him out. As things were, though, the shock of it woke him from his alcoholic stupor. His eyes opened. Trolley wheels, legs, and a bed all cluttered up his foreground vision but that did not matter. It was what was in the background that mattered.

The door caught the deadpan voice's attention because it was moving. It took the merest moment for the deadpan voice to recognise the figure that looked in and then a lifetime of malice and crime focused itself like a laser beam through the alcohol that filled his head. The beam fell on Dot.

'Get her!' yelled the deadpan voice and he hurled himself up from the floor and at her.

The piercing command tore the light, boyish voice from his trolley and dragged him in his colleague's wake. His hands closed round something hard and unyielding.

'Oh, hullo,' said a woman's voice as he finally woke up. 'Haven't we met before?'

The main doors of the hospital opened. A man strode in.

'Alright then.' He looked around as though he owned the place. 'Where is he?'

A woman entered too. She moved diffidently as though she owned nowhere of her own and was dependent on other people to provide her with everything she had. Which was the case. But in spite of her cowed nature, there was a light in her eyes. It was the kind of light that shines in the eyes of people who think that their problems are about to be solved once and for all.

'Er, Rupert...' began the woman.

'Deirdre.' Rupert's demeanour softened. 'Right then. We'll just find him and get him sorted and everything will be alright. A nice little place of your own. A bit of money

214

to keep you going. What more could a woman want, eh?'

On the spur of the moment Deirdre could think of several little things she might like to add to the shopping list that she and Rupert had worked out on their way to the hospital. But she was a prudent woman. She would take what she could get and not push her luck. She smiled.

'Oh Rupert, I couldn't want anything more than to just leave it all to you. You'll see me alright, I know you will.' On the other hand, she smiled again at the thought, there was no point in closing down her options, not when things were going so well.

'And you know what the best thing is?' Rupert rubbed his hands together in anticipation. 'The Boss will enjoy giving it all to you. Positively enjoy it. Just you see if he doesn't.'

'I'm sure you're right, Rupert,' sighed Deirdre. And then she became more practical. She looked around. 'And now, maybe...' she hesitated diffidently, avoiding appearing too pushy. 'Maybe we should find the Reception or something. They ought to know where the Boss is, oughtn't they?'

'Good idea.' Rupert looked around for a sign to show them where the Reception was but there were no signs. That did not stop Rupert though. He pointed away to the right.

'This way,' he said firmly and that way they went.

'So you,' said a soft, compelling voice close by, 'are Rudge then, are you?'

Startled, Rudge span round from where he had been watching Rupert and Deirdre. His hand rested on the hilt of his knife, ready for anything.

'Don't worry with the knife, Mr Rudge. I'm not going to hurt you.'

And now that he saw the owner of the voice, Rudge believed her. He would have believed anything she told him. In the normal way of things women like this only spoke to him in dreams. Good dreams. His, not theirs.

215

'Yes, I'm Rudge,' he said. He straightened his tie and did not know what to do or say next.

'Pleased to meet you, Rudge,' said Poppy. 'I've heard so much about you.'

'Er,' said Rudge. 'Right,' he began. 'But how did you...' And then a different thought occurred to him. 'And how did you know...' He glanced down at his coat where the knife lay hidden.

Poppy laughed. It was a laugh that made Rudge feel warm and wanted.

'That was easy. You see, I'm a mind reader.'

'Ah,' said Rudge. 'Right. I see.' And as fast as it had come his warmth was gone. Just his luck. She was mad. A complete fruit cake. Ah well. He had other things to do than stand around here. He had a diamond to find. And then maybe, later on, he might meet up with Rupert too. He'd like that. He wandered disconsolately in the direction that Rupert had gone. Pity though. He glanced back over his shoulder. She really was...

'If you're serious about the Diamond,' said Poppy, 'then your best bet's letting me help you.'

Rudge stopped dead in his tracks.

'And as far as Rupert goes, you can do what you like about him, just so long as you let me at him first.'

'But... How...'

'Though of course,' Poppy went on, 'you needn't bother with me at all, if you don't want to.'

'Who...' Rudge was finding it difficult to cope with what he was hearing. 'Who are you?'

'It's probably best,' replied Poppy, 'to try and think of me as your fairy godmother.'

Rudge tried.

'Good,' said Poppy. 'And very nice too.'

Florien was pushing Dave on his bed along the endless corridors.

'I think it's left now,' he said. 'I'm sure it is. It must be.'

'Left,' said Florien. Her voice cracked slightly. 'Left it is then.' She swung the bed in a wide sweeping turn round the corner and hurtled on towards wherever Dave was directing her. She hoped it was the main exit but she did not really care. Any exit would do just fine. And the sooner the better.

'Whoa!' said Dave. 'Take it steady! We're together Flo...'

'My name is not Flo,' grated Florien through clenched teeth.

'...remember? So no need to panic. Eh?'

'And I am not panicking.' She was of course. She was panicking like hell. But she couldn't admit that to Dave, however bad she felt. There was such a thing as self-respect, after all.

Florien knew all about self-respect. It was what was helping her to cope with the panic. Self-respect said it was fine to panic if there was plenty to panic about. And there was.

Away from the Casualty Department the hospital was in a worse state than Florien could ever have imagined. There was no one about. There were holes in the walls. The signs were all over the place. And that was just to begin with. The worst thing of all was the atmosphere. It was warped. And it crept right inside you. And it made it difficult to... to... She swallowed hard, holding back the torrent of fear that rose in her throat and made her feel sick.

Around a corner, far ahead of Florien, two figures appeared. One of them was wearing a nurse's uniform and, seeing her, Florien finally gave up altogether.

'Help me!' she screamed but there was only a dry crackling at the back of her throat. She let go of the bed, held her arms out piteously and subsided to her knees. Tears rolled in hot torrents down her cheeks.

'Help me!'

217

'Hey hey, hold on Flo girl.' Dave sat up anxiously on the bed. 'Don't go giving up now. Not when we were doing so well and all.'

'This is the right way?'
'Yes. It's the right way.'
'And you're sure we haven't been here before?'
The Runt stopped forging ahead of Hubcaps and turned back to wait for him. He was looking at a bent metal sign he had picked up from the floor.
'What are you doing?' she said.
'Oh nothing.' Hubcaps twisted a corner of the sign backwards and forwards until it grew hot in his hand and broke off. Then he dropped the sign and put the broken bit into his pocket.
'Shall we go on?' he said. Considering the circumstances he was surprising himself with his own cheerfulness. The circumstances were all completely wrong but if the Runt was not mentioning it, then far be it from him...
'Alright,' said the Runt. 'But do try to keep up.' Without waiting for a reply she turned and walked away round a corner. Hubcaps followed.

By the time that the Runt reached her, Florien was just a small sobbing heap on the corridor's red tiles. She reached out and hugged the Runt's ankles.
'Help me!' she muttered over and over again. 'Help me! Help me!'
The Runt looked at Hubcaps. He shrugged.
'You're the nurse,' he said.
Florien looked up into the Runt's face.
'Help m...,' she began and then her expression changed. It became fierce and terrible beyond all the restraints of polite social intercourse.
'You!' she screamed. She leapt to her feet. 'You!' She drew back her fist and punched the Runt on the chin. The

Runt's eyes went blank and she fell limply to the floor.

'Ha!' shrieked Florien triumphantly. 'Got you back! So there!' With another shriek she jumped over the Runt's prostrate body and ran away down the corridor. Hubcaps watched open-mouthed until she was out of sight and then he turned to Dave.

'Er. What...' he began but that was as far as he got. Dave had left his bed and was standing behind him with his fist clenched. Hubcaps felt a straight left connect with his jaw.

'Friend of hers were you?' said Dave. He poked at the fallen Hubcaps with his foot and, getting no response, he too ran away down the corridor as fast as he could manage, what with the pain in his chest and all.

'Wait for me!' he shouted in a thin, strained voice. 'Hey, Flo, wait for me.'

Mad Harry raised his head as footsteps approached. A man was running towards him. Harry had seen him earlier and he had looked like a crook then, solid and heavy with a gang of thugs around him. But now he was no longer solid and heavy. He was not solid at all. He had his hands over his ears and he was bouncing from side to side along the corridor like a beam of light trying to escape from a strand of fibre optic.

'Can't you hear it?' screeched the man as he ran past Mad Harry. 'Can't you hear it? It's gone bad.' But he did not wait for an answer. He ran on and away and disappeared round a bend. Harry watched him go. There was a puzzled expression on his face.

Hear what? he thought. There was nothing to hear. The hospital was as silent as, he groped for an expression, but he had never heard a silence like it before. All there was, filling every available channel of his senses, was the agonising search beam of the Diamond. It was louder now and more confident than ever. And, listening to it, Harry realised how little he had known about hate. Until now.

219

Well, well, well. The Diamond closed down its search beam and smiled to itself. This was quite a collection - as desperate a cross section of humanity as it had seen in one place for a long time - which made this a very special moment, a rare opportunity for some real fun. And with Harry beaten and dispirited, at least for now, the Diamond felt quite secure about taking time out to make the most of it.

It began to think. It might even be possible to turn the whole thing to its advantage and rid itself of Harry once and for all. It smiled again. Who knew where things might lead, if these people really got stirred up?

Fear, that was the key. For a bit of real fun there was nothing like fear to really get people going. And the Diamond was not thinking about the sort of fear that the hospital was now awash with — that vague, ill-defined kind of fear that only gets people running around like headless chickens. No. What the Diamond had in mind was the good, solid, highly directed kind of fear that people believe they can overcome if only they are determined enough, move fast enough and fight hard enough.

The Diamond had played this game before. The first step was to tell the participants exactly what was going on and for that it preferred to use a voice other than its own. It gave the game more impetus if the voice came from everywhere at once. So, and the Diamond smiled as it began to creep insidiously into the mind of the corridors, what better voice to use than the one closest to hand? And these corridors, they must surely have quite a voice.

The first ambulance driver walked round the corner back into Dot's street. She was looking for her crewmate.

'Ah, there you are.' There was tension in her voice. 'Had a good rest then, have you? Feel up to sitting still now, while I drive us back, do you?'

The crewmate yawned and stretched as he eased his bulk away from the wall. He felt tired which was unsurprising really, he looked at his watch, considering the time

'I suppose I can manage that,' he said. He stretched and investigated a small itch behind the leading lip of his left ear. 'I mean, it's my job isn't it, when all's said and done?'

'You don't say?'

'I do say it.' The crewmate's hide was thicker than the skin on cold custard. 'And I've got no objections to doing my job. As you know. What I can't be doing with is...' But his driver was no longer there. She was disappearing rapidly in the direction of the High Street. Breaking with the tradition of a lifetime the crewmate shambled into a run after her.

'What I can't be doing with is messing with what's none of my business.' He pressed on harder as the gap between him and his driver widened.

'Because...' Unaccustomed to vigorous exercise the crewmate found himself having difficulty shouting. 'And you mark my words girl. Because...'

In the High Street the convoy of ambulances was drawn up pointing in the direction of the hospital and ready to go. The first ambulance crewmate appeared around a corner and all the other crewmates watched from out of their windows as he delivered his last word on his driver's folly.

'Because no good won't come of it! It never does!' In the relief of finishing his run the first ambulance crewmate's last words came out in an uncontrolled roar that filled the High Street silence. He looked round challengingly but no one said anything. They just watched him. Fixedly. The first ambulance crewmate scrambled into his cab with undignified haste.

'You mark my words,' he grumbled defiantly before slamming his door. 'No good won't come of it.'

'Well then,' said the first ambulance driver, 'if you're quite ready.' She let down the handbrake, let out the clutch and let rip.

WOOooo! WWOOOoooo! WWWOOOOooo! A brigade

222

of ambulances carved the silence of the night with a torrent of noise to gladden Hubcaps's heart.

'Aah,' sighed the first ambulance driver. 'Listen to that.' She wound down her window to hear better. 'Don't you just love it?' Her face softened as she spoke. The tension was visibly draining down from out of her.

'No,' muttered the crewmate huddling in his seat and trying to keep his feet out of the growing pool of tension which was sloshing around the floor. 'I hate it.' He scowled at his driver. 'It gives me a headache.'

Once the Diamond was inside the mind of the corridors it did not immediately try out their voice. It could not. It was too overawed by what it found. And for the Diamond to be overawed was a phenomenon on an epic scale.

Mad Harry believed that the architect who designed the hospital's maze of corridors was a genius. He must be. His creation had defeated Harry for the best part of a day.

A different point of view has been taken by the many mathematicians who have been invited to investigate the geometry of the hospital's corridors. They believe that the architect was mad. Or, to be more accurate, they would like to believe he was mad but they know in their hearts that madmen are never employed to design anything. Of course. Which leaves the mathematicians in an impossible position. They are working hard on it, though. Because anything beats looking too closely at those corridors.

And now, inside the mind of the corridors themselves, it was the Diamond that had unearthed the truth. If it was any judge then the man who produced the corridors had been bright and ambitious, certainly, but no genius. He had merely been high. Although 'merely' was a less than adequate word, under the circumstances. It must have been something terrifyingly powerful that had tuned the young architect's head into the alternative reality where the corridors lurked, a reality beyond the mundane world of

223

Euclidean geometries and Newtonian physics.

It would have been a fun place, the Diamond thought enviously, that alternative reality – though this would have been no consolation to the architect through a confused and painful later life – it would have been packed with pretty and fascinating baubles. There had been these corridors, to begin with. And maybe there had also been monkeys writing great, original drama.

Like all tourists throughout time the architect had brought a bauble back with him. And like many tourists throughout time he had found that there was nowhere at home to put it. But unlike other tourists, the architect could not give his bauble away to the church bazaar – not corridors compounded of infinite volume in finite space – they would have had the vicar in fits.

While the Diamond was making its discoveries about the corridors, around the corridors themselves there was less fear than there had been earlier. This was not so much because the trembling had stopped. It had done that often. It was because now there was no feeling left lingering that it was about to start again.

Florien halted in her headlong flight and looked around wonderingly. Dave cannoned into her from behind and screamed.

'What did you want to stop for?' he asked angrily once the worst spasms of pain had passed.

'Because I'd forgotten why I was running,' answered Florien, reasonably enough she thought.

The Axe and the Sailor rounded a corner and saw a small bewildered figure ambling aimlessly towards them.

'Boss!' cried the Axe loudly. 'Boss, you're alright.' The Sailor gave a grunt of pleasure.

'Er, yes.' The Boss felt himself vaguely. 'I think so.' He

turned his head cautiously from side to side. 'But my neck's a bit stiff though. And...' he looked down at himself. 'Why am I wearing pyjamas?'

The Runt sat up and groaned. She fingered her jaw and it was a mistake. But it is a common enough mistake and so she did it again.

'What happened?' she murmured but there was no reply. Hubcaps lay motionless beside her. She shook him and he stirred and groaned. 'What happened?' she asked again.

And so it was all round the hospital. People looked dazed and relieved, as if they were waking from bad dreams. At the main entrance Rupert and Deirdre came up behind Rudge and Poppy. Without signs to guide them they had come full circle and ended up where they had begun but they did not seem to mind. And Rudge even managed to look pleased about meeting Rupert again after so many years.

Dot stood between the deadpan voice and the light, boyish voice and beamed at them.

'Right, so you've got me. What now?' she said.

'Er,' said the deadpan voice.

'Um,' said the light, boyish voice.

'Then maybe you should just let me go, eh,' said Dot. Much to everyone's surprise they did.

'Thanks,' said Dot. She smiled, blew them a kiss and went.

In Burns and General Surgery the doctor started laughing.

'What now?' said the nurse, but the acid had gone from her voice and she started giggling. 'What is it now?'

'Don't you feel it?' said the Doctor. 'It's like...' He started fumbling for words.

225

The nurse rested her hand on his arm.

'Ssh,' she said, 'Yes I do I feel it. And thank god for it too. You've been being such an idiot.' The doctor's face froze but only for a moment. 'I know,' he said and he nodded. 'I know I have been.'

'Er,' began the Diamond. Then it stopped and coughed as if to clear its throat. The corridor's voice was rusty with disuse.

'Er, right then. I hope you're all listening.'

'What do you think,' muttered Poppy to herself, 'when the walls start talking? Of course they're listening.' Fortunately for Poppy the Diamond was paying her no special attention. It had other things on its mind.

'Well, I had intended to invite you all to a party,' went on the Diamond, 'but, um... But then...' It hesitated again, collecting its thoughts. They had a disturbing tendency to scatter inside the mind of the corridors.

'But then I decided just to drag you all in anyway.'

And now there began to be strength in the voice. Poppy noticed the change immediately and she was not alone. No one listening was in any doubt that the voice could do exactly what it said. And no one liked the idea. Throughout the hospital fear was reborn, but it was a new kind of fear, fear like a spur. Deirdre leapt into action.

'No!' she yelled. 'NOoo!' She made a grab at the main doors but they would not budge. She shook and rattled them but still they would not budge.

'There's no point even trying,' said the voice. But although Deirdre could see that indeed there was no point since the edges of the door were all sort of smeared over, she kept on trying anyway. She was only human, after all. Rupert watched her transfixed. So did Rudge. But Poppy was concentrating on something else. She was watching the walls.

'Hey Boss! Look at the walls!' said the Axe far away in the depths of the corridors.

'What walls?' said the Boss. It was a sentiment that echoed and re-echoed around the hospital for the next several milliseconds, although it felt longer.

'Oh yeah,' said the Axe. 'What walls? There aren't any.'

The Diamond was impressed. Really impressed. After all, there it had been, for it did not know how many millions of years, unable to do anything... Oh it could stir people up, sure, and cause things to happen but it had never been able actually to do anything. And now... Now things had changed. Now it had the means to...

'I say 'come' and thou comest,' intoned the Diamond and its voice sounded really impressive in this... This place. Whatever it was.

'I say 'go' and thou goest.' And boy are things going to be different now, it thought. Being a king-maker, well that was all very good, and entertaining enough, in its own way. But to be a king. Well...

The Diamond surveyed the small crowd of people standing in a frozen huddle in front of it. So, from the back, did Poppy. They were all there, everyone who had been in the corridors when... She glanced around her. When the corridors had changed into this... this arena, or stadium or whatever it was.

Someone coughed.

'Er,' said the Axe hesitantly. 'Just now. Didn't you say something about a party?'

'A party?' said the Diamond scornfully. 'A party?' Maybe it had, in another lifetime, but who cared? Now? 'Is that really important?'

'Er,' said the Axe. He hesitated because of course it wasn't. Not really. Thinking about the impossible things that were happening all around him, that was important.

227

And thinking about what to do about them. That was important too. But thinking about those things would mean that... He looked at the red-tiled floor to avoid seeing the... The whatever it was that he did not want to believe was true. Not yet. Not ever. His feet shuffled involuntarily. 'It's just,' he said, 'I like jelly. That's all.'

'Jelly?!' said the Diamond in a voice that Ivan the terrible would have loved to posses. 'Jelly?!'

To avoid any confusion, what the Diamond has created by reshaping the corridors is simply a big space. It is very big since although it has finite boundaries it is, as the Diamond has already discovered, infinite in extent. In its present form it resembles nothing more closely than a roofed-in Olympic stadium with deviant parallax.

The Diamond itself is positioned at the centre of this big space and it too is big, uncannily big, even in an alternative reality. It has made itself look this big by bending the space around it and, given the people it is dealing with, this is a thoroughly sensible precaution. Even the Sailor and the Axe would need to think twice before grabbing at a Diamond the size of a bus.

Now that the initial silence had been broken, the crowd began to be less frozen and was taking more interest in its surroundings.

Hubcaps caught sight of something on the floor that looked familiar. He stooped and picked it up, a hospital direction sign with a corner broken off. He fumbled in his pocket and took out the small, broken piece of metal he had put there earlier. It fitted into the broken sign making a perfect match.

'So what exactly does that tell you?' said the Runt in a tart tone of voice. She was right beside him.

Hubcaps dropped the pieces of metal and watched them fall to the red tiles.

'It tells me we're here,' he said gloomily. He looked round to avoid meeting the Runt's eye. 'And so is everyone else, it seems.' And everyone else was talking too. There was a regular chorus of 'What are we doing here?' and 'What is this place?' and 'Don't tell me that's the Diamond. How on earth do we carry it?'

'Shut up!' shrieked the Diamond in an access of rage. This was not how terrified subjects were supposed to behave in front of their king. No one paid its shrill voice any attention so it tried again, aiming at a more regal tone.

'Shut up!'

The general hubbub began to die down until only one lone voice remained.

'It's mad you know.' Harry Devine was explaining to Dot what he knew about the Diamond. 'Completely mad. It wants to rule the world.'

Oh yeah, the Diamond felt like saying, well hark at who's talking. But that would be bad for its credibility. Instead it said, 'If you're quite ready, Mister Devine.'

'Who me?' said Harry brightly, 'Oh sure. Don't mind me. You just carry on.'

'But what about our party?' muttered the Axe darkly.

'Look.' The Diamond was not angry any more. The fine passion had fled and like a patient adult after five minutes with children it was now just cross and scratchy.

'There is no party. I changed my mind. Alright? No party. No jelly. No cake.'

'Oh?' This was the doctor now. 'So what then?' He looked at the nurse with the briefest of smiles, wanting her to notice how brave and clever he was being. 'I rather liked the idea of a party.'

'Enough!' cried the Diamond and, in what registered only as a momentary flicker to the human eye, the alternative reality shifted its boundaries and the doctor was gone.

The small crowd fell suddenly still.

That's shut them up, smirked the Diamond to itself. In a

manner of speaking.

'So,' it said, 'He's gone. Does anyone else want to go then?'

There was a thoughtful pause.

'Well yeah.' This is the Axe again, bolder and more confident now. 'I wouldn't mind.' He turned contritely to the Boss. 'I mean, Boss. We can't just grab it and run, can we?' He glanced towards where the Diamond was lowering over them. 'And if there's no party neither...'

'Yes, Mr Axe. Yes.' The Boss sounded old and tired and dispirited. He kept glancing out of the corner of his eye to where Rupert was standing smiling at Deirdre.

'You go. I go. We all go.' He looked up at the Diamond. 'Alright with you?'

'But... But...' The Diamond did not know what to say. This was not the reply it expected. 'But you don't now where he's gone.'

'Oh. I'll take my chances on that,' said the Boss.

'Can't be worse than here,' added the Axe. 'there could be jelly.'

In reality the doctor had not gone far. Only to the other side of the boundary. Out there the hospital was intact, but without corridors. They had been commandeered.

A patient raised a head full of drugged sleep.

'What's up Doc?' he said in a creaky voice to the doctor who had mysteriously materialised at his bedside. The patient laughed as his head fell back onto the pillow. 'Always wanted to say that,' he muttered as he drifted away again. 'Always wanted to say that.'

The atmosphere in the ward flickered again and standing beside the doctor were the Boss, the Sailor and the Axe clad in hospital pyjamas.

'Hey Doc,' said the Axe. 'You wouldn't know where our clothes are, would you?'

Down at the near end of The Borough High Street there was calm. But only for the moment. Not so far away there was a strident wailing and howling that announced the approach of a convoy of ambulances. On the pavement there was a battered little car with paint scrapings and dents along its side that suggested it had recently been closely involved with something big and white. The little car was not listening to the noise of the approaching ambulances. It was brooding over its own grievances and muttering to itself.

Hubcaps was a car man. Clearly he was a car man. The little car had never been driven by anyone with a touch like his. And he had called the little car beautiful. So ever since he had driven the little car into that ambulance it had been dreaming that he would return to restore it and maintain it and generally love it to death. But Hubcaps had not come back. So if Mohammed would not come to the mountain, and the mountain knew where Mohammed had gone...

The little car started itself up and began backing out into the road. The hospital was to the right, it thought as its back wheels dropped down off the kerb, and it was not very far away.

The lead ambulance of the convoy swerved violently onto the wrong side of the road to avoid the little car that had just backed out in front of it. Unfortunately for the lead ambulance the other side of the road was occupied by the lead car of a convoy of emergency health staff who were on their way home after being stood down at the hospital when the ambulances failed to arrive.

'There,' said the crewmate in the lead ambulance as his driver mounted the pavement and grated along three shop windows in a row before halting the ambulance, 'I said no good wouldn't come of it.' There was a deep satisfaction in his voice. 'And it's a good job them windows was boarded up,' he observed. 'Might have done some damage else.'

All around them there was a cacophony of noise. Tyres squealed. Horns blared. Sirens wailed and were cut off short. Voices were raised in anger. The first ambulance driver waited hunched in her seat as she anticipated the groaning of tortured metal that would herald the moment when vehicles began slamming into each other. Tension was visibly flooding back up into her from the puddle on the floor.

'Be dry soon, that will,' said her crewmate brightly. 'And that'll be another good job, won't it?'

Around the Diamond the whole crowd was clamouring now to be allowed to go as the doctor and the Boss and his boys had gone. It occurred to the over-inflated gem that at this rate there would be no one left to rule. And if there was no one to rule...

'Er...' it began but the hubbub continued. 'If you'd just let me get a word in edgeways...' Gradually people quietened down and looked expectantly at the ruler of the alternative reality.

'No one is going anywhere. Alright?'

'But...' began several voices, 'what about...' A rapid flickering of the boundaries silenced them. The doctor, the Boss and his boys were back among them.

'No one is going anywhere,' repeated the Diamond. 'No one. Anywhere.'

'So what then?' It was Dot who spoke now. 'What instead?'

What it really wanted to do, the Diamond knew the moment it heard Dot's querulous voice, was murder the lot of them. It had expected being king to be fun. And it would be, it was sure, if only... It sighed, exasperated. There must be easier people than this to rule. People who said 'Yes, your Majesty' a lot and listened when you spoke. It was just a question of finding them, surely. The Diamond sighed again. But even if they could be found, it would still have to put up with a world filled with people like these. People who...

'Well?' said Dot. 'What then?'

Which was when the Diamond had its idea. It was king. It did not have to put up with anything. It could surround itself with whatever people it chose, and as for the rest of them...

'I'll tell you what then,' it said. 'You're going to play a game.'

'Ah,' echoed the Axe in the background. 'A game. What's it's name?'

The Diamond allowed the crowd to settle into an expectant hush before speaking again. And then it spoke in imperious tones.

'The name of the game, Mr Axe, is Murder.'

The groaning of tortured metal never came. Slowly the
driver relaxed. Her shoulders came down. Her knuckles
turned from white to pink on the steering wheel. She began
to breathe again. The crewmate watched the floor anxiously, expecting to see the flood reappear but it remained dry,
which was yet another good job.

From outside came a pathetic 'Parp parp.' A small battered car in the middle of the road was trying to edge its
way in an embarrassed fashion out of the chaos it had
created.

'Oh no you don't,' said the first ambulance driver. She
leapt down from her cab, sprinted over to the little car and
hauled the driver's door open. Or what would have been
the driver's door if there had been a driver.

The first ambulance driver stared aghast at the empty
driver's seat and then sank to the ground and began to sob.
This shouldn't be possible. It was all too much. Too much.
Too much. Too much.

'What's happening?' she groaned. 'Whatever's happening?

There was a brief silence after the Diamond pronounced
the name of its game. But it was not the fear-filled silence
that it had aimed for. It was more polite than fearful.
Vernon broke it.

'Oh yes?' he said. 'Murder. Is that the game where someone goes out of the room and the lights go out and when they come back on again the person comes back into the room and finds somebody murdered and no one is allowed to lie except the murderer and the person has to find out who did it by asking questions?'

'No!' said the Diamond tersely. 'It isn't. And now...'

'Then,' said Rupert, 'is it the game where there's this ball and two walls and one team has to carry the ball to one wall while the other team tries to carry the ball to the other wall and there aren't any rules because if it is then it's really one for youth clubs and I really think, that at our age...' He looked around him taking in Dot and Deirdre and the Boss.

'No,' said the Diamond, 'it's not. And if you'll just let me...' But no one was listening any more. A lively discussion was in progress.

'Oh silly.' The Runt was taking the role of discussion leader. 'That's murder ball.

'Murder's the game where there's this board with rooms on it and six murder weapons and you have to find out who done it even though you never know who was done.'

'No it's not,' chimed in Deirdre with an authority born of long hours playing board games. 'That's... Oh. What's its name? That board game. It's called... It's on the tip of my tongue. Begins with a C.'

'Killing?' said the Axe.

'Nah!' Rudge was scornful. 'It's more likely to be CID.'

'Or Crime?' said the deadpan voice.

'Or what about Carnage?' said the Axe.

'Carnage?' said the Boss in a dismissive voice, 'For heaven's sakes. How many people get seen to in this game?'

'Lots,' said the Diamond eagerly, 'I hope.' But no one listened.

'Is this the game now, then?' enquired Dave the ambulance crewmate. 'Guessing the name? Because if it is...'

Florien plucked at Dave's sleeve. She could feel the

couched lance of the Diamond's attention turning their way and she did not like it.

'Only I want to be sure, you see.' Dave ignored Florien and carried on regardless. 'Because if I say the name first and this isn't the game yet, then I could lose later if this becomes the game instead of whatever it was you said.'

'Murder,' said the Diamond. 'That was what I said.' The word tried to fill the big space and dominate it but it was up against stiff competition.

'Cluedo!' said Deirdre excitedly. 'I knew I knew it. Right on the tip of my tongue it was.'

The big space resonated with the noise of people clucking their tongues, clicking their fingers and generally trying to convey the impression that they had known the answer too. Really. If they had been given time.

'Bleeder,' muttered Dave. 'I knew it all along.'

'Play it all the time I do,' he confided to Florien. 'With my little girl.'

'She wins I expect,' said Florien sarcastically.

'Listen!' The Diamond was really rattled now. 'I said "listen!"'

Cold, polite faces turned in the Diamond's direction.

'Look.' The Diamond was almost pleading. 'The game is Murder, right? It's not Crime, or Killing or Carnage or Culprits. And it's not the game where one person goes out of the room and turns off the light and only the murderer can lie.'

Once the Diamond got going it began to feel better. People were paying attention.

'And nor is it the game with two walls and a ball. Or the game with a board and six murder weapons and you've got to guess who done it even if you don't know who was done.'

'Look.' Dot Coulson interrupted. She was getting cross. 'Whatever this game is, can't we just get on with it? The night's not getting any younger after all.'

236

The Diamond decided just to ignore Dot.

'The lights will go out,' it said in sonorous tones. 'The lights will come on. And the last one living, wins. Now. Are you ready?'

'We...ell,' said Hubcaps. 'That just depends, doesn't it?'

'Depends on what? Mister Hubcaps.'

'On what kind of a game it is. Are we working alone or is this a team game?' His voice became confiding. 'Because, you see, I'm not very good at team games.'

'That's right,' said the Boss without a trace of irony. 'He's not.'

In the High Street the first ambulance crewmate sat in the cab of his ambulance with a gleeful expression on his face. The object of his joy was the sight of his high and mighty driver crouching beside a small, battered car, breaking her heart over the chaos and confusion that had descended on the High Street.

'Eat dirt, Lady,' the crewmate muttered as he reached into the glove compartment for his newspaper and the cool remains of tea in his flask. 'I said no good wouldn't come of it.'

The Runt's car was feeling embarrassed and ashamed of itself. It was ashamed because it could not think what had come over it. Normally it prided itself on being a model road user, an inconvenience to no one. And yet, its headlights flickered as it had a quick, guilty look round, this had been no accident.

The car had to think this. It's favourite dictum was 'There's no such thing as accidents, only people getting it wrong.' Only sometimes, it seemed, it wasn't just people who got it wrong.

But, however bad the little car felt, it didn't make it any better the way this ambulance driving woman was going on. She was really embarrassing. The Runt's car was not used to the sight of grown women crying. What it was used to was grown women thumping its steering wheel and kicking its doors when it had only been doing its best. And that, when it came down to it, was what it wanted most right now. For once in its life it really needed a good kicking. It would make it feel very much better.

Whether the first ambulance driver could sense the little car's embarrassment it could not tell but this was just the moment she chose to start pulling herself together. She rocked back on her heels and looked to see if anyone had been watching her. In the cab of her ambulance the crewmate hurriedly turned his attention back to his newspaper.

'Come on now, pull yourself together girl,' muttered the first ambulance driver. She wiped her eyes on her sleeve and left a dirty smear on her face. 'Up you get. You're not beaten yet.'

She stood and began to take in the mess around her. It made her cross. She hated messiness. But there was one thing at least to be said for this mess. She turned a baleful eye on the Runt's car. There was something to blame and, she kicked hard, something she could about it.

'Aaah.' The car's sigh was almost audible. That was better. Pretty soon everything would be back to normal.

In the Diamond's alternative reality time is standing still. That's what happens when a crowd of minds all work together to avoid believing what they are seeing.

'Right then, if we're all ready, we should just get on with it,' says the Diamond.

'This isn't happening,' the crowd of minds thinks.

'When I say go,' the Diamond says.

'Things like this don't happen to me.'

'Last one living after the lights go out, wins.'

'What does this thing take us for?'

'One.'

'Nah. It'll never do it.'

'Two.'

238

'And no one'll play, anyway.'

Three.'

'It can't be serious.'

The lights go out.

'Go.' Without even an exclamation mark. The Diamond is as serious as hell.

Very few people have experienced the total darkness caused by the complete absence of light. A dark night means that the stars are dimmed by a layer of heavy cloud. A dark house is one lit only by the glow of the street lamp outside. Or by the little red indicator lamps that indicate how much electricity is being wasted. So total darkness comes as a shock.

In the Diamond's alternative reality no one moves. No one breaths. Every one listens. Every one thinks. Every one hopes that no one else will do anything. Well almost everyone. The Diamond sighs windily. It has given these people a licence to kill. What more do they want?

There is a crumpling sound. A woman collapses from holding her breath too long. It sounds like a woman, any-way. Or a small man. Whatever. The first victim has been located. There is a quick rush of footsteps. People close on the noise. Then there is silence again. People realise that by moving they are giving their own positions away.

A dull thud. A murderous blow by the sound of it. Then silence again.

The Diamond relaxes. This is better. Battle has been joined. And now that one has gone down they will all smell blood.

Battle has been joined and among the first to find each other are the Sailor and the Axe. They waste no time on expressions of friendship. They do not relive the good times. They get right down to business. Under the cover of their straining, their battering and stamping, their tearing and retching and groaning, people begin quietly jockeying for position. Most of them aren't very good at it. Some pay the price. The air begins to be filled with terrible dying groans and even more terrible localised silences.

It is only a subjective impression of course, but to Dot it seems that the big space is growing smaller. There is something in the quality of the sounds around her that make the boundaries seem closer than they were. The Diamond is squeezing them together, ruling out any avenue of escape. The very idea is horrible.

A flailing hand strikes Dot across the back of her head. A sharp sigh passes by her ear and a solid thump suggests that a wicked knife has passed into someone's ribs. A knife? Dot bites back the yelp of pain she is about to let out. What knife? But she knows. Instantly she knows.

Rudge. And he must be close.

And, crazily, Dot remembers for the first time the gun in her hands. The gun she did not let go in that brief moment when the deadpan voice and the light, boyish voice held on to her – and what has happened to them she wonders briefly.

Dot raises the gun in the air, twiddles the little lever on the side, just as she practised, and pulls the trigger. A ragged spear of flame lances into the blackness of the big space and casts deep shadows all around.

The flame dances and keeps on dancing – time, remember, is standing still – the shadows echo the movement. Spectral orange faces leer up from out of the black, they are demons interrupted in their work by a greater devil than the one that drives them.

The flame flickers out but the crashing of the gun's explosions continues to reverberate around what is, quite clearly now, the claustrophobic smallness of the big space. But the shock has set time moving again. And people can breathe freely once more.

Down in the High Street there was beginning to be less confusion.

It was marvellous, thought the first ambulance crewmate as he watched his driver in action, just what that woman was capable of when she put her mind to it.

And what was marvellous too was the way she approached things. I mean, thought the first ambulance crewmate, take him now, if he had the job of clearing up this mess, which thank heavens he did not, not his job this wasn't, but if it had been his job then what she was doing was not the way he would have set about it. He had to admit that. To be honest. Start in the middle he would have done and worked outwards from there. And now that he saw the job being done properly he could see that it wouldn't have worked. He had to admit that. Only fair that was. Only honest really.

At which point in his thoughts the first ambulance crewmate brought himself up short. Crikey, he thought, I'll end up admiring her if I'm not careful. Whatever next, eh? He turned back to his newspaper. Catch him admiring her? He turned the page. Just let them try. That's all. Just let them try.

'Stand still!' said Dot. Her voice was small beside the terror she had unleashed. 'Everyone! Stand still!'

Everyone obeyed. Everyone who could. Who wouldn't?

'Right then.' Dot stood sweeping the gun from side to side in front of her in case anyone should try to rush her.

'That's it. Enough. Turn the lights back on! This game is sick.'

'I take it you're addressing me?' said the Diamond.

'Of course. Who else?'

There was a pause, busy with thought.

'And what if I don't?'

'Eh?' It was not the reply Dot was expecting. Not with a gun in her hands.

241

'What if I don't? What will you do then?'

'Then I'll kill the lot of them!' said Dot without thinking. She considered this for a moment.

'Er...'

'Oh will you?' The Diamond's voice was rich with smugness. Then it sounded sad.

'I hoped for better things from you,' it said.

There was a gentle pattering as the bullets that Dot had fired came raining back down on to the red-tiled floor. Suddenly overwhelmed by the futility of even trying any more, Dot let the gun slip from her fingers, allowed her legs to fold under her and gave her head leave to bow to the floor.

There was a soft sighing through the space where Dot's heart had just been and another crunchy thud sounded behind her. A body fell. A limp hand groped feebly at her heel and became still.

Down in the High Street the first ambulance crewmate's attention wandered away from his newspaper and towards where his driver was busily sorting things out.

Catch him admiring her? Hah!

But he was having difficulty keeping his attention inside the cab. There was a problem with his newspaper which made it difficult to read. He looked closely at the page open in front of him. Bad print, was it? All the words slightly fuzzy around the edges?

The crewmate's attention wandered out of the window again.

The first ambulance driver was in her element.

'Oi, oi, oi, oi!' she yelled. 'Whoa!' She banged on the boot of the car that she had been guiding out of the tangle that blocked the High Street.

'Right then, doctor.' She leant down beside the driver's window. 'You're clear to go now.'

'But I wanted to go that way.' The doctor pointed back towards the tangle.

'Well.' The first ambulance woman looked where the doctor was pointing. 'Don't see how you can really.'

'But...'

'Besides, you're emergency call out aren't you?'

'Yes, but...'

'Well we're the emergency and we'll be moving again soon. We're going to need all the help we can get. But...' The first ambulance driver stood up. 'I suppose you must do what you think's right.' She moved to the next car and knocked on the roof.

'Alright? Ready? Oh, hullo sister, you stood down too?'

I've been stupid, thought the first ambulance crewmate as he watched. He was looking wide-eyed and youthful as if scales of worldliness had fallen from his eyes.

I mean, his thoughts went on, just look at her. Poise, tact, diplomacy and command. Above all, command. And she wasn't bad looking neither, now that he came to look. If he had been twenty years younger...

He wasn't though. But it was still all mighty admirable. Admirable through and through. And since it was stupid not to admire what was admirable, then he had been stupid. But he could make amends. He could begin right now.

The first ambulance crewmate jumped down lightly from his cab and moved towards his driver with a spring in his step.

'Aye aye!' came a voice from one of the other ambulances. 'Good old No-Good's on the move. And he's in a hurry.'

'Call of nature, then,' came a second voice. 'Only thing that hurries him.'

There was a chorus of laughter.

'Oi, oi, oi, oi,' shouted the first ambulance driver waving her arms as she directed the car in front of her from out of its hole. 'That's it sister, keep on coming.'

A movement caught the first ambulance driver's attention. She looked over her shoulder, still waving the nursing sister's car back towards her.

'Bill?' she said, surprised. Her mind was no longer on the job in hand, but it forgot to mention this to her arms. They kept on waving.

'Didn't expect to see you out here. What is it? Call of nature?'

'I've got something to say,' said Bill. 'I've been...' But the first ambulance driver never got to hear what Bill had been going to say.

There was a low grunting whine from the nursing sister's car as the nursing sister's left foot slipped off the delicately feathered clutch. The car leapt backwards pressing the nursing sister's right foot down more heavily on the accelerator and this made the car jump further and faster. There was one brief scream and then silence. The car stalled.

'Netty?' said Bill. He could not believe his eyes. 'Netty?' His eyes filled with tears. He reached out, but he could not move. He was frozen to the spot. Around him the world was dragging to a standstill as if time was standing still.

Slowly Bill raised his eyes to the stars lost somewhere beyond the dank, dark clouds and the street lights' glow. Slowly his mouth opened. And he roared.

'NEEETTYYYYY!'

Loud and long.

In the darkness of the big space the Diamond surveyed the scene around it. It needed no lights – when a thing has no eyes, light is a superfluous extra – and it liked what it saw. This was turning into an interesting experiment.

After all, it thought, take a random bunch of people and give them a licence to kill and you might expect more than one to resist the unpleasantness. Weren't people meant to have scruples, after all? Wasn't that why they claimed to be set apart from the beasts?

244

Well now it was time to tighten the screw. It would crowd them all in further and make the cocktail of paranoia and claustrophobia more potent still. It turned its attention back to the mind of the big space but it found that the space was occupied.

'More than one,' said the occupant.

'Eh?' said the Diamond.

'I said "more than one",' said the occupant. 'There is more than one who will resist you. I am the second and now it is time to stop.'

Bill's roaring ended.

The other drivers and crewmates were clustering around Netty's body. They looked up at Bill and shook their heads. And they waited to see what he would do next. Him. Good old No-Good.

He looked about with a new, fierce determination. What would Netty have done? he asked himself, because it was up to him now to do it for her. And the answer was that she would have got things moving. She would have got things done.

'Alright then, you'd better pick her up. We'll take her back with us.' He turned away from Netty's body and nodded in the direction of the distraught nursing sister who was repeatedly accepting full responsibility, in direct contradiction of the terms of her insurance policy. 'And see to her too. Shock.'

'Alright Bill,' said the voice that had earlier on been commenting on Bill's bladder. 'And what are you going to do?'

'Me?' said Bill. He looked hard at the voice who wilted beneath the weight of something new in No-Good's manner.

'I'm going to get things moving, that's what I'm going to do. I'm going to get this job done.'

He moved down the street and banged on the roof of a car.

'Alright then, doctor?' he said, bending down to peer

inside. 'Ready to go are we? Ready to run?'

'And who,' said the Diamond, 'are you?'

'Poppy,' said the lurking thing.

'Well let me tell you, little flower...'

'I am no flower.'

'Then little thing, whatever you are.'

'I am no thing.'

The Diamond pounced.

'Oh yes you are,' it snapped, 'you've got to be, because...'

'Alright! Alright. What if I am? What are you going to make of it?'

'Mincemeat.'

There was an ugly pause which ended with the thing's still being there.

'I think we could do with some light, don't you?' it said

Light? What was this thing that it needed light? It was the Diamond's turn to be frightened now, with the fear of the unknown.

The lights came on.

'We don't need light,' said the Diamond. The lights flickered and went out briefly but then came on again.

'I prefer it this way,' said the thing.

'Alright,' said the Diamond. 'Alright. But who are you?'

With the lights on the big space did not seem so big any more, only about the size of a decent living room. And it was a good thing that the floor was red. A couple of people vomited.

The only living being unaffected by the sight of the big space was Poppy. She was not looking at it. She was standing apart from everyone else and appeared to be concentrating on something in the distance. As for the rest of the living beings, they felt the direction of the Diamond's attention and gradually they too turned towards Poppy. Hope filled their eyes.

'You?' said the Diamond. 'You're Poppy?'

'I am Poppy,' said the thing from inside the mind of the big space.

'But you're human.'

'As you pointed out, I can't be. I became a thing. And frankly, just at the moment, it doesn't seem so bad after all.'

'But you do have a body?'

'And I'm told its not a bad one.' The conversation was becoming almost chummy.

'Then I shall crush it,' said the Diamond. It did not intend chumminess to become the keynote of the moment.

The boundaries of the big space lurched violently inwards. It caught everyone by surprise and they all jumped. Including Poppy. But she was quick-thinking, was Poppy. Too quick for the Diamond.

'Oh no you shan't.' The motion of the boundaries was suddenly arrested.

'Oh yes I shall.' The Diamond sounded strained as the boundaries inched inwards.

'Shan't.' The boundaries halted and then crept outwards.

'Shall.' Inwards.

'Shan't.' Outwards. And now the combatants became too strained to talk.

Sweat covered Poppy's face in a glistening sheen as she concentrated on throwing back the Diamond's power.

Far down in the Diamond's grossly magnified depths sparks flashed slowly and dully in angry colours as it strove to crush Poppy, body and mind.

The survivors of the Diamond's game watched the battle intently. They did not understand what was happening, but they understood alright that if this young woman did not win, then they would all be dead much sooner than they would wish.

'Who is she?' said Deirdre in a wondering voice.

'Poppy,' replied Rupert. 'Her name is Poppy.'

'She's Poppy? But she's...' A spasm of anger gripped

248

Deirdre's features. And then self-interest took charge.

'Well come on Poppy,' she said quietly. The next moment she was yelling fit to burst.

'Get on with it, Poppy!'

The boundaries moved out one inch.

'That's it Poppy! Give it all you've got!'

And the cry was taken up all around.

'Come on Poppy!'

'That's it, go for it!'

'Poppy! Poppy! Poppy!'

Poppy was trembling now and felt as if she was about to break. The strain was too much. She could not sustain it much longer. And her opponent would never grow tired. The Diamond could keep this up for ever. So there had to be something else she could do. There simply had to be.

The boundaries crept in an inch. Then two. Then three.

The crowd groaned and the vigour of its support was broken. The shouting became sporadic.

'Come on Poppy!' That was Rupert. But his voice was weak, like a boxing fan who sees his man reeling.

Poppy was dismayed by the slackening support but then, contrarily, it strengthened her resolve. She must not let these people down. They were depending on her.

As if she was carrying the weight of the world, Poppy raised her foot. Struggling to stay upright she reached forward with her leg and put the foot down again. She had taken one step. But she needed another. And another. And then another. Because there was something else she could do. If only she could do it in time.

The mercy convoy arrived at the hospital in grand good order. At the head of it was Bill driving the Runt's car. Gravel flew as he screamed in at the hospital gate and came to a halt with locked wheels outside the hospital's main entrance. Behind him, ambulances formed an orderly queue outside Casualty. In the staff car park, the convoy of emergency staff began sorting itself out.

Even as sirens faded to silence and engines cut out, Bill was on the job.

'Come on!' he yelled. 'Chop chop! There's work to be done. Plenty for everyone.'

Spurred on by Bill's enthusiasm, one of the emergency staff began running. It was contagious.

'Come on,' they called to each other. 'Work to do. Let's not keep it waiting.'

But – there is always a 'but' just as things are getting going – when strong hands shook the doors of Casualty, they had no effect at all.

'Hey Bill!' called the shaker. 'Some idiot's locked these doors.'

'What?' said Bill. 'Locked Casualty? Never.' He crossed, shook at the doors himself and then looked more closely.

'They're not locked,' he said. 'See for yourselves.'

People looked. Jaws fell open.

'Coo,' said someone.

'Gosh,' said someone else. But Bill was not listening. He was already looking at the main entrance doors.

'All sort of smeared across,' he said thoughtfully. 'Just like Casualty.' He explored further. 'The windows too,' he said to no one in particular and it was then that feeling took over from thought. Bill looked up at the hospital.

'If I can't get in now,' he told it, 'I'm going to be cross. Really cross.'

He kicked at the main entrance. The doors did not budge. They did not even rattle.

'That's it,' said Bill. 'That's bleedin' it.' He stormed away and climbed into the Runt's little car. Ambulance crews and emergency staff clustered round him.

'What are you going to do, Bill?'

'Take it easy Bill.'

'Don't do anything silly Bill.'

But Bill did not hear them. He was winding the little car's

250

engine up to an unheard of pitch.

'Eat your heart out Formula One,' the little car muttered nervously as it wondered what was going to happen next.

Bill waved away the clustering crowd of people.

'Stand back!' he shouted. 'I'm going in.'

You're going in, thought the little car. *You're* going in? And then Bill dropped the clutch and the car was working too hard to think at all.

The boundaries of reality trembled. Poppy was nearly there. Her hand reached out. But she was attempting the impossible. That tiny hand. That enormous Diamond.

No one was saying anything. Everywhere breath was bated. On and off.

Poppy completed another step. Her hand reached further forward. It passed into the distorted space around the Diamond and became the size of a house. Everyone exhaled. It was just an illusion then. Optical trickery. The realisation seemed to bring the danger down to size. Poppy's fingers began to close...

And then she faltered.

'Hah!' snarled the Diamond.

Poppy's knees trembled.

'Hah!' snarled the Diamond again.

Driven down by an insupportable weight Poppy buckled towards the red tiles.

'Hah! And Hah! And Hah!' At each word Poppy was driven lower. Her hand left the distortion and returned to its natural size. The boundaries of reality began to fold inwards.

It was all over.

'Vernon?' Dot said quietly. She had discovered the giant on the floor, lying close behind her. The black knife was in his chest. He must have been protecting her the whole time then. And it was good to think that. There had to be good somewhere. She picked his hand up, looked at the collapsing boundaries and tried to think of some apposite last words.

'Thanks anyway,' was the best she could come up with. And 'It was nice knowing you.'

The lights went out. The world went black.

Which set the scene nicely for the entrance of the Runt's car.

Headlights blazing, horn blaring and with a grim-faced Bill at the wheel it appeared in the middle of the big space looking the size of a skyscraper. It had a bus-sized Diamond sitting on its roof and a Parliament-sized door frame wrapped around its bonnet.

Behind the Diamond a gaping hole in reality had appeared. It was lit by the burning light of stars shining through a dense layer of cloud and was framed with a ring of puzzled faces.

'Everybody out!' grunted Poppy. 'The whole thing's going.'

The next moments were extremely long but very, very confused. An attempt should still be made to summarise them though, for the sake of the historical record.

There was some panic and a good deal of the knee in the face variety of scrambling which implies, more or less inevitably, that chivalry is dead. But then Dot knew that already. She had kissed it where it lay, still on a red-tiled floor.

There were survivors, whole and wounded, but no bodies. The alternative reality took everything with it as it sighed its way out of existence through the gaping hole in itself. This is topologically impossible, the cynics will sneer. But cynics, huh, what do they know?

People stood motionless on the gravel outside the Casualty Department. There was a ragged tear in the hospital wall where once the main entrance had been and there was silence.

The Sailor broke it. It was the first time he had spoken since being invalided ashore from sea.

'Boss?' he said. There was no answer. The Sailor will never speak again, he thinks, until there is.

'What now then?' Rupert looked at the diamond that Poppy had placed in his hand.

'Build a new villa,' said Poppy. 'It should fetch enough.'

'A new villa?' Rupert was puzzled.

'The old one burnt.'

'Oh. I see.'

'And marry Deirdre. She'll be good for you.'

'And you? What about you?'

'Things to do.' Poppy was gone but the echo of her voice came back. 'Thing to undo.'

'The doors are open now,' said the duty doctor with a new-found briskness. He was standing by the entrance to Casualty. 'Can we get on?'

'Let me help,' said Hubcaps. 'It's time I started making myself useful.'

'But weren't you... Earlier...' began the doctor. Then he finally gave up being officious for good. 'Yeah, alright,' he said, 'Thanks very much.'

'And you...' Hubcaps looked at the Runt. 'What is your name? I can't go on calling you "Runt" forever.'

The Runt bridled. It was something she was good at.

'Who says you'll be calling me anything for ever? And "Runt"'s always done till now. It was Aunty's name for me when I was a baby.'

253

23

'Which brings me to another question,' said Hubcaps much later. 'Where is Aunty?'

The shabby old woman tapped on the window of the shiny, new, red Mercedes.

'Could you please think about not parking on the pavement,' she said, 'it's for people not cars.'

The pock-marked, pale-faced driver of the new car wound down his window, took the cigarette from his mouth, looked at the old woman and blew smoke into her face.

'Not you again,' he said, 'What the hell do you think you're doing?'

'Cleaning up,' said the shabby old woman. 'Just cleaning up.'

'Whatever,' said the pale-faced driver. 'Eff off anyway.' Then quite suddenly his expression changed from arrogant contempt to fear. He stubbed out his cigarette, hurriedly wound up his window and drove off without a backward glance.

'Aah, progress,' sighed the shabby old woman. 'At least I'm making progress.'

'We're making progress, I think,' said a large mellifluous voice behind her.

'Vernon?' Dot froze. Very, very slowly she turned round. It was Vernon certainly, large as life and with all his hair back. 'But...' she protested. 'But...' She looked at the space on his chest which, last time she saw it, had been occupied by a dagger. Instinctively she reached up to touch it. There was nothing there. 'But...' She looked in puzzled wonderment up into Vernon's face. It smiled.

'But you were...' She took him in from head to toe, still looking doubtful. 'I mean...Weren't you?'

Vernon caught her hand and held it. 'Well now I am not, 'he said. 'I one hundred per cent am not.'

'But how...'

Vernon smiled. 'It's these alternative realities,' he said. 'Almost anything can happen.'

Dot looked puzzled, and frightened.

'Alright then,' said Vernon. 'I used to be a theoretical physicist, before I dropped out. States of being were my specialism.'

Dot looked less frightened, but still puzzled and now Vernon smiled broadly.

'Okay, okay. You want the truth? I cheated. Alright?'

Dot smiled. That she could understand. Then she looked cross. 'But cheating, that's not very chivalrous is it?'

'Am I so very chivalrous then?'

Dot nodded. 'Yes,' she affirmed. 'Yes you are.'

'I see.' A long pause. 'Well chivalry has its limits then. I guess,' said Vernon finally. He brightened.

'And now we'll never finish cleaning this place up, will we, if we simply leave that getaway car undisturbed?' He nodded in the direction of a hot-looking car sitting on the pavement outside a jeweller's shop. Its engine was running and its driver was looking around nervously.

'You know though,' said Dot as she and Vernon walked sedately along the High Street, 'I don't think that I'd ever really want to finish.' She hugged his arm warmly to her breast.

'I'm not sure that's the point.'

END

FANTASY FICTION
from Colin Smythe

Terry Pratchett's first Discworld novels, still available in hardcover

THE COLOUR OF MAGIC

On a world supported on the back of a giant turtle (sex unknown), a wickedly eccentric expedition sets out. There's Rincewind, an avaricious but inept wizard, Twoflower, a naive tourist whose murderous luggage moves on hundreds of little legs, dragons who only exist if you believe in them, and of course, the Edge of the Discworld, and its circumfence. . .

'Pratchett is very good indeed' - *Standard*

0-86140-324-X Hbk 206pp £13.99

THE LIGHT FANTASTIC

In this sequel to the much-acclaimed *The Colour of Magic*, Rincewind, Twoflower and the many-legged luggage return to the Discworld with the help of the Octavo and overcome the attempts by the wizards of the Unseen University to capture them, and then save the Discworld from an invasion from the Dungeon Dimensions.

`Marvellous sequel... pure fantastic delight.' - *Time Out*

0-86140-203-0 Hbk 218pp £13.99

THE FIRST DISCWORLD NOVELS

containing *The Colour of Magic* and *The Light Fantastic* in a single volume, with a new Josh Kirby cover.   For publication in Spring 1999.

ISBN 0-86140-421-1   £16.99

CHRONICLES OF AN AGE OF DARKNESS
by
Hugh Cook

Although the ten volumes in this series form part of a vast fantasy epic, each is a complete and spectacular tale in its own right.

The paperback editions of the Chronicles listed here are copies of the Corgi editions we bought from Transworld. To avoid confusion, they have been allocated new International Standard Book Numbers now they are only available from us.

THE WIZARDS AND THE WARRIORS
The opening volume in the series.

'I ask all of you here to join me in pledging yourself to a common cause,' said Miphon. Elkor Alish laughed, harshly: 'A common cause? Bewteen wizards and the Rovac? Forget it!'

And yet it had to be. Though Alish never accepted the alliance, his fellow warrior Morgan Hearst joined forces with Miphon and the other wizards. The only alternative was the utter distruction of their world. They faced two perils, each of which could bring about their end: the Swarms, and a power that turned living things to stone, and brought rocks to life.

Published in the USA as *Wizard War*.

'Superior Sword and Sorcery. A stylish and horrific fantasy adventure awash with heroic derring-do and some of the most ingenious magic I've come across in many a moon.'

Julian May, author of *The Pliocene Exile*

'a big fat novel chockablock with magic, action, and probably the single cleverest use of magical devices I've come across in fantasy... two bottles that are much, *much* larger inside than they are outside, and what happens when one of them gets inside the other. The handling of the permutations of this circumstance is fiendishly clever.'

Baird Searles in *Isaac Asimov's Science Fiction Magazine*
ISBN 0-86140-244-8 352pp. hbk £14.99

THE WORDSMITHS AND THE WARGUILD

The second volume in the series. Unfortunately out of print in both paperback and hardcover. Published in the USA in two volumes, entitled *The Questing Hero* and *The Hero's Return*.

THE WOMEN AND THE WARLORDS

'Lord Alagrace said you'ld help.'

'Any oracle can give you a reading,' replied Yen Olass.

'I told Alagrace an oracle couldn't help me,' said the Ondrask. 'I told him I wasn't interested in a reading. But he told me you'd do better than that. He told me you'd fix it.'

'What?' said Yen Olass. She was genuinely shocked, and it took a lot to shock her.

So begins Yen Olass' involvement in the life-long feud of the warlords of the Collosnon Empire. She was to witness war, madness and wizardry, and would play a greater part in the events of her time than a mere oracle had any right to expect. Published in paperback in the USA as *The Oracle*.
ISBN 0-86140-294-4 284pp. hbk £13.99

THE WALRUS AND THE WARWOLF

'You're right,' said King Tor. 'Those were but boyish pranks. So I'll let you off lightly. We'll have you birched in public today. You spend tonight buried up to the neck in the public dungheap. Tomorrow morning, we'll put you on a boat. Three leagues from shore, you'll be thrown overboard. That is my justice.' Drake knew he had got a good deal.

What he didn't know was that this was only the start of a long journey that would take him far from his home and his love – and that he would have to endure far worse before either could be regained. The fourth in the series. The first eighteen chapters were published in the USA as *Lords of the Sword*.

ISBN 0-86140-294-4 hbk iv, 486pp £14.99
ISBN 0-86140-395-9 pbk 780pp. £6.99

THE WICKED AND THE WITLESS

The action of the fifth volume of the Chronicles takes place just before that of *The Wizards and the Warriors*. The young Sean Kelebes Sarazin, returning to Selzirk after a long period as a hostage, expects to play a major role in the city where his mother, Farfalla, is the kingmaker. But his hopes are rudely dashed: His comfortable life as a hostage had left him ill-prepared for a life of war, intrigue and wizardry. Nevertheless, he has a vision: he sees himself as the legendary figure of prophecy, Watashi, and sets out to make that vision come true.

ISBN 0-86140-396-7 460pp. pbk £5.99

THE WISHSTONE AND THE WONDER-WORKERS

Shabble. In appearance, a miniature sun, though coloration tends to be changeable and idiosyncratic. In voice eccentric, speaking at will in any of the accents ever heard on Untunchilamon, even those implacable foreign accents otherwise voiced only by the conjuror Odolo. In behavious feckless, for Shabble has scant regard for consequences. That is Shabble.

While Shabble is still hanging there in the air, a massive energy drain affects all of Injiltaprajura. Lights darken. Fires go out. Candles die. Then, to Shabble's horror, Shabble feels Something trying to seize Shabble's own energy. Shabble squeals in fright and flees down the nearest drainpipe. The drainpipe (naturally) leads Downstairs. Downstairs! There is horror down there, and Shabble fears in greatly. Yet the alternative is death.

What has caused this massive energy drain? It is left to Chegory Guy, an Ebrell Islander, to find out. This in unfortunate as his chief skills are as a knifefighter and a rock-gardener. And yet it is he who finally holds the future of the entire, equatorial island of Untunchilamon in his hands.

Although it is the sixth volume of this vast fantasy epic, this volume is a complete and spectacular tale in its own right.
ISBN 0-86140-397-5   448pp.   pbk   £5.99

THE WAZIR AND THE WITCH

The Hermit Crab, a being with powers at least equal to those of any wizard or sorcerer, dwelt on a small island in the harbour of Untunchilaamon's capital city. The Crab took exception to the violent political disputes that had disturbed the peace of its domicile; to restore the peace, the Crab commanded Justina and Varazchavardan to declare a truce and resolve their differences. This they did. Had they disobeyed, they would have been turned inside out by a wrathful Crab, therefore the matter of their compliance is scarcely a mystery.

This is the true history of the final days of the rule of Justina Thrug over the island of Untunchilamon, and it is the only such history which is worth the price of the fooskin upon which it it is wrtten. And remember, your historian was there.
The seventh volume in the series.
ISBN 0-86140-398-3 448pp. pbk £5.99

THE WEREWOLF AND THE WORMLORD

'You travelled by night.'
Alfric kept his face blank. This was no time to show impatience. But Alfric liked to do business in an efficient manner; and not for nothing was the king known as He Who Talks In Circles.

'Night is a strange time to travel,' continued King Dimple-Dumpling. 'Particularly when night is Her chosen time.'

'My duty bids me to rule the night,' said Alfric. 'I cannot permit Her forays to keep me from the dark. I am a Yudonic Knight.'

'Who fears nothing,' said the king.

When one hears dry irony from the lips of an ogre, it is hard to credit one's ears. But Alfric, who knew ogres better than most of his kind, did not underestimate them.

On occasion, Alfric Danbrog, a banker by profession, found it hard to live up to his Yudonic heritage. Yet he was called upon to face not only ogres, dragons, assassins and She Who Walks by Night but – worst of all – more senior bankers.

The eighth volume of the series.

ISBN 0-86140-399-1   352pp.   pbk   £5.99

THE WORSHIPPERS AND THE WAY

'Enemy behind us,' said the singlefighter.

So Hatch slammed the fighter into a wrenching turn, a turn so savage he had to tighten his stomach muscles to keep himself from passing out. And there was his enemy. In his sights. The enemy for real? Or a drone? Hatch hesitated, just for a moment, and a moment was far too long.

Asodo Hatch and Lupus Lon Oliver had already established themselves as the best of the best at the Combat College, which was designed to produce Startroopers for the Stormforce of the Nexus. IN just under a year, they would face the terminal examinations that would decide which one of them attained the lucrative position of instructor. There was only one instructor's position. And to win it, one would have to defeat the other in combat within the illusion tanks.

ISBN 0-86140-400-9 380pp.   pbk   £5.99

The tenth book in the series, *The Witchlord and the Weaponmaster*, is unfortunately out of print.